M000233679

The Amish
Princess

Patrick E. Craig

The Amish Princess

First Edition eBook: 2016
First Edition Paperback: 2016
ISBN (ePub): 978-0-9965334-7-8
ISBN (Paperback): 978-0-9965334-6-1

Published by P&J Publishing
Caldwell, Idaho
In cooperation with NCC Publishing (www.nccpublishing.com)

Cover by Garborg Design Works, Savage, Minnesota
Cover Photos © Chris Garborg, Bigstock / Voy
Author Photo by William Craig, Craig Prographica

20161211

Dedication

This book is dedicated to my grandmother, Nettie Patrick Craig, a true Irish *seanchaí* who imparted her gift of storytelling to many of her descendants, for which I am very grateful.

Acknowledgements

To my wife, Judy, for her tireless efforts in proofing and editing *The Amish Princess*.

To Lindsay A. Franklin for her excellent substantive editing and advice with this book.

The Amish Princess

Contents

A Note from Patrick E. Craig

The Hershberger family has been the center of my writing endeavors since 2010 when I wrote my first Amish tale, *A Quilt for Jenna*. Since then, I've told the stories of three generations of Hershberger women, Jerusha, Jenny and Rachel in four books. Now this book, *The Amish Princess*, goes back in time to tell the story of another woman, Ruth Hershberger, whose life profoundly affects the history of the Hershberger family. The setting for this story is the period of American history from the coming of the first Amish families to America until the middle of the Nineteenth century. Many of the events and characters are historical, but the story is fictional, as are the main characters.

Here's the set-up: In my first book, *A Quilt for Jenna*, Jerusha Hershberger's grandmother, Hannah, gives Jerusha a small, plain-bound book. It is the story of her great-great-great-grandfather, Joshua, and his twin brother, Jonathan. In the book, Jerusha learns of the choices the brothers made after Indians massacred their family near Fort Henry on the Ohio River in 1770, and the effect those decisions had on generations of Hershbergers. One brother, Jonathan, forsook the Amish way of life, and he and all his descendants went out into the world. The other brother, Joshua, kept his Amish faith, even under the most difficult conditions. It was because Joshua stayed true that Jerusha's family came to be in Apple Creek.

Then, in my second book, *The Road Home*, Jerusha's adopted daughter, Jenny Springer, meets Jonathan Hershberger, a hippie and an atheist who stumbles into Jenny's life "by chance". Together, they uncover the incredible tale of Jonathan's great-great-great-grandfather and-grandmother, Jonathan and Ruth Hershberger. And there was a lot to the story, because Ruth was a full-blooded Delaware Indian princess who had come to the Lord through many trials and Jonathan was Joshua's missing brother, the Amish man who left his faith and suffered greatly for it…

But then if I go on, I'll tell the whole story…

Part One

A Tale of Two Families

The Amish are direct descendants of the Anabaptists, a branch of the Radical Protestant Reformation of sixteenth century Europe. What set the Anabaptists apart was their rejection of child baptism. They believed a person should not be baptized until they were old enough to know the meaning of their commitment to Christ. When the Anabaptists rejected this practice, the mainline Protestants and Catholics, with the help of the secular authorities, began to persecute them terribly.

Out of that persecution, two distinct movements arose. One group took the path of resistance and fought their tormentors. The other group, followers of a man named Menno Simons, took the path of non-violence. As they read the Bible, they were convinced that Jesus taught men not to kill or hurt other men. The Mennonites became the predominant Anabaptist sect. Then another group, led by a man named Jacob Ammann, left the Mennonite church, adopted the practice of shunning, and became the Amish. Because of their adherence to non-violence, the Mennonites and the Amish were easy prey for the mainline Protestants and Catholics and were almost wiped out because of their stand.

At the same time in America, a noble Indian tribe known as the Lenni Lenape, also called the Delaware Indians, lived in their historical territory along the Delaware River Watershed, Western Long Island, and the Lower Hudson Valley. The Lenape had fierce war chiefs. One of the most renowned of these warriors was Wingenund who became the father of Opahtuhwe, or White Deer, our ancestor, the woman called the Amish Princess.

The Lenape also had Leaders known as Sachems who were chosen for their behavior, skill in speaking, honesty, and ability to make wise decisions. The Sachems were initiated in the mysteries of the shamanistic religion and led their people in the ancient rituals and ceremonies.

The Lenape called their land "Lenapehoking," or "Land of the Lenape." As part of the Eastern Woodlands, Lenapehoking *had many rivers, streams, and lakes and was densely forested and rich in wildlife. The Lenape lived in villages of up to two hundred people and governed themselves with wisdom and equality*

In 1682 William Penn received all of Pennsylvania from the British Crown as payment for a debt to his father, even though the land belonged to the Lenni-Lenape. Because he was facing persecution and jail as a Quaker in England, Penn decided to come to America and start a colony. When he arrived, he wisely made treaties with the Lenape and paid them for their land. But he needed settlers to populate his colony, so he sent emissaries to Europe, especially Holland and the countries along the Rhine River, asking people to come. The people that were the most interested were the Anabaptists, because Penn promised them religious freedom. Over the next one hundred years, thousands of them came to America and settled in Pennsylvania.

Our Amish ancestor, Jonas Hershberger, arrived in Philadelphia with his father, Mathias and his mother in 1737 when he was six years old, the youngest of five sons. Mathias bought land in the Northkill Settlement and established a prosperous farm. Jonas was the youngest son and, since there was not enough land to be shared between all the brothers, he left Northkill in 1764 when he was thirty-five years old. Jonas brought his wife and five children and settled near Fort Pitt, later the site of Pittsburgh, Pennsylvania.

While this was happening, the Lenape, like many Native Americans, were decimated by European diseases; their homeland was overrun, and the survivors had been driven into western Pennsylvania. During the French and Indian War, the Deleware tribe, led by Wingenund, allied with the French and fought against the British and the settlers, who were pushing into their new territory. When the French lost the war, Wingenund took his wife and daughter and moved further west. They had been settled in the Ohio wilderness for several years by the time the Hershbergers, with their three sons and two daughters, arrived in western Pennsylvania.

As Charles Dickens once wrote, "What connexion can there have been between many people in the innumerable histories of this world, who, from opposite sides of great gulfs, have, nevertheless, been very curiously brought together!" And that is certainly true of the Hershberger family. For from that point, our history took an interesting turn. Out of that turning came my family, the Hershbergers of Apple Creek, and my husband Jonathan's family, the Hershbergers of Long Island. One family remained true and faithful to its Amish roots, and one family was sundered from its faith and lost to the order. It would take over two hundred years and the hand of God to bring them together again. The Amish Princess is the story of the beginning of that journey.

Two Families
From The Journals of Jenny Hershberger

Chapter One

From Death to Life

The smell of death was everywhere in the steerage area of the schooner *Charming Nancy*. Jonas Hershberger gagged at the stench as he made his way up from the hold. He could not stand being below decks one minute more—seeing the white, tear-stained faces of grieving fathers and mothers and hearing the moans of the dying. He passed by *Bishchopp* Kauffman on his way forward. The once-energetic leader of their flock now sat silently, staring at the shroud-wrapped body of his youngest child. The *bishchopp* looked up at him and shook his head. He whispered something to Jonas.

Jonas leaned closer. "What, *Bishchopp*?"

The man took hold of Jonas' arm with a painful grip. "He let loose on them his fierce anger, wrath, indignation, and distress, a company of destroying angels."

Jonas pulled his arm away and stood, staring at the man for a moment, and then he turned and blindly groped his way to the ladder that led upwards toward the fresh air and escape from the horror below.

The Amish people on board the ship had not expected such trials when they left Lomersheim near Wurtemburg that spring. Indeed, the Hershberger family and those who traveled with them had been full of joy as they prepared to depart. After the Palatinate and nearby areas had been repeatedly invaded by the French, the Anabaptists living there had struggled with the devastation and famine that followed, as well as the constant threat of religious persecution. When the man who represented William Penn came to their village and told glowing tales of Pennsylvania—the rich farmland, the mighty forests, the rivers teeming with fish, the abundance of game and most of all, the freedom from tyranny and death at the hands of other Christians, Jonas' father, Mathias, had leapt at the chance to emigrate.

So the Hershbergers set out on their journey with others from their village. In the spring of 1737, they journeyed to Rotterdam and there they joined a group of Amish people who were to board the *Charming Nancy* and set sail for the new world. But trouble found them before they even started. On the twenty-eighth of June, while they were still in Rotterdam getting ready to set out, *Bishchopp* Kauffman's daughter, Zernbli, died. On the twenty-ninth the ship went under sail but enjoyed only one and a half days of favorable wind. Then on the seventh day of July, early in the morning, the Zimmerman's son-in-law died. The travelers landed at Plymouth, England on the eighth of July. During the nine days the ship remained in port, five more children died.

And so it went. As the endless days on the gray-green sea crept by, the list grew longer. Lisbetli Kaufmann died, followed swiftly by four more. On the first of August another of the *Bischopp's* children, Hansli, died, then five more children died. On the twenty-eighth Hans Gasi's wife died. During the voyage of eighty-three days, one in nine of the passengers succumbed, and the *Charming Nancy* became a death-ship. Jonas had watched his father and mother work themselves into exhaustion, nursing the sick and praying for deliverance. And now, at last they were coming to Pennsylvania.

Jonas climbed up the last steps of the ladder and staggered onto the deck. The ship was slowly making its way against the current. He felt the fresh wind that was moving them upstream and smelled the fields that lay on both sides of the great river.

His hair whipped in the chill breeze, but he did not want to go below deck again, not ever. It was so good to see land again. He closed his eyes and breathed deeply. Then he opened them and began to look more closely at the shoreline. As the ship rounded a promontory, he saw a small figure on the bank. It looked like an Indian boy with a basket slung over his shoulder. He wore a breechclout and leggings that covered his nakedness. The boy stood silently, staring at Jonas as the ship passed. Jonas waved to him, but the boy did not wave back or make any sign. Then the boy turned and disappeared into the tall grass lining the shore. A step on the deck drew Jonas' attention, and he turned to find his father, Mathias, standing behind him. His father's face was drawn and lined with pain.

Jonas pointed toward the shore. "Father! I think I saw an Indian, just there. His skin was dark and he didn't have any clothes."

Mathias Hershberger did not answer. He stepped to the rail and stared silently at the water. He put his face into his hands, and Jonas could see his father's shoulders shaking with sobs. "So much death, Jonas. *Hat du lieber Gott aufgegeben wir*?"

Jonas put his hand out to touch his father's arm. "God wouldn't abandon us, would he, Papa?"

Mathias shook his head slowly and then lifted his eyes to the heavens. "So many have died lieber Gott. We fled death in the Palatinate only to find it on the sea. Why? What did we do to bring your anger?"

Jonas stood silently, staring at his father. Mathias was usually a happy man, satisfied with his lot in life and a strong follower of the Amish way. To see him like this was troubling for Jonas. Finally, Mathias wiped his eyes and turned to his son. "Forgive me, Jonas. I sound as though I am questioning the will of *Gott*. Far be it from me to challenge the things that *der allmächtige Vater* plans for our lives. I am just troubled by the many deaths on our voyage, especially among the children."

Jonas took his father's hand. "I know it is hard, Papa, but all of us are still alive."

Mathias frowned. "We should not rejoice that none of our family died, while so many have lost loved ones. The *Bischopp* lost three of his *kinder*."

The rebuke stung and Jonas was silent for a moment. Then he whispered, "I am sorry, Papa."

"No harm, my son. It is just that we must always think of others first. That is what the Lord commands, and we must see that we obey."

Jonas tried to turn the conversation away from death. "Will we have a large farm, Papa?"

Mathias smiled at his son. It was the first time he had smiled in many days. "Yes, Jonas. We have seven mouths to feed, and I have brought enough silver to pay for a goodly piece."

"Where will we live, Papa?"

His papa pointed to the west. "We will go to the Northkill settlement. It is west of Philadelphia and slightly north. Some of our people went ahead to get things ready there and more Amish are coming. We will have a farm and live among our own kind, free from the persecution of the Lutherans and the Catholics."

"They hate us, don't they, Papa?"

"Yes, my son. When we refused to baptize our infants, it deprived them of tax revenue. And so they drove us out in the name of protecting the true faith, but it was really only about money. For the love of money is the root of all evil: which while some coveted after, they have erred from the faith and pierced themselves through with many sorrows."

"That's from the Bible, isn't it, Papa?"

"Good, Jonas! Yes, it is First Timothy, verse six. And now, show me where you saw the Indian."

Eighty-four days after leaving Rotterdam, the *Charming Nancy* sailed slowly into the harbor at Philadelphia. The surviving settlers crowded onto the deck, cheering and weeping as the city came into view. Jonas stood by his father and mother as

Bishchopp Kauffman came slowly up from below and made his way to the railing of the ship. After several minutes, he turned to his flock. He had grown gaunt and pale during the voyage and his hands shook. His wife stood by him as he removed his hat and looked up at the sky.

"*Das Lieben des Gottes*, we look to You today for strength and comfort." He stood silently for a moment and then turned to the people. "Many of us have suffered greatly on this journey. I have buried three of my children in the cold waters of the Atlantic Ocean. *Mein Herz ist mit dem Kummer schwer, und ich werde dasselbe nie sein.* But we must put our sorrow aside. Today we stand at the doorway of a new life, free from tyranny and oppression. We will live in a new land, flowing with milk and honey. As we come into our promised land, I put before you the charge of Joshua to the people of Israel. 'Now therefore fear the LORD and serve him in sincerity and in faithfulness. Choose this day whom you will serve, whether the false gods they serve in the land beyond the sea, or the one true God who has led us through sorrow and suffering to a new day. Many of you may fall away, lured by the treasures of this new land or defeated by trials. But as for me and my house, we will serve the LORD.'"

Jonas' father stepped forward. He looked around at the somber faces. "Our desire for acceptance, for approval, is strong, and we don't always live up to the convictions that we have chosen to live by. As we come to this new land, we must repent of that, for the world cannot know of its brokenness and hopelessness without a people who show a holy way of life. The world cannot know that there is an alternative to violence and war without a people of peace making peace. The world cannot know that God cares for the weak and the vulnerable without a people practicing a lifestyle centered on ministering to those who are in need. As we go forward from this day, we move from death to life, from shadow to sunlight, from despair to hope. Let us always remember that we are Amish, and we serve a God of peace. The world cannot know the unsurpassable worth of human life without a people who consistently work to protect life— the life in all people, even those who call themselves our enemies. *Mai segnet der Lieben-Gott und begünstigt uns in dieser neuen Welt.*"

The settlers nodded in agreement. From the back of the group, someone began the slow chant of *Das Loblied*, the hymn of praise. The chorus swelled as the people joined in.

> *O Lord Father, we bless thy name,*
> *Thy love and thy goodness praise;*
> *That thou, O Lord, so graciously*
> *Have been to us always.*
> *Thou hast brought us together, O Lord,*
> *To be admonished through thy word.*
> *Bestow on us thy grace.*

Jonas felt the strong grip of his father's hand. As the words of gratitude and thanks for God's goodness lifted toward heaven, he made a promise to himself.

I will always follow the way of peace.

Chapter Two

Wings on the Wind

A young boy stood on the shore of the great river and watched the gray-green waves rush in and out between the stone sentinels, ceaselessly, tirelessly as they had since before the time his people came to *Lenapehoking*. The strap of his basket chafed his brown shoulder as he stepped from one wave-washed stone to another, looking for the mussels that clung to the rocks, hidden among the matted seaweed. He was far out from the sandy shoreline, wending his way among the pools that lay exposed at low tide. He hated this task. He longed for the day when he would be allowed to go on hunts with the warriors and join the elders at the council fire to plan raids on their enemies.

He heard a splashing sound from a pool in front of him and crept slowly to its edge. A large fish, stranded by the rapidly receding tide, lay thrashing in the shallow water. The boy waded into the pool and scooped the gasping creature onto the rocks. His mother would be pleased at this prize. Now his basket was full, and he could return to the village.

The cries of the gulls filled the air as he made his way back to the shore. They, too, were hunting the mussels that covered the rocks like black stone knives set on edge. White wings flashed in the morning sun, and the haunting sound of the birds troubled the boy and filled his heart with a strange premonition.

"Wingenund, Wingenund," the gulls seemed to be crying, "all is going away." He paused to look up at the great flock circling above the rich fishing grounds. As he looked, his gaze was drawn out over the swells to the middle of the great river. A large two-masted boat with white sails full of the morning wind was beating its way slowly against the current toward the settlement at Philadelphia. It was another of the white man's ships from *Gamenowinenk*, on the other side of the great sea.

More and more of the strangers had been coming to *Lenapehoking* and what land they could not buy from the chiefs of his tribe, they had taken outright. The hunting grounds of the tribe had been slowly shrinking, and there was much anger among the people of the Wolf Clan toward the settlers. As he stood watching, he saw someone on the deck waving to him. He did not respond but stood for a long while watching the ship move away. The unfamiliar foreboding gripped him again, and his heart was dark as he found the trail leading back to his village and began the long walk home.

When Wingenund returned to his village, he could sense something was amiss. There was much agitation among the people. When he went into his wigwam, he found his mother crying.

"Why do you weep, Mother?"

His mother lifted her head. "We must leave our village."

"But why?" This is our home."

His mother rose slowly and looked around at the articles inside the tent she would need to pack.

"I asked you why, Mother."

"The *Swannuken* have come and told us that they have found an old treaty between William Penn and the Lenape. They say the Lenape gave them the land between the two rivers as far west as a man could walk in a day and a half. Then they sent men who traveled twice as far as our sachem understood the treaty to mean. Now we must leave the Land of the Dawn."

Wingenund threw down the basket. "Are the salt-water people to rob us again? Will not the Iroquois join with us and challenge them?"

His mother shook her head. "The Iroquois are angry that our tribe signed a treaty without their permission. They have always feared us, and they are happy to see us go. They will not join with us, so we must leave the land."

"But where will we go? This is *Lenapehoking*, the land of the Lenape. We have lived here since the Lenape came from the far west to find the Land of the Dawn. What man has the right to take it from us?"

Wingenund's mother laid her hand on her son's shoulder. "We will travel toward the setting sun, into the great forest on the other side of Blue Mountain. Many of our people live there already, and we will join them in the great village of *Kithanink*. We will have new lands and better. We will forget these cheaters and liars and live among the true people."

Wingenund grabbed up his father's tomahawk and sank it into the ground at his mother's feet. "I will never forget. From this day, I declare war on all the white men. They will come to fear the name of Wingenund."

A shadow darkened the doorway of the tent. Wingenund turned to find his father, Buckongahelas, frowning at him. Buckongahelas strode forward, pulled the tomahawk out of the ground and held it in front of Wingenund. "And who are you to declare war when you have not even gone on vision quest? I am the war chief of this clan. Only when I am gone will you become chief. And only when you are chief will you have the power to say when the Wolf Clan goes to war."

"But the whites always cheat us, Father."

Buckongahelas put an arm around his son's shoulder and pointed to the doorway. "Come, walk with me, my son."

The two went out into the chill of the evening. Around them, women were preparing meals on open fires. Children ran, playing among the lodges. From deep in the woods came the sound of a courting flute as one of the young warriors of the village serenaded his intended bride. Above them the sky was rapidly shading toward dusk, the clouds marked with golden edges that were slowly fading to rose and then to purple. A flock of geese crossed the sky, their honking dim in the distance.

Wingenund walked beside Buckongahelas who was silent for a long time. Finally, his father spoke. "It is true that the white men cheat us. When the Dutchmen first came to our shores, they asked for a piece of land to grow vegetables and raise herbs. They said they needed only as much land as the hide of a bull would cover. They spread a bull hide on the ground before the Lenape to show its size. Thinking this was a reasonable request, the Lenape agreed. Immediately a Dutchman took a knife and, beginning at one place on the hide, cut it into a rope no thicker than the finger of a child. When he was done, there was a long rope. The Dutchman drew this rope out to a long distance and then brought the two ends around so that they would meet. He then claimed all the land inside the rope. The Lenape were surprised at the intelligence of the Dutchman, but since they had far more land than they needed, they granted his request."

Wingenund started to speak, but his father continued.

"We should have recognized the deceitfulness of the white man then. The Dutchman did not plant seeds on the land he took from us; he planted great guns instead, and drove the Lenape away. Then when Penn came to *Lenapehoking*; he tried to be honest with us. He offered us money for land that he said had been given to him by the king of *Gamenowinenk*."

Wingenund looked up at his father. "But how could that king give Penn land that did not belong to him?"

"That is the way of the *Swannuken*, my son. The land where they come from is divided into kingdoms, and a king rules each. The men who left there to come here have a burning desire to set up their own kingdoms and be a king here. They consider themselves to be superior to all men, and so they do not recognize that we are people also. They do not see that we have our land and our ways, and though we may be different from them, we are not less than them."

"But cannot we fight them, Father? We are strong; we could drive them away."

Buckongahelas put his arm around his son's shoulders. "The way of war is simple. Any child can make war. But wisdom is greater than war. When you are chief you will need wisdom more than you will need a warrior's skill. The lives of your people will be in your hands, and you must make decisions for all of them, not just for yourself. Consider the white man's way of war. The Indian who goes to war against another Indian fights with honor. They meet, they have one battle, and the outcome decides the quarrel. But the white man is not defeated by one battle. Instead, he sends more men and fights again. He keeps coming even when the Indian goes to his winter camp and is caring for his people. He will always keep coming. So we may win one battle now, but the white man will come back again and again until we can fight no more."

"But is there not a time when we say they will take our land no more?"

"Yes, my son, but this is not the time. We will go over the mountain to a new home. The British have promised that no white man will come there. We will see if they are telling the truth. If they are not, then we will fight. I have seen it in my dreams. The path of war is before us, but we must find a safer place for our women and children. When you have a vision, my son, then perhaps you, too, will know what lies before us."

Suddenly, Wingenund remembered the cries of the gulls. "But I did have a vision, Father. Today when I was hunting for mussels I heard the gulls. They were crying to me. I heard their voices on the wind. 'Wingenund, Wingenund, all is going away, all is going away.' I did not know what it meant, but my heart became cold. Now I know and I hate the white men for stealing our land."

Wingenund saw his father looking at him intently. Then Buckongahelas spoke. "My son, you are destined to be a great chief. I am the war chief of the Wolf Clan, and you will follow after me. Already I see strength and wisdom in you. But do not stain your life with bitterness and hatred. We must do what the sachem tells us. Tanteque marks our trails before we are even born. So it is useless to push against our path. We go to the west. Make yourself ready."

Wingenund dropped his eyes and remained silent. But inside him his heart was crying out.

I will take vengeance upon these lying whites. They will not escape my wrath.

Chapter Three

The Land and the People

Wingenund ran up the path to the sachem's wigwam. He was angry and troubled and needed to speak to the old man, to receive his wisdom.

Owechela will tell me what my vision means. He will tell me my destiny.

As he came into the small clump of trees where Owechela's wigwam stood, Wingenund stopped.

I have not brought the sachem a gift!

Quickly, the boy looked around, then he remembered the piece of maple sugar he carried in his belt from the fishing trip. He snatched it out just as the old man came out of the door of his hut. Wingenund knew that the old man never tired of his visits, especially when he brought gifts. He held out the sugar and the old man smiled. "Ah, Wingenund, my bold warrior. Bringing sweets for an old man. Come, boy, and sit by the fire with me while I warm my bones."

He motioned toward the door and ushered the boy inside. The sachem lived in a longhouse that befitted his status as great

Chief of the Lenape. Owechela pointed to one of the benches along the wall that was directly in front of one of the fire pits that ran down the center of the lodge, and Wingenund sat down. The old sachem sat next to him. The smoke from the fire drifted out through an opening in the ceiling. Corn and herbs hung from the roof, drying in the warm air. They were silent for a long time as the old man gazed at Wingenund's face. Then he spoke. "My son wears a long face. He grieves for *Lenapehoking*, the Land of the Dawn. He wishes to punish the saltwater people for stealing the land given to us by the Great Spirit."

Wingenund looked in wonder at the old man. Owechela always seemed to know everything about him, about all the children of the village. In fact, he had given Wingenund his name. The old man saw the look on the boy's face and smiled. He stretched out his hands toward the fire. "Do you know why I gave you the name, Wingenund?"

The boy shook his head.

The old man reached for his pipe. He rolled a coal out of the fire with a stick and pushed it into the pipe to light the tobacco. Then he began, "Long ago, the Lenape lived far to the west in a place by the Yellow River. They lived well until a great drought seared the land and brought much suffering and hardship to the Lenape. The great Chief Tamerand was very wise, and he knew that one day drought would come again to destroy his people. So he sought the guidance of the Great Spirit for wisdom. The Great Spirit told him to send three men, Maskansisl, Machigoloos, and Wingenund, to the Land of the Dawn where they would find a beautiful new home. Their names meant Strong Buffalo, Big Owl and Willing One. Wingenund, or Willing One, was chosen because he was willing and a priest."

The old man tapped the boy on his forehead. "I gave you the name Wingenund because willingness is what you lack most. You are not willing to do what is needed to protect your people, but it is the one character trait you must develop if you are ever to come into your destiny and be a great chief."

The boy turned to hide his frown, but the old man took Wingenund's face in his hand and turned it back until the two were looking eye-to-eye. "You turn away because you know I am right. This is a time of trouble for the Lenape. The *Swannuken* come from across the great salt water and buy and steal our lands. The Iroquois have become our enemies and are pressing us from the north. We must go over the mountain, into the great forest and build new villages for our people. I shall not live to see this great change, but you will live through a time of great trouble, and our people will need strong warriors who are also wise and willing–willing to do whatever is needed to preserve our nation."

Wingenund's mouth went dry. The thought of losing the old man hurt. "Please, Owechela, you must stay with us. We need you; I need you."

The old man smiled but said nothing and smoked his pipe quietly. After a while, he took a piece of coal out of the fire and began to write upon the floor. He first drew a circle, a little oval, to which he added four feet, a head, and a tail. "This is a tortoise, lying in the water around it and so, at first, was the world. Then the tortoise gradually raised its back up high, and the water ran off of it, and thus the earth became dry. And there grew a tree in the middle of the earth, and the root of this tree sent forth a sprout and the sprout grew into a man, who was the first male. This man was then alone, and would have remained alone; but the tree bent over until its top touched the earth, and another root came out and there grew upon it the woman, and from these two were all people produced."

Wingenund listened intently. The old man was a master storyteller and had told him the story of creation many times. In fact, the boy could recite many of the stories exactly as the old man told them. As he listened, Wingenund suddenly realized that Owechela was training him. Just then, the old man reached forward and placed both his hands on Wingenund's head. Owechela's eyes were closed and his lips moved, but there was silence in the wigwam. Wingenund held still, motionless, as the old man continued to pray silently. Then Owechela spoke.

"A mist surrounds each of us when we come into this world. As children and youth, we begin to see through the mist and look into the past to find out who we really are and where we came from. We learn of our ancestors and the past opens to us.

We learn of the forces that surround us. Because we are limited within our flesh we cannot see clearly. So we only see part of what is there. Struggles come upon us whether we want them or not. Storms rage and tear at all that we hold to be true. In turn, we fight the forces that rage around us, or we yield and are conquered by them. Our one path is the path of truth. Even though we cannot see clearly, from time to time a seed of truth appears in the mist, and we must reach out to grasp it and then plant it in our hearts. We must always seek truth. Only truth can free us from ignorance and darkness and let us see what lies ahead."

The old man paused; his hands still on Wingenund's head, and then the soft voice spoke again. "I see the path that lies ahead for this one. He shall be a defender of his people and a force for life and hope. Blood and death shall rage about him, but he shall not be killed. Strange ones shall come to him. He shall have a child that he will love as he loves his own life, but the child will seem to turn away from the path of the Lenape. But the Great Spirit is guiding all, and one shall come to the 'willing one' who shall make all the stories and all the legends of the Lenape become clear at last. The child whom he loves will lead him to the greatest truth and, though all seems dark around him, a great light will shine in his heart. The arrow and bow shall fall from his hand and his voice shall be the voice of peace, for he shall speak the words of the greatest one who shines through all the darkness. And then this one shall use the truth as a hunter uses the sight on his gun. He shall aim his life by the truth. But before he knows the truth, he will know great pain, sorrow, and loss. For he is the 'willing one', and, in time, he will learn to be willing to bear the burden of his people with a true heart."

Owechela stopped. He took his hands off Wingenund's head and smiled. "Now you are a man, Wingenund, and your life will not be the same. I have taught you the stories so that the Lenape will depend on you to preserve their past. You must remember every story I have taught you and never forget. But you must also become a hunter and a warrior. You must learn the tongues of the saltwater people who have come to our land so they cannot offer friendship with one hand and lies with the other. Tomorrow you will leave *Lenapehoking* for the dark lands to the west. You will never return. Your path will lead through fire and battle, but you must remain strong and remember all that I have taught you. And in your time of greatest sorrow, you will remember the words I spoke to you today. You will remember old Owechela and the day that I spoke the words of manhood over you. And in the end, you will find the peace that you seek."

The old man turned to the fire and spread his hands again. Wingenund knew that all had been said and it was time for him to go. Silently, he rose and went out from the wigwam. Owechela did not turn or ever speak to him again.

The gray of dawn was pushing the stars back to their resting place, and the indigo heavens were surrendering to the slowly awakening sky. Wingenund stood at the door of the family wigwam, listening to the voices of *Lenapehoking* speaking around him. The first blush of pink began to spread over the land, and the trill of a songbird broke the solemn stillness. Far off on a hill, an elk bugled and finally the top of the sun rose over the hills to the east, and all of nature took its first breath. A small breeze shook the leaves of the ackmatuck trees, but Wingenund's heart was heavy within him. It had been two days since Owechela spoke over him, and now the old man was dead. He had passed a few hours after the boy had left him, and his voice would never touch the councils of the Lenape again. He heard his mother stirring inside the hut as she gathered the last few possessions and wrapped them up for the journey. Then she appeared in the door of the wigwam with the large bundle on her back, the tumpline that supported it already digging into her forehead. Wingenund picked up his bundle and together mother and son walked out of the village. Behind them the rest of the women and children followed. The men had gone ahead to blaze a trail and their path headed straight toward the west. Behind them, the sun rose into the sky, but the chill fall wind kept it from warming them. Silently, the procession made its way into the forest. Wingenund walked alone at the head of the people, his thoughts turning over the many words Owechela had spoken:

"Days of war and bloodshed lie ahead, great sorrow but also great light."

Wingenund kicked at a pebble.

Ah, this morning I feel the mist gather about me, and I cannot see my way.

Wingenund sighed and tried to concentrate on the trail before him. Then the hatred for the whites rose in his heart again until he almost choked. He knew the bitterness would displease Owechela, but the old man was no longer there to warn him. The miles fell behind them, and after many hours, Wingenund did not recognize the forest they were walking through. Soon they reached a point where Wingenund stopped and looked back one last time, but he could no longer see where his village lay.

So passed the Lenape from the blessed homeland of *Lenapehoking.* As he turned to the west, the boy spoke out loud. "Oh, Owechela, how I wish you were here to guide me. I do not have the wisdom of Chief Tamerand or the willingness of the first Wingenund. I feel that I will fail my people. Can't you speak to me from out of the mists and tell me what I must do?"

But no answer came. Only the crunching sound of the fallen leaves beneath his feet as he walked the path of sorrow.

Chapter Four

The Land and the Promise

The setting sun was disappearing below a sheen of blue mist that hung along the ridgeline of the mountains. Glorious streams of orange lit the undersides of the higher clouds as if an unseen hand had layered the brilliant colors across a heavenly canvas. The tops of the mountains were slowly darkening, and the thick forest began to blend together along the rocky heights until all was blue and mysterious. Far to the north some errant rain clouds drifted a mist onto the forest below, but directly above, all was clear. There was a bite in the air that presaged another storm to come, but this day was marking its departure with a magnificent display. The rain from yesterday still dripped silently from the branches of the white pine trees, and the ranks of maple trees among the hemlocks and pines set fire to the somber silence of the woods.

Jonas Hershberger walked along the banks of Northkill Creek. Behind him lay the small settlement of the Northkill Amish. The mighty bulk of the mountain ran away to the north and south along the creek. Beyond the mountain was the Indian land, but settlers were already pushing to the west and Jonas had heard his father talking in hushed whispers to his *maam* about the possibility of trouble with the natives. Jonas followed the creek's course up toward the gap in the summit of the ridge. He often thought about what lay on the other side, but his *daed* had forbidden him to go anywhere outside the valley where their new home lay.

He was thinking about the day they had come to the Northkill settlement along with other passengers from the *Charming Nancy*. A few hours after they arrived, Jonas and his father walked along Northkill creek. Every few steps Mathias would dig at the soft soil with his shoe or look around at the healthy crops that the earlier settlers had put in during the summer. At one point, Mathias picked Jonas up and set him on his big shoulder. He pointed down the valley. "This is a rich land and the fields are white for the harvest. The corn is tall and strong, and the vegetables are healthy and large. *Es ist sehr gut.*"

Mathias began to explain how they would rotate the crops from year to year to keep the soil fertile. He bent down and scooped up a handful of soil and held it up for Jonas to smell. It was rich and dark and smelled of forest and grass and manure.

"It almost smells sweet, Papa."

Mathias smiled as he tossed the handful of dirt away. "The land here is full of promise. It will help us continue our old world way of life, but it will also provide stability in our new land. As long as we have the land, we can provide for our families, and our way of life will go on and on. We become one with the land, working hard, pushing our bodies to the limits, and yet, even as we struggle, we rejoice in the power we have as masters of our world; a world given to us by a loving God who shows us the way and walks before us—a cloud by day and a pillar of flame by night."

Jonas looked up at his father in surprise. It was not often that Mathias waxed eloquent, and the boy began to feel his father's connection to the land and through his father, his own connection. "Will I be a farmer too, Papa?"

Mathias set his son down and turned back toward the settlement. "That is for *unser liebender Gott* to decide, *mein sohn.*

You are so young; it is hard to know what your destiny holds. This new country holds great promise, and for now, it seems to be in farming, but we cannot tell what the future holds."

Jonas had been puzzled by his father's vague response to his question. *Of course I will be a farmer! What else is there to do?*

That had been two months ago, but his father's answer had not left his mind. So today, as he walked along the creek bank, his mind was not fully on his task. Jonas had been looking for Lotte, the Hershberger's wandering *kuh*. Somehow the cow had figured out how to get the gate to the simple corral open. This was the third time Lotte had escaped, and Jonas, as the youngest, had been assigned the task of finding her. He had followed the animal's tracks out of the barnyard and down along the stream, and he knew that she was not far ahead for her leavings were still steaming in the cold air. After their arrival, his family had purchased two hundred acres along the creek from Melchoir Detweiler, and the cow had come with the land. Already, with the help of neighbors, the Hershbergers had erected a one-room cabin where the whole family slept and ate. *Maam* had hung blankets to give some degree of privacy, and the family had fallen into the never-ceasing cycle of early rising, working on the land, sitting together over a plain but nourishing supper, and going to bed long after dark.

Jonas' papa had managed to save enough silver from the sale of their gristmill in Lomersheim to purchase supplies for the winter when they arrived, so with that concern out of the way, Mathias and his older sons were concentrating on felling trees and cutting boards to add more rooms to the cabin and frame up a building on the creek. The elder Hershberger planned to grind flour for the settlers, so he had plenty of willing helpers.

Jonas loved their new home. The forest was filled with wild animals, and often at night he heard the mournful scream of a mountain lion on the hunt. The settlers often found deer and elk grazing right in their fields, which meant fresh meat on the table. Jonas' father was a crack shot with the rifle, and he was already teaching his youngest son the way of the hunter. Jonas' brother Amos had already bagged an elk and the hide was being stretched and dried on the side of the cabin. On Sundays, all the settlers met at the Detweiler cabin since it was the only one large enough to accommodate all the families. One of the brethren would bring out the *Ausbund* and the congregation would sing *das loblied*, the ancient hymn of praise. Jonas loved the sound of the slow unaccompanied singing of the hymns. His father had told him that their songbook was over two hundred years old and was a symbol of God's grace in protecting their order down through the years. The music and the history of his people stirred Jonas deeply, and as he walked along, he began to sing the hymn of praise.

> *O Lord Father, we bless thy name,*
> *Thy love and thy goodness praise…*

Jonas was so intent on watching for signs of Lotte that he did not notice how far he had gone along the trail. A sense of heading downhill broke into his reverie, and the words of the hymn faded on his lips. The trail dropped away below him. He had crossed over the forbidden line of the ridge top and was now on Indian lands. Then, just ahead, he heard the clang of Lotte's bell. He hurried around a corner in the trail and lurched to a halt. The cow stood docilely under a stand of larch trees. Beside her stood a young Indian boy. The boy had looped a braided leather thong around the cow's neck and was pulling the resistant animal toward the woods. A hot flush rushed over Jonas' face. He yelled at the top of his voice.

"Hey, that's my cow."

The boy jumped in surprise and slowly turned to Jonas. He stood silently and then shrugged his shoulders. Then he said something in his own tongue and continued to lead the cow up the path. Jonas ran up, grabbed the thong, and jerked it.

"You can't just steal someone else's property. That's a sin."

The boy's eyes narrowed and he pointed back down the trail. *"Kta! Kta!"*

Jonas didn't know what do to. He was about the same size as the Indian lad, but the boy did not appear ready to release the cow, and Jonas did not know if he could make him. He felt anger slowly filling his heart like the tide coming in. He raised his fists and advanced toward the boy. "I don't know what you are saying, but that is our cow and I'm taking her back."

The boy reached into his waistband and then a dangerous looking knife was in his hand. He beckoned to Jonas with the other hand. "*Mahtake!*" The meaning was perfectly clear.

Jonas glanced around and saw a stout looking branch lying on the ground. He grabbed it up and then the two boys were facing each other with their weapons in their hands, breathing heavily. They slowly began circling each other, looking for an opening. Suddenly, they heard a twig snap in the woods. The Indian boy glanced away and Jonas took advantage. He rushed in and swung a hard blow at the boy's head. Just in time, the Indian boy leaped away, but as he did, Jonas' club caught him on the shoulder and tumbled him onto his back. Jonas rushed forward, planted his feet, and raised the club above his head.

"Jonas, stop!"

His father's voice cut like a knife and Jonas froze.

"What are you doing to that boy?"

Jonas slowly lowered his club and turned to his papa. "He was stealing Lotte, Papa."

Mathias took the branch from Jonas' hand and threw it down. He took Jonas by the shoulder and the grip of his strong hand hurt. "And you were going to resort to violence to solve the problem? That is against everything we know. You must not fight with anyone; it is forbidden by the *ordnung*."

The Indian boy had jumped up and there was hatred in his eyes. He pointed to the cow. "*Ni yuni.*" He held the knife up.

Jonas looked around for his club, but his father's foot held it to the ground. Mathias held out a hand in a gesture of peace. "What is your name, boy?"

The boy shook his head.

Mathias pointed to himself. "Mathias, Mathias." Then he pointed to Jonas. "Jonas, Jonas." Then he pointed back to the boy.

The Indian lad drew himself up. "Wingenund." He brandished the knife.

Jonas twisted in his father's grasp, but he could not break free. "Papa, that is Lotte, our *kuh*. He has no right to steal her. You must take her back."

Mathias looked down and Jonas could read great disappointment on his papa's face. His father looked at Wingenund. "You will not give us the cow?" He held out his hand.

Wingenund shook his head. "*Ntayalëmska!*" He turned and walked out of the clearing and back down the trail that led into the heart of the Indian territory. Lotte followed docilely along.

"Papa!!"

Mathias watched the cow disappear into the forest. He sighed and then turned back toward the settlement. "No matter what, *mein sohn*, you must never use violence to get what you want. The Lord commands us so, and if you want to follow our ways, you must obey. Now come."

Jonas looked after the Indian once more, but the lad and the cow had disappeared. A great anger came over him, but then shame followed. He was being unfaithful to Jesus and his commandments. He took a deep breath. "I am sorry, Papa. You are right. Violence is not the way."

Together the two Hershbergers walked down the hill into the darkness.

Part Two

Drums Along the Border

In 1754 a bitter conflict over territory between the French and the British erupted into open conflict. The war was fought primarily along the frontiers between New France and the British colonies and was centered in western Pennsylvania. The English made allies of the Iroquois Indians, traditional enemies of the Lenape, and the Lenape, including Wingenund's tribe, allied with the French.

Over the next nine years, fire and death raged along the border. Finally, the English defeated the French, and Wingenund's family was forced further west into the Ohio territory. Once the war was over, Jonas, his wife, and five children moved to Fort Pitt in western Pennsylvania, near the Ohio border, to set up a gristmill and take up land.

It is in this setting that the families of my ancestors became irrevocably bound together in an inspiring tale of love and hate, bitter, sorrow, and great joy.

Drums Along the Border
From The Journals of Jenny Hershberger

Chapter Five

The Arrows of War

Wingenund stood before the gathered tribal leaders—men and women of the Lenni-Lenape. The fire burning in the center of the great longhouse cast dancing shadows on the walls. Wingenund was now a great chief. Although still young, he had achieved renown as a warrior. Since he had come to the town of Kithanink, his skill with the rifle, the bow and arrow, and the ways of war had made him a leader. When his father, Buckongahelas, had been killed in a raid against the Iroquois, the role of war chief had fallen naturally upon his shoulders.

In the years since he made his first coup against the whites, he had grown tall and strong. He stood before the people with a long gray mantle trimmed with wolf fur wrapped close about his striking figure. His war bonnet, which trailed to the ground, was made of white eagle plumes with black-pointed tips.

Silence fell on the people as they waited to hear his judgment. At his side sat an Oneida chief, Scarrooyady, and a Mohawk, Cayanguileguoa, from the Six Nations of the Iroquois. They had come to tell the Lenape of a treaty they had made with the whites and to enjoin them to bury the hatchet and make alliance with the British. Wingenund looked at them and then spoke. The contempt was plain in his voice.

"Wingenund's ears are keen; they have heard a feather fall in the storm; now they hear the hiss of serpents. Wingenund says to his people, 'Do not bury the hatchet!' These men before you have smooth tongues. Their words speak of peace and comfort; the words flow easily like the mighty river that flows beside our great village. But Wingenund does not hear their voices or their words. He hears the voices of his warriors who lay dead in the forest, their eyes put out by whites to keep them blind in the afterlife. He hears the heart of *Lenapehoking* crying to him. 'I am your homeland. Why have you abandoned me to the saltwater people?' He hears the lament of the women for warriors who will never return. He hears the voice of the gulls on the shores of *Lenapehoking* warning him to beware of the white man."

Wingenund turned and pointed to the two Iroquois chiefs. "These men speak of peace. In the days of long ago, when Wingenund's forefathers heard not the paleface's axe, they lived in peace. They waged no wars. A white dove sat in every wigwam. *Lenapehoking* was theirs, given to them by the Great Spirit, and they were rich. The paleface came with his sickness, his burning firewater, his ringing axe, and the homeland of the Lenape was stolen forever. Wingenund has grown to be a man among his warriors; he loves them; he fears for them. Wingenund says to his people that our day is over, and if we must die, we will not die as women, but as men; defending our homeland, fighting for our women and children, and standing before the white man and these dogs of Iroquois and saying you may take no more of our land unless it is over the dead bodies of the Lenape nation."

Wingenund stepped back into the shadows and there was great silence in the longhouse. Then the renowned chief, Glickhican, rose from where he was sitting next to Shingas, the great Lenape chief. His eagle eye swept the gathered people, and then he walked slowly to where Wingenund stood. He turned and faced the Iroquois chiefs. His words rolled from his tongue with power and dignity. "We are the Lenape. We were a peaceful people. When the saltwater people came, we sat in council with our friends, the Iroquois of the Six Nations. There was much talk and many promises. The whites offered money and told us they only needed some land by the great salt sea to grow their crops and establish trade with us. We sold them some land, but they claimed we sold them much more than we intended. They cheated us. And then more settlers came in ships and soon *Lenapehoking* was overrun. Our brothers, the Iroquois, betrayed us and helped the *Swannukens* steal our land.

"Then these settlers pushed their way to the west, and soon the Kittochtinny Valley was taken from us. Now they invade the Juniata Valley. We made complaint of the aggressions. The Six Nations, pretending to be our brothers, stood up in council with the whites and declared that taking the lands they had guaranteed to their cousins, the Lenape, as a sacred hunting ground, was a breach of faith, and that the settlers must be removed or the Lenape would take up the hatchet against them. The white government issued proclamations, warning squatters to keep off these lands, but they did nothing to stop them. This stealing of land and the arrogance with which the settlers treated us now grows to grind us like a heavy stone. These Iroquois come, again telling us they are our brothers. They say they will make a great treaty for us. But they are liars and dogs that care not for the Lenape. Our French fathers have defeated Washington and they ask us to join them in the fight against the British. We will join our French fathers, who are strong, and bury the hatchet of war in the heads of the British. We will burn their forts and drive their settlers from our land."

Glickhican reached out and took up a large war club leaning against the wall. He stood before Scarrooyady and Cayanguileguoa, staring down at them. Wingenund watched as the great chief swung the club down with a terrible force at the feet of the Iroquois. His voice rang out. "Death to the British!"

One by one, the leaders of the Lenape came forward: Shingas, then the war chief, Captain Jacobs, followed by others. Each one took up the club and swung it into the ground at the feet of the visiting chiefs. "Death, death, death."

It was many months since the great council of war. Wingenund stood on the battlefield on the banks of the Monongahela. Around him were scattered bodies of British soldiers. One of his braves approached. The warrior had a bloody cut on his face and held a sword in his hand. "Braddock is defeated. I took this from him. Washington has carried Braddock's body from the field. Our French brothers joined us in a great victory. The rest of the British have fled to Great Meadows. Should we follow them?"

Wingenund gazed across the field. "No. Let Washington take his troops and depart. He will tell the story of the might of the Lenape and their French brothers. They will not soon return. Now we will go south to Juniata Island and drive those men back to the east side of the mountains. Come!" Wingenund turned and strode away. His warriors, some of them wearing the red coats of the British and holding up fresh scalps, followed him into the woods.

Wingenund stood before a group of cowering captives in the great longhouse at Kithanink. They were women and children and a few men. Wingenund held up a tomahawk and shook it before their faces. The men cried out and the women and children gave shrieks of terror. Wingenund laughed and turned to his braves. "There is no difference between the men and women of this fallen race. We have burned their fort and killed many settlers. They have fled the valley of the Juniata like the dogs they are. We will take these captives and send them to our French fathers at Fort Duquesne. Now the saltwater people have learned of the terrible wrath of the Lenape."

Just then a warrior burst into the longhouse. "Soldiers, many soldiers are attacking the village."

Wingenund looked at the captives. He turned to the warrior. "Take these to the French fort. We will defend the village." He beckoned his other braves and ran outside. Gunshots sounded from the east side of the village. The chief, Shingas, and Captain Jacobs came around the end of the hut. Shingas pointed toward the sound of the rifles. "Wingenund, they are too many for us. You must take your wife and go to the French fort. I will follow. Captain Jacobs will stay and hold the soldiers as long as he can."

Wingenund gripped his friend's arm. "I will not flee; I will stay with you and die like a warrior."

Captain Jacobs shook his head. "No, my son. You are the greatest of our warriors. You must take the young men and flee to fight another day. Go with Shingas. I am old and my voice among the people grows soft. Lead our people and take vengeance upon these whites." Captain Jacobs turned back and rallied a few of the older men around him. They rushed off toward the sound of firing.

Wingenund ran to his wigwam. His wife stood at the door with a hatchet in her hand and a grim look on her face. Wingenund took her by the arm. "Spring of Water, you must gather our things and come with me. We are leaving Kithanink. The soldiers are too many for us."

Spring of Water went into the wigwam and began packing their most needed goods. Wingenund stood by the door watching for soldiers. The sound of gunshots was drawing nearer. Spring of Water came to the door with a bundle on her back. A few tears were running down her face. They did not look back as they walked quickly out of the village. Other warriors and their families joined them as they went. Wingenund could hear shouting and suddenly there was a great explosion. He paused at the top of the hill and looked back. A great plume of smoke was roiling up from the part of the village where Captain Jacobs' hut was located. Wingenund shook his head sadly. "That explosion was the powder stored in Captain Jacobs' lodge. I am afraid our great chief has died defending the village."

Wingenund and his wife stood silently, watching as the village began to burn. They could hear the screeches of the warriors and the shouts of the soldiers. Soon, a great cloud of smoke hung over the valley. Spring of Water took hold of her husband's arm. "I was hoping that our baby would be born in this peaceful place."

Wingenund turned to his wife. "Our baby?"

"Yes, Wingenund, I am with child. The midwives say that it will be a daughter."

Wingenund frowned. "And how do they know?"

Spring of Water pointed to a blemish on her face. "The old women say that a girl baby steals your beauty. That is why I have this spot on my cheek."

Wingenund turned to his warriors. "Even in death, the Great Spirit gives us promise of life. We will go to the land of the setting sun. Our brothers in Ohio will welcome us. My daughter will be born, and she will be a princess of our people. I see a great future and a great family that will spring from her loins. Now let us go into the forest and live to fight another day." Then, for a moment, he paused.

Spring of Water looked at him. "What is it, husband?"

Wingenund was remembering the words of Owechela, spoken over a young boy so long ago.

"The child whom he loves will lead him to the greatest truth and, though all seems dark around him, a great light will shine in his heart. The arrow and bow shall fall from his hand and his voice shall be the voice of peace, for he shall speak the words of the greatest one who shines through all the darkness."

Wingenund turned to go. "It is nothing, nothing…"

The Indians filed silently onto the trail, and one by one they disappeared into the woods. Wingenund was the last to leave. He stared down on the great village of Kithanink that had been his home for so long. A great sadness filled him. He remembered his vow on the day his family had been driven from *Lenapehoking*. "I will never forget. I will bury my hatchet in many settlers and take many scalps. My name will be feared all along the frontier. Owechela was wrong." He shook his fist at the soldiers gathering below and then turned and vanished into the forest.

Below in the village, more buildings exploded. The remaining warriors put up a stout defense but soon they were overwhelmed. Captain Jacobs was killed and scalped after jumping from his home in an attempt to escape the flames. Even as Wingenund sought refuge in the forest, the remaining defenders were rounded up and shot. The battle ended when the entire village was engulfed in flames. The soldiers set about scalping the dead Indians and rounding up the livestock and stores. By midday the village of Kithanink was no more.

Chapter Six

Sons of Thunder, Daughter of Peace

It was late spring in 1753. Jonas Hershberger paced back and forth in front of the plain log cabin. From inside came the shrieks of his wife. Jonas' face was pale and sweat ran down from his brow. His brother, Amos, took him by the arm. *"Für ängstlich sein, nichts aber in allem, was mit Danksagung…"*

Jonas shook him off. *"Ja, ja, ich weiß*, Amos. Be anxious for nothing but in all things with thanksgiving… Well, that's not your wife in there screaming!"

Amos laughed. "They all sound like that. It's the curse of God on women to have trouble in childbirth. Eve should have left that fruit well enough alone. Now we men have to stand outside and hear them yell as they bring our children into the world." Amos pushed Jonas away from the house. "Would you please go milk your cow or tend your crops—anything to keep your mind off this. I promise you it will be over soon."

Jonas wiped his brow with a cloth from his pocket and smiled. *"Ja, Amos, du hast Recht.* It's just that it's my first child, and I am worried for Martha."

Just then there was a great howl of anguish from inside the house and then silence. Jonas rushed toward the door, but Amos grabbed him. Suddenly, the silence was broken by the cry of a baby. Amos slapped Jonas on the back. "You see, brother, all is…"

Before he could finish, Martha cried out again. This time Jonas pulled himself away from Amos and ran into the house. The midwife was standing by the bed with a screaming baby wrapped in a blanket. "My baby…my wife…what has happened?"

"Your babies, husband."

Jonas turned to Martha. She too had a bundle, but this baby lay quietly in Martha's arms.

Jonas stared in amazement. "Two babies? *Was ist denn hier los?*"

The midwife brought the screaming child to Jonas. "Yes, Brother Hershberger, you have two fine sons."

Jonas took the baby into his arms, but his son continued to yell lustily. The midwife shook her head. "This baby was born first, but it was very strange what happened."

Jonas looked at her. "Tell me what happened."

The midwife pointed to the other baby in Martha's arms. She walked over to the bed and lifted the baby's arm. There was a piece of string tied around it. "I have been watching Martha these past weeks, and I noticed a struggle in Martha's womb, but I did not know there were twins. I just thought the baby was restless, but it was the two babies fighting. When Martha was about to deliver, one of the babies put out a hand. I was reminded of the story of Pharez in the Bible so I tied a string around the baby's wrist. Then the baby pulled back and the other baby with no string on it came out first." The midwife picked up the quiet one. "This baby should have been the first born of your sons, but the other usurped his place."

Jonas puzzled over the woman's story. He knelt down by the bed and laid the crying baby beside Martha. Then he took his wife's hand. "*Wie fühlen Sie sich, Frau?*"

His wife was pale and her hair was plastered to the sides of her face, but she squeezed his hand. "I am fine, Jonas—very tired, but fine. The midwife did a good job. Your sons are born and they are strong." She held out her arms and the midwife placed the quiet son back into them. Martha pulled the crying baby close to her, and he began to quiet. She looked at both her boys and held them close. "Now, we must choose names for them."

Jonas looked at his sons. He thought for a moment and then he spoke. "The quiet one shall be named Joshua after he who came first into the Promised Land. The unruly one shall be named Jonathan, after the bold son of Saul. It was Jonathan who climbed the cliff and won the battle against the Philistines with only his armor-bearer to help. This one has already proved that he is impetuous and headstrong. I pray that his brother shall be a guide to him in the days to come, for I feel that Joshua will live in wisdom and peace. It was Joshua who told the people, 'as for me and my house, we shall serve the Lord.'"

Martha smiled her approval. "Yes, husband, those are fine names. Now go about your chores while I feed them."

Jonas left the house and began to walk down the path, looking up at the heavens. His brother caught up with him. "And so, brother, the baby is fine?"

"Not baby, Amos, babies, for there are two fine sons."

Amos' mouth opened in surprise and then he laughed. "Two fine sons to help in the fields."

Jonas frowned. "I am the youngest son, brother. There will be no fields for me here, for Papa cannot divide his land among all five of us. No, I must go west."

Amos grabbed his brother's arm and stopped him. "Surely you will not go now. The border is aflame. The Delaware have joined with the French and already they bring fire and death on the settlements to the west of us. No, you cannot take your family there."

Jonas looked toward the pass, over the mountain. He could see the place where Wingenund had taken the cow from him all those years ago. "I know I must wait, brother, but all wars end. At some point the British will defeat the French and the Delaware will be forced further west."

"How do you know this, Jonas?"

Jonas shrugged. "There are only 75,000 French in all of the colonies. The British supporters number over two million, from New York to the Carolinas. No, the French cannot win this struggle."

"Still, Jonas, it will take the British a while. It is reported the governor is sending George Washington to demand that the French give up their claims and their forts. We will see what happens then."

"I think you are right, Amos. I do not think the French will give up so easily. And the Indians hate us so. But still, one day the British will be victorious, and then I will go."

"Well, until then, we should give thanks for the birth of your sons and the health of your good wife."

The two men knelt by the path to pray for Jonas' sons. As they knelt, Jonas had a strange feeling, like a voice in his spirit. "Your house will be divided, and your two sons will each find a different path." Jonas looked around but only his brother was there. He returned to prayer, but his heart was troubled.

A soft rain muted the sounds of the forest and a hush was on the valley. The first rays of the sun broke through the morning fog and lit the woods with a golden light. Streams of mist rose from the beaver pond and the vapor was cool and refreshing upon Wingenund's skin as he made his silent way between the trees. Above him, a black squirrel barked a warning and the warrior stopped and held still. In the soft ground before him were the clear outlines of a deer's hooves. Fresh droppings still steamed, and Wingenund knew he was close behind his prey. The squirrel ceased his chattering and leapt away among the branches. The birds were singing their songs, and peace lay upon the land. Wingenund walked on until he came to a glade. The majestic oaks mingled with the tall pines and spread a wonderful canopy over the small meadow. The freshness of spring filled the air, and Wingenund's heart was unburdened for the moment.

As he stepped into the glade, he looked ahead and then stopped in amazement. At the end of the grassy swale stood the deer he had been tracking. But this deer was not the tawny brown of the deer he hunted so often in the wilderness of the Ohio. The deer was a doe and it was pure white, from the tip of its nose to the white tail, raised like a flag. As Wingenund watched, unmoving, the deer looked up, then slowly picked its way across the glade until it stood directly in front of the warrior. A great stillness came upon the woods as Wingenund stood staring into the deep pools of the white deer's eyes. The bow and arrow dropped from his hands. The lovely animal looked up at Wingenund without fear, almost as if she were speaking to him.

They stood that way for a long time. Then the deer turned and stepped off the trail into the woods and slowly moved away among the trees. A small breeze sprang up and the sun burst over the horizon, directly into Wingenund's eyes. He was blinded for a moment, and when he recovered, the birds were singing brightly; the mist had fled before the wind, and the white deer had vanished. Wingenund stooped to pick up his bow. On the ground was a tuft of white hair. He picked it up and stared at it in awe. Then he gathered up his weapons and hurried back toward the village.

As he made his way toward his lodge, one of the women came to him. "It is Spring of Water's time. The baby is coming."

Wingenund shook his head. "But she is early. The old women said she was not due until the coming of the full moon."

The woman smiled. "Be that as it may, my chief, the baby is coming now."

Wingenund felt a strange chill pass over him. He walked quickly into the village with the woman trailing behind. At the door of his lodge, Glickhican, the great sachem of the Lenape, stood with his arms crossed. The old man stopped Wingenund. "There are great portents in the air today, my son. Your daughter is being born on a very auspicious day. I had a dream last night. A white deer came to me and told me of a princess who would bring the way of peace to her people."

Wingenund stared at the sachem. "A white deer? I saw a white deer in the forest this morning, and she had no fear. When

I saw her I knew that something of great importance would happen today."

Glickhican nodded. "Did the white deer speak to you?"

"No, but somehow I knew her coming was about my daughter."

The old man sighed. "Yes, that is what the deer in my dreams said. Your daughter has come to us at a great junction in the trail of the Lenape. Her own life will be difficult, but she will show the way of peace to our people, and she will answer the question the story of our people asks of the whites."

"What question, my sachem?"

"The *Wallum Olum,* the book of our people, ends with the coming of the whites to *Lenapehoking* and asks, 'Who are they?' It is said in the book that the men with pale skin will offer two paths to the Lenape—the way of life, or the way of death. If the Lenape will not listen to the way of life, then our people will be uprooted and sent to a far land by the pale skinned people. It is your daughter who will see both faces of the white man—the way of life and the way of death, and it is she who will offer this choice to our people."

Glickhican turned and walked away, leaving Wingenund at the door of his lodge. Suddenly from within, came a woman's scream and then a baby cried. But the little one cried only for a moment. Wingenund entered. His wife lay on the bed of boughs and skins, the baby by her side. The old women of the village began a chant of greeting to the new one. Spring of Water held up the baby, and Wingenund took her. The baby was perfect, and already a crown of raven-black hair covered her head. But the baby's most striking feature was her eyes. They were the same dark pools that Wingenund had looked into that morning when he met the white deer. He held the baby up, offering her to the Great Spirit. "Her name shall be Opahtuhwe, the White Deer of her people. She will help us to find the true path of peace. She will show us who the white man really is. And her people will love her."

Chapter Seven

The Bonds of Destiny
April 1764

Jonas Hershberger stood at the top of the hill and looked down on the Northkill Settlement. Below him, the road wound back through the trees. The forest was alive with songbirds, and the morning breeze stirred the palette of wildflowers that were in bloom everywhere. Pink clouds floated above him as the morning sun touched the day with streamers of golden light. Jonas could hear the gobbling of a flock of wild turkeys in a stand of hemlocks away down the hill, and several deer were stepping gracefully across the meadow at the top of the rise. In between the dark pines, Jonas could see flashes of red from the peeling, shaggy bark of the cedar trees.

Jonas had grown to love this beautiful valley. He had spent many happy hours hunting in the forest or climbing the mountain behind their farm. He had toiled in the fields alongside his brothers and learned to take pride in abundant harvest. He had labored long at his father's mill. The beauty of the fall and the mildness of the winters, the bursting forth of life in the spring and the long peaceful summers were etched upon his memory indelibly. Thirteen years earlier, Bishop Jacob Hertzler had arrived and their community became the leading Amish settlement in all of Pennsylvania. It had been the only home he really remembered. He had grown up here.

This place had once been forbidden Indian Territory, but now white settlers mostly populated it. It was here that the boy named Wingenund had taken his cow, and the fruit of that confrontation had been Jonas' unyielding decision to follow the non-violent ways of his people. He sighed as he recalled that day. His reverie was broken when Martha called to him from the wagon.

"Jonas, you love this place. Why are we leaving?"

He looked over at the wagon. The canvas sides were rolled up, and his twin sons were up on the driver's seat. As usual, they were arguing: this time over who was to hold the reins. Aaron, his youngest son, was playing with the dog next to the wagon. The four red oxen stood patiently, waiting to be on the move again. Martha sat in the back with his daughters. He could hear the girls sniffling as they wept quietly. It had taken many months for Jonas to persuade his wife and family to leave their home, and now he turned with a frown and walked back to the wagon.

"Martha, I've explained this many times. I am the youngest of five sons. I have no inheritance here. My only future is as a hired hand on a farm belonging to my oldest brother or working in my father's mill."

"But, Jonas, my father would divide his land between you and my brother. Wouldn't that satisfy you?"

"Your father's farm is smaller than my father's. What will we do when our sons are grown? I want to go where there will be room for them to take up land. Martha, look down there."

Jonas pointed to the valley. All along the creek and out onto the land surrounding it there were cabins and houses. Smoke from the chimneys clouded the bright spring air. As far as Jonas could see, the land was under cultivation.

"It's all gone, Martha. There is no room for our sons to grow and have their own farms. They would have to leave here, so we might as well go first and blaze a trail for them in a new land. We have an opportunity at Fort Pitt. Many settlers are moving in, and they need a miller. There is much open land along the Ohio. We can have a large farm and my sons can be part of the building of a new country."

Jonas climbed up on the wagon seat and shook the reins. The oxen started and the wagon began to roll down the old trail, now a broad road into the once-forbidden land of the Lenapes.

"Aren't you afraid of Indians, husband?"

Jonas shook his head. "No, Martha, the Delaware tribes left years ago. The white people treated them very unfairly, and now the Indians are gone. The treaties that Penn made with the tribes long ago were set aside or broken by his sons. With the help of the Iroquois tribes, the British have pushed the Lenape far out to the west."

"But, Jonas, won't they give us trouble when we get there?"

"Martha, we are not going that far. We are going to a British fort that is still in Pennsylvania; Fort Pitt. A new city is springing up there, and it is a fertile area where there is much land available for settlers. They have soldiers that defend the incomers and the Indians have withdrawn into the wilderness."

"But, Jonas, we are Amish. Won't they ask us to take up arms to defend ourselves?"

Jonas turned to his wife and put his arm around her. "So many questions, my dearest. There are many settlers and traders moving through and they need flour. We can build a mill on the river and have our homestead right there within a short distance of the fort."

Martha shook her head. "It makes me very anxious, Jonas. I don't like change at all."

Jonas sighed. "'Be anxious for nothing, Martha, but in every thing by prayer and supplication with thanksgiving let your requests be made known unto God. And the peace of God, which passeth all understanding, shall keep your heart and mind through Christ Jesus.'"

Martha nodded her head in agreement with Jonas' words. "I try not to be a *zweifler*, Jonas, but I can't help doubting sometimes. I need to trust you are hearing from *Gott* and put my fears aside."

"*Ja*, my dearest, that it is exactly so. *Sie müssen Ihre Ängste beiseite.*"

Jonas shook the reins and the oxen picked up their pace. They had many miles to go.

Many days later they halted their wagon at the top of the hill above Fort Pitt. From the high bank where they stopped, the land ran downhill and narrowed gradually until it ended in a sharp point that marked the last piece of land between the Allegheny and Monongahela rivers. Here, the two streams merged and formed the broad Ohio. The newborn river flowed around a wide curve and disappeared between heavily forested banks. On the narrow point of land commanding a view of the three rivers stood the long, low pentagonal fort built of earth and brick. The massive fortifications, the surrounding ditch filled with water from the river, and the small gun ports cut into the brick-faced walls gave the structure a reassuringly impregnable look.

It had been a hard journey, and their difficulties were compounded when their youngest girl fell sick with fever. The Hershbergers were forced to stop and camp along the trail until the child was better. While they were there, a group of settlers who were going to build a settlement a few miles downstream from Fort Pitt traveled by, and the Hershbergers joined their wagon train. When Jonas explained that he was a miller, the settlers enjoined him to become part of their group. And so the Hershbergers arrived at the fort with a call and a commission.

As they stood on the bluff, they could see many log cabins below them. There was much activity around the dwellings, but beyond the encampment and across the river, the dark, primeval forest loomed in quiet and solemn majesty. Horses were grazing on the short grass around the fort, and oxen munched at hay that had been thrown to them. Smoke from many fires curled upward, and women dressed in the linsey garments of the pioneer stood stirring the contents of steaming kettles in front of the cabins. A man swung an axe with a strong arm, and the clean, sharp strokes rang in the air like bells pealing. From where they stood they could see a group of soldiers in their distinctive red coats drilling on a small parade ground inside the walls of the fort.

Jonas turned to his wife. "Here is the fort, dearest wife. As you can see, there are many people and many soldiers. Fort Pitt is well built and strong. Why, it withstood a two-month siege by the Indians during Pontiac's war. Just to look at it makes me think this fort could stand forever. We will not be many miles down the river, and if any of the Indians arise, we can flee here and be completely safe. And there is word that another fort is to be built near our farm."

Jonas' enthusiasm was lost on Martha. "I hope you are right, husband. But still, I wish we had never left Northkill."

The twin boys clambered down off the wagon. Jonathan pulled off his hat and tossed it into the air. "Huzzah! We are in our new home. Just imagine how many deer roam those woods. I'll be the hunter for the family and keep us in fresh deer meat, wild turkey, and elk."

Joshua was quick to respond. "Not without me, brother. I will provide more meat for I am the better shot."

Jonas could sense a storm brewing, so he grabbed both boys by the shoulders. "The main focus of our life here will be the farm and our crops. After that you will help me in the mill. Then, and only then, if there is time, you will be able to hunt."

Joshua nodded his assent. "Yes, *daed*, you are right. We are farmers and I will help you grow the best crops in all Pennsylvania."

Jonathan scowled. "But I don't like farming, Papa! I want to be in the forest, hunting and fishing. Someone will have to supply meat for us. Why can't it be me?"

Jonas smiled. His two sons were so alike and yet so different. Jonathan, the warrior, and Joshua, the peacemaker. Joshua always put the betterment of the family first, but Jonathan was self-centered and truculent. Jonas sighed and looked toward heaven.

Ich werde deine Hilfe brauchen, lieber Gott! I will need you help with this oldest son of mine.

The next day, the two boys were given time to explore the fort while Jonas went down river with the men to visit their new home. "I must see the land where our farm will be, and then I will make arrangements for lumber, a millwheel, and a grinding stone to be delivered to the site. You boys may look around, but do not stray into the woods, and keep your mother informed as to your whereabouts."

The two boys could hardly hide their excitement. "Yes, Papa!"

Jonas smiled. Sometimes the boys were so linked that even their answers sounded like an echo.

After Jonas left, Jonathan and Joshua began their exploration. They asked a sentry if they could go inside the fort, and they spent a few hours walking the battlements. Jonathan imagined himself to be a soldier defending the fort, but Joshua was reluctant to join in games of war. Jonathan smirked at him.

"It's a different world out here, brother. We may not be able to stick to the peaceful ways of our people."

Joshua frowned. "You should not speak this way, Jonathan. The Bible says…"

Jonathan interrupted. "The Bible, the Bible… That is all we ever hear. Well, the Bible was back then and this is now. We face many challenges and great danger here on this frontier, and we must be ready to defend ourselves."

"I will never forsake the ways of our people, Jonathan."

"Then you may end up a dead peace-lover, little brother."

Joshua pushed his brother. "I am not your little brother. *Maam* said I put my hand out first."

"Yes, Joshua, but I beat you, as I always do."

In the early afternoon the boys were making their way back to their camp when they heard a commotion along the riverbank. They pushed through the crowd and saw a group of Indians coming out of the woods and down to the encampment. They led packhorses loaded with furs.

Joshua stopped. "They must be here to trade, Jonathan."

"Or spy out the defenses of the fort."

The Indians were led by a tall, imposing man with a long rifle. He had a headband with three feathers, a long cloak draped around his shoulders and buckskin leggings tied with thongs. His powerful muscles rippled as he walked. His face was impassive, yet he radiated power and leadership. Behind him walked a pure black horse. Seated bareback on the animal was a young girl. She had coal-black hair and was dressed in a white beaded, leather dress. The girl's most amazing feature was her eyes. They were deep brown pools set in a beautiful light-skinned face. She did not look like the rest of the Indians in the group. A scout that had been with their wagon train was standing close to them. He pointed to the tall chief and the lovely child. "That 'ere is Wingenund, the greatest of the Delaware chiefs. And that be his daughter, Opahtuhwe, the White Deer."

Jonathan frowned. "I thought we were at war with the Delaware."

"Aye, but Wingenund is here under a flag of truce. He wants the British to enforce their laws about further settlements in Ohio. There is to be a big council, and all the chiefs are coming."

Joshua pulled the man's arm and pointed to the girl. "Why does she have pale skin?"

The man laughed. "She's part French. They say she is the granddaughter of a great French general. When the general was visiting America years ago, the Injuns stole his ten-year-old daughter. She grew up with the reddys and married a great chief. Spring of Water, Wingenund's wife, was their daughter and Opahtuhwe is Wingenund's child."

Joshua couldn't take his eyes off the girl. Although she was young, the bloom of a coming loveliness rested lightly on her features. The boys crowded closer and Joshua caught the girl's eye. She glanced his way and then Joshua was lost in the deep pools of her eyes. She looked at Joshua for a long moment and then Jonathan caught her attention. She looked back and forth between the two brothers, so alike as to be indistinguishable. The beautiful eyes widened for a moment and then a shy smile stole across her face. She turned away quickly. The Indians passed and Joshua stared after the girl. Jonathan punched him on the shoulder. "What's wrong, brother? Cat got your tongue?"

"She's the most beautiful girl I ever saw."

Jonathan spit on the ground. "Aw, she's just a kid! And she's a reddy."

But Joshua and Jonathan had looked upon the White Deer of the Lenape. And they would never be the same.

Part Three

Lives Entwining

I remember the day I first met Jonathan Hershberger. He was dressed in the strangest clothes, his hair was long, and he was driving an old hippie van. I had never seen anyone like him. But there was something in his eyes that caught me, and from that moment, I belonged to him.

I imagine that the first time White Deer saw her Jonathan it was like that. And like me, she faced many trials and great sorrow in the days that followed. But unlike me, she never knew the joy of the life that comes when a husband leads his wife in the way of peace or the fulfillment of the hope that was born in her heart that day.

Lives Entwining
From The Journals of Jenny Hershberger

Chapter Eight

Scar

It was a bright spring day in 1770. The woods along the Ohio River were green and lush with the luxuriant growth of April. Oaks and maples had put forth their leaves only weeks before, and the lime green of the new growth added an otherworldly luminescence to the scene.

Jonathan and Joshua Hershberger crept silently through the thick growth, crawling flat on their bellies. They held their long rifles pointed ahead. Jonathan was in the lead and Joshua came close behind. A moss-stained rugged rock with water trickling down its sides lay to their left. On the right, a hillside covered with tangled ferns sloped down to a small pond surrounded by lush fronds and dotted by the swift movements of water bugs. The deer ahead of them had been drinking at the pond when she raised her head and moved off into the woods, disturbed by a slight scent on the wind. Now the animal stood stock still in the trees ahead, sniffing the wind and trying to find the thing that had caught her attention. When the deer moved, the boys lay absolutely still until the birds began their songs among the trees, and the crickets and other noisemakers resumed their calling. The dancing, dimpled brook that flowed away out of the pond lent its own voice to the symphony of sound.

When the two boys first caught sight of the deer they had circled around until they were downwind, and it was only an errant current on the breeze that had brought the hint of their scent to the deer. Jonathan tapped his foot on Joshua's outstretched hand, a signal for the blond lad to move up beside his brother.

The fifteen year old twin brothers bore an amazingly close facial resemblance. The only difference between them was in their clothing and their coloring. Joshua moved noiselessly until he lay even with his brother. At a slight nod from Jonathan, the two rifles began to slowly lift together, imperceptibly moving until they were leveled at the creature ahead. Jonathan nodded again and the two rifles spoke as one. The deer leaped straight into the air, took one or two stumbling steps, and then crashed to earth in a thicket of laurel. Leaping to their feet, the Hershberger boys ran to the spot where the deer lay. Jonathan knelt down and examined the deer's side. Two small holes marked the otherwise smooth skin, one slightly ahead of the other.

Jonathan pointed to the bullet hole closest to the heart. "That one is mine."

Joshua shook his head. "I think not, brother, for mine was the truer aim."

Jonathan chuckled. "I knew you would contest my skill, so I notched my ball."

Joshua frowned at his brother. "*Mox nix.*"

Jonathan grinned. "Ah, brother, but it does make a difference. I think you will find my notched ball lodged in the center of the heart when we skin the beast."

The two lads took a coil of rope from a knapsack on Jonathan's back and set about hanging the deer from a majestic oak that stood by. Working swiftly with sharp hunting knives, they gutted and bled the deer. When they pulled out the entrails, Joshua dug in them until he found the heart. He carefully cut it open and disclosed two bullets lodged in the flesh. One, indeed, was dead center. The other was so close behind that a knife blade could not have been slipped between them.

Jonathan held up the truest ball. There was a notch in it. "Once again, the master hunter edifies the apprentice."

Joshua gave Jonathan a friendly buffet on the arm.

"You've not always bested me, and we shall have many more opportunities to prove who is the better marksman, I am sure."

They cut the hide into pieces and then swiftly cut up the meat, laid it on the pieces of hide, and rolled the whole package into bundles. Then they tied the bundles with twine. When they were finished Joshua stood up and looked at the sun.

"Not more than an hour to kill, skin, and pack. Father will be pleased."

The two boys set off in the direction of the river. They were both tall and lithe, but though they looked very much alike, they were different in many ways. Jonathan wore the deerskin clothing of the borderman, with fringed shirt, smooth leather leggings and moccasins. His long black hair was pulled back and tied at the nape of his neck. Joshua was dressed in settler clothing, with a dark shirt, homespun breeches and leather shoes. He wore his blonde hair cut shorter in the Amish fashion.

They headed down the trail and soon came to the swiftly flowing green water of the Ohio. They walked down the trail that ran along the bank until they came to a clump of willows growing out over the water. Jonathan stepped into the water and pulled a birch canoe from its hiding place beneath the willows. Together they loaded the bundles of meat into the canoe and set off upstream. The current was strong but so were they. They stayed in close to the bank and moved slowly upstream until, in an hour, they came to a well-marked landing place. Jonathan leaped out, grabbed the nose of the canoe, and pulled it up onto the bank, while Joshua unloaded the guns and bundles and set them on the shore.

They each grabbed their rifle and a bundle and walked up the trail. After a few minutes, the path opened up into a broad meadow. Set upon a knoll in the middle of the meadow was a low log cabin. Spread around the cabin was outbuildings, a barn, and a small corral. Away at the top of a distant ridge, the boys could see the rough beginnings of the fort the men who had settled in the vicinity had started. There had been no trouble from the Indians for two summers, and so work on the fort had languished.

The boys walked to the front door of the log cabin. A wide veranda ran along the front and a sloping roof provided cover for the pile of wood and tools lined up against the wall. A younger, dark-haired boy came around the side of the house and noticed the bundles that Jonathan and Joshua laid on the porch. He poked at them with his foot.

"Did you get one?"

Joshua smiled at his younger brother. "Yes we did, Aaron. There are two more bundles down at the landing, if you would be kind enough to fetch them. Jonathan and I have to get this hung up in the drying shed."

Aaron headed off toward the dock. As he did, the boys' parents came out of the house.

Jonas looked at the bundles on the porch. "Fetched home a deer, did ye? Who shot him?"

Both boys answered at once. "I did."

Then Jonathan grinned. "It's true that we both shot at the same time, but mine was the shot that killed the deer."

"Aye, Father," Joshua retorted. "His bullet was dead center in the heart, but mine was not a knife blade behind."

Their mother looked at her two sons. "You boys. Always competing, so alike and yet so different. Well, take out some steaks and then get the rest ready for drying. I'll start the fire and we'll have venison tonight. Girls, come out and help your mother!"

The twins sorted through the bundles and handed their mother several slabs of still-bloody meat. Then they headed around the back of the cabin to the drying shed.

Jonas Hershberger watched his two tall sons as they left. He was proud of his boys and his daughters. He was raising a fine family here by the Ohio River, and despite many hardships, he was perfectly satisfied with the land he owned and the farm he had built. His mill was successful, and the settlers around them were grateful they didn't have to travel long distances to get the corn ground into flour. The last two summers had seen the marauding Indian tribes move farther to the south, and they had experienced little difficulty in that regard. Jonas hoped that the rest of the summer would be the same. Jonas looked up as two bright and talkative girls came out on the porch.

"Abagail, Charity, help your mother to get the stove going and then fetch some potatoes from the cellar. We'll ..." He trailed off as he looked at the girls. They were staring toward the river with frightened expressions on their faces. Jonas turned. Aaron was coming up the trail carrying two bundles. Behind him came six Delaware Indians. They did not wear war paint, but their faces were grim, and they all carried rifles and tomahawks.

Jonas stepped off the porch and walked toward the oncoming group. "Get in the house, girls. Mother, stay here while I see what our red brothers want."

Aaron was walking stiffly and held his chin high, but Jonas could see his son's lips quivering. Behind him, the Indians walked in single file. They made no sound but looked about them with obvious interest at the newly planted fields and the corral with horses and a cow. Jonas motioned to Aaron. "Stand ye here, lad, while I speak with these folk."

Aaron edged around behind his father and set the bundles on the ground. The Indian leader stepped forward. He was tall and carried his rifle cradled in his arms. His head was shaved on his forehead and the sides. The hair on the back of his head was pulled up into a scalp-lock, and it was decorated with feathers. His eyes were piercing black, and a woolen blanket was draped around his shoulders. His face had some tattooing, as did his arms. A nasty scar ran along his jawline. The rest of his band was just as formidable looking.

Jonas stepped in front of the leader. "What can I do for you, brother?"

The scar-faced one motioned toward the two bundles Aaron had dropped and said a few words. It was obvious that he wanted Jonas to give them the meat. Jonas paused for a moment. It was the first meat the boys had brought home for quite a spell, and their larder was running low. Just then came a cry from the porch.

"Go on with ye, you beggars!"

It was his wife. He looked around in alarm. His wife was motioning at the Indians and pointing back down the trail.

"Jonas, send them away. I'll not have them taking meat off our table."

"Martha, be careful what you say. We don't know if they are dangerous or not."

Martha scoffed. "Dangerous! Look at them! They are nothing but a band of beggars. I'll not have them depriving my children."

She motioned again, pointing down the trail, and her meaning was not lost on the leader. He scowled and started to raise his weapon. Just then, Jonathan and Joshua walked around the side of the house, carrying their rifles. The scarred leader stopped and looked at the rifles the boys were carrying. He said something to his men and then made what looked like an obscene gesture at Martha. One of the Indians made a gesture like a throat being cut and then they turned and walked back down the trail.

Jonathan strode to his father's side. "What is it, Father?"

"Just some Indians, Jonathan, begging for meat. Your mother seems to have run them off."

Jonathan lifted his rifle. "More'n likely it was the sight of our rifles that ran them off. Perhaps we should stand guard tonight."

Jonas shook his head. "Boys, I'll not be having you worry about shooting these Indians. Our Lord tells us that it is wrong to kill, and we'll not raise our hand against them."

Joshua nodded. "Father's right, Jonathan. We'll just trust the Lord to send them away."

Jonathan stared after the departing Indians. "Seems foolish to me. So I'll be keeping an eye peeled, no matter what you say."

"Leave it at that, Jonathan. We'll be fine. Now hurry up to the house and get your chores done before supper."

The three boys walked up to the house while Jonas stood and looked down the path after the Indians. Trust in the Lord or not, he could not still the uneasy feeling that gripped him.

Chapter Nine

Death's Turning

After a fine dinner of venison grilled on the fire, the Hershberger family was settling in when the family dogs raised an alarm outside. Jonas looked at his youngest son. "Go see what ails the dogs, lad."

Aaron went to the door to see what was the matter, and when he opened it, there was a flash and the report of a rifle. The boy screamed and fell back into the room with blood pouring from his leg.

Jonathan sprang to the door, slammed it shut, and dropped the bar into place before the Indians could enter. There were several loaded guns on the walls, and he grabbed one. Quickly, they doused the lamps. The girls were whimpering. Jonathan laid his finger to his lips. "Hsst, girls. Get down in the corner and make not a sound."

Joshua went to the window and opened the shutter a crack. "I can see them. It's bright as day in the moonlight out there. They are out by the corral. That big, ugly one is making signals and talking to his men."

Jonathan quickly tossed a rifle to Joshua. The look on his face was grim. "We've got plenty of guns and ammunition. You girls get ready to reload as we fire. There ain't an Injun in the world can stand against a fierce rifle volley. They'll not gain entrance here."

Then Jonas stepped between his son and the door. "No, son, we'll not fire upon them. I cannot give my consent to harming other human beings."

Jonathan's mouth fell open in amazement. "Are you mad?" he hissed. "Those reddys will kill us all and worse to the girls."

Jonas shook his head and placed his hand on Jonathan's rifle. "We must place our trust in the Lord for I cannot take the path of violence."

Joshua looked in his father's direction. "But, Father, what will happen to Mother, the girls, our farm? We must defend ourselves."

"A man does not give up what he believes, simply because the test is too hard. I will not give my consent to fire on the Indians. They are our brothers."

Jonathan tore his gun loose from his father's grasp. He shouted at his father, "You doddering old fool! Let us defend our family! I cannot stand by while you show yourself a coward."

"My son, you are welcome to leave, but as you are under my roof, you will obey my wishes. I have said all in the matter. You will not raise your weapon against those men."

Joshua looked at his brother and then at his father and then laid down his rifle. "Father is right, Jonathan. The Lord commands us to love our brothers, no matter what. If a man smite thee on the cheek …"

"Do not quote the Bible to me, Joshua! Go ahead and stand with him. You've always been a soft-heart. I know well what the Bible says, for this craven dog has shoved it down my throat all my life. I am going for help. There are men not half a mile away who will come and defend our family, even if you will not."

His mother raised her hands toward her son. "Jonathan! You would leave us?"

"Only to rescue you from death or worse, Mother." He grabbed another rifle and ran to the back of the house. "I will return with help." He opened the back window, hoisted himself through, and was gone.

After Jonathan left, the family huddled together in the dark. The bullet from the Indian's musket had passed through the fleshy part of Aaron's leg, and Mother Hershberger bound up the flowing wound. From outside they could hear an occasional whoop and taunting call. Some of the braver warriors began running past the front of the house. As they ran, they would discharge their weapons into the log walls. When no rifle fire was returned, they grew bolder. They began to break into the storage buildings, carrying out the provisions the Hershbergers had labored to put away. Then the family heard a commotion out by the barn.

Aaron dragged himself to the window. He turned to his father with tears running down his face. "Father, they've set the barn on fire!"

Soon the ghastly light from the burning barn lit the clearing. The Indians were gathered in front of the house, no longer afraid of the guns inside. They were whooping and keeping up a great commotion, and their bloodthirsty yells froze the very blood of those inside the cabin.

Just then, Joshua gave an alarm from his position by the front door. "Father, they are coming with torches. They mean to burn us out."

There was a thump on the roof and then another. Soon a crackling could be heard and then the smell of smoke began to fill the cabin.

The youngest girl, Charity, began to shriek. "Father, we shall burn to death!"

Jonas bowed his head. "Many of my forbearers stood in the flames for their Lord. Shall we do less? We will go to a better world where Christ is King and men live in peace."

But even as he spoke, the smoke grew so thick and the heat of the flames so fierce that they could bear it no longer. They flung open the front door and stumbled out into the yard. The Indians crowded around them, yelling and whooping and making threatening gestures. The leader nodded to one of his men who went off into the darkness and soon returned pushing someone in front of him. It was Jonathan! A stream of blood ran down the side of his face. Jonathan looked at Martha. "I am sorry, Mother. They had a guard in the woods behind the house. He clubbed me down as I ran by."

The leader of the savages stepped in front of Martha. He had an evil smile on his face. "I am Ehèntawisèk." He pointed to his face. "Scar came from long knife of General Braddock when I put him under the hatchet. My chief, Wingenund, strongest of the Wolf Clan warriors. We are better people than you; you treat us like dogs." He reached in his shirt and pulled out a piece of venison that he had gotten from the smokehouse. He pulled out his knife and thrust the meat in Martha's face. "Now, you eat."

Jonathan struggled in the grasp of his captors as he watched the red giant torment his mother. She shook her head and whimpered. Then Scar put the knife to her throat. "You eat!"

Mother Hershberger saw death in his eyes. She opened her mouth to scream, and the big Indian shoved the meat into her mouth. His knife flashed, once, twice, and she fell lifeless at his feet. He kicked her as she lay and spit on her. The other Indians crowded around and stabbed her repeatedly. One bent down and then stood up with a whoop. He held up Martha's long hair. It shone red in the moonlight. Jonathan cried out but the braves held him tightly. Charity shrieked and Aaron turned his face away, sobbing.

Then Scar turned to the girls who were now speechless with terror. He nodded to his men, and they began dragging the girls toward the woods. Realizing their fate, the girls began to scream and beg. "Father! Father! Please help us!"

Jonas watched in horror as the men pulled his girls into the bushes. He covered his face with is hands. "Be with them, my God."

Their piteous cries filled the night and soon turned to awful shrieks as the Indians tormented them in the woods. The boys, held tightly by their captors, were forced to listen as their sisters screamed and begged for death. After a while, there was only silence.

Scar took Aaron by the hair and pulled him forward. He looked at the bloody bandage tied around Aaron's leg. "Young one, no walk, make us slow," he said grimly. Swiftly his tomahawk flashed in the light of the burning cabin, and Aaron fell without a sound. Joshua struggled free and dropped to his knees by his brother's body. He looked upon the beloved face, weeping. "Aaron, oh, Aaron."

Then Scar turned to Jonas. His cruel face was impassive as he stared at the older man. "You not warrior. Not fight for woman and children. You will be slave to Lenape. You slave to Indian till you die. You will do the work of our women for you are a woman in your heart. I will take your sons, make them mine, teach them warrior way, not like you."

Jonathan looked at his father. Hatred burned in his eyes. "Yes, Father, you are a slave. You are a slave to your ignorance and to a God who cannot help you." He pointed to the bodies of Martha and Aaron. "Look what you've done, you fool," and he spit in his father's face.

Jonas stood silent before his son, but Joshua leaped up to defend his father. "Jonathan, you must not! He is your father."

Jonathan stared in disgust at his father's face, streaked with tears and spittle. "No! He is no longer my father. I renounce him and all his ways. I will gladly go with this Indian, for murdering savage that he is, he is still more of a man than this pitiful creature. But I tell you this, brother. I will not forget this day; neither will I forget what has been done here." He glanced meaningfully at Scar. The big Indian laughed and slapped Jonathan on the shoulder. "Good! You hate. Make strong, make warrior. You and brother live with us, know the warrior path."

Scar turned to Joshua, but Joshua shook his head. Then he looked his captor straight in the eye. "No, I will not learn the way of the warrior. I will follow my father in whatever fate befalls him. I will never take up the weapons of war."

Scar stared at the lad for a long moment. Then he frowned. "Then you be slave, too. I make your brother Lenape warrior, adopt him into Wolf Clan. You will be lowest in the village."

The chief motioned to his men, and they shoved their prisoners toward the woods. Jonathan whispered to his brother. "You fool! The only way to escape them is to play along."

Joshua shook his head. "You have dishonored our father and our faith. Our *maam* and sisters are in heaven with Aaron. They are better off. 'For I reckon that the sufferings of this present time are not worthy to be compared with the glory which shall be revealed in us.'"

Jonathan's face twisted in rage. He struck his brother and knocked him to the ground. "Do not quote that wretched book to me, Joshua, for it has been the death of my family."

Joshua rose slowly to his feet, his fists raised. The Indians gathered around the two brothers, laughing and pointing. One of them pushed Joshua toward Jonathan, who shoved him away. Jonathan shouted at his brother. "Come on, Joshua. You've always wanted to beat me. Now is the time, here's your chance!"

Jonas struggled with the braves that were holding him and cried out. "No, Joshua! Do not respond in hatred! Remember your faith; remember our Lord as he suffered on the Cross."

Joshua stared at his brother for a long time. Love rose in his heart as he stared at Jonathan's tragic face. He lowered his hands. "No, Jonathan. I will not fight you." Then he turned away.

Quickly, the Indians bound the hands of the Hershbergers. They gathered up as much of the stolen provisions as they could carry. Then they shoved the three captives down the path into the woods. As the grim procession made its way toward the river, Jonathan looked back at the lifeless forms of his mother and brother lying in the clearing, their bodies twisted grotesquely in death.

"I swear revenge, Mother," he whispered. "I will not rest until all of these murderers are dead and their scalps hang drying on the wall of my cabin. I swear it, by all that is holy ..."

Chapter Ten

Shawnee Town

The Indians pushed the three prisoners ahead of them down to the banks of the river where there were several canoes pulled up along the bank. Scar motioned for Jonathan to get into one and pushed Jonas and Joshua toward another. The rest of Scar's braves began stacking booty from the Hershberger farm in the remaining canoes. Behind them the sky was bright from the burning barn and house. Joshua whispered to his father. "Perhaps the men from the settlement have seen the fire and are coming." But his father only shook his head, terrible grief etched into his face. Scar climbed into the lead canoe and his men followed. They pushed out into the current and were quickly swept downstream. The green Ohio carried the canoes into the wilderness. Behind them the dreams of Jonas Hershberger drifted away into the dark night on wings of fire.

By the next morning they had traveled far down the river. Joshua, whose heart was heavy with sorrow, did not notice the beauty of the ever-changing scenery. The rugged gray rocks on one side of the stream contrasted with green-clad hills on the other. Above all, hung an ambiance of deep solitude and loneliness. All along the shore different animals and birds watched without fear as the travelers drifted by. A sand hill crane, stalking along the shore, lifted his long neck from his hunt for frogs and then stood still and silent as a statue until they disappeared from view. Blue herons spread wide wings and lumbered away along the shore. Crows circled above, cawing raucously. Deer waded knee-deep in the shallow water and when they saw the silent procession sweep by, instantly became motionless, staring at the travellers with wide, curious eyes. Joshua saw a buffalo on a level stretch of the bank, but the huge beast was not afraid and tossed his shaggy head, seeming to resent the coming of strangers into his kingdom.

They traveled for long hours that day. Joshua stayed beside his father in the middle of the canoe. Late in the afternoon he heard whispered words from Jonas. "Martha, my dearest, death isn't the greatest loss in life. It's what dies inside of us while we live."

All day the canoes drifted swiftly down the river. Grief-blinded eyes did not notice the densely wooded hills, the broken cliffs, the long reaches of sandy bar that glistened golden in the sunlight, nor did they comprehend the flight and call of wildfowl above.

The intense blue of the wilderness sky above began to pale, and in the west, a few stray clouds, painted golden and purple for moment and then crimson for another, finally grew gray and darkened as the sun sank behind the mountains. Soon the red rays disappeared, a pink glow spread over the sky, and as gray twilight stole down over the hills, the full moon rose majestically in the southeast, serene in glory, the guardian of the night and far above the cares of the wretched captives below.

Just before it was completely dark, they came to an open meadow on the northern bank that broke the dark, forbidding ranks of trees and swept down to the water's edge. Scar grunted and motioned toward the bank. The braves pulled their canoes toward the shore, and leaping into the shallow water, they heaved them onto the sandy bar that fronted the river. Scar motioned to Jonathan to get out. The other two prisoners were jerked roughly from their seats and flung down on the sand, much to the amusement of the Indians.

Jonathan seemed totally indifferent to the plight of his father. Joshua looked at his brother in anger. Jonathan smirked. "So, my peace-loving brother, I see hate on your face. Having difficulty staying with your creed?"

Joshua turned away and lifted his father from the sand. Overnight, Jonas had changed from a strong capable man to a pitiful shadow of his former self. He clung to his son like an old man. Any movement the Indians made frightened him, and the Indians seemed to take delight in lurching at him to scare him or shaking their knives in his face. Joshua led his father up the bank and helped him sit down by a large tree. Scar gave some orders and the Indians came over and cut their bonds. Scar looked at his captives. "You will not try to escape now for you do not know the way back."

Joshua stretched his cramped muscles. Jonas sat as one with no hope, his head hanging, his hands limp at his sides. Joshua knelt down beside his father. *"Papa, müssen Sie nicht das Sie zerstören lassen.* You must not let this destroy you."

Jonas looked up with watering, uncomprehending eyes, and Joshua could see that sanity had passed from his father's mind. Jonas was a ruined man, and Joshua's heart broke.

Joshua heard a step behind him, and then Jonathan was standing beside him. Contempt was in his voice. "Look at him; he's lost his mind. He let his family be murdered, and now he can't face up to his cowardice so he hides in insanity. And you, brother, stood by while these butchers tomahawked your younger brother. I hope you can sleep at night. At least I tried to bring help."

Joshua shook his head. "I know you don't understand, Jonathan, but as father said, a man doesn't give up his faith just because he faces trials. I am sorry that Papa's ways seem hard to you, but when we stand before Jesus…"

Jonathan turned and knocked his brother sprawling. Then he stood over him and pointed at him. Jonathan began to speak in

German so the savages would not understand. "*Ich werde lernen, ihre Wege, und dann wird ich sie alle zu töten. Keine reddy wird von mein Messer sicher sein.*"

Joshua stared at Jonathan. Then he answered him in German. "*Sie würden ein Mörder wegen der Rache werden. Aber es, wird Jonathan verboten. Sie werden die Qualen des verdammten ertragen.*" Jonathan glowered down at his brother. "I'm only going to say this once, Joshua. Don't you ever again mention the name of Jesus to me, or tell me that I must follow the Amish way. I'm done with it." He lowered his voice. "No Indian will be safe from my knife. I will become the destroying angel of the frontier. My life will be about exacting terrible justice on these red savages. Always in my mind I will see the knives that stabbed my mother, hear the screams of my sisters as these animals raped them in the woods and then slit their throats. And I will never forget Aaron's face as he died under the hatchet of him." He pointed to Scar. "On that one I will exact my greatest revenge. I will let him think that he is my new father, but when the time is right, he will feel the bite of my blade in his heart."

Joshua looked intently at Jonathan. He did not know him. The face before him was not the face of the brother that he loved, but the face of a madman. Joshua stood up and brushed himself off. "You say Papa has hidden in insanity, but it is you that is insane. The devil has entered into your heart, for he is the father of murderers."

Jonathan smiled a strange smile. "If the devil has entered me, then so be it, for I will need his strength to carry out my life's mission. From this day I live only to see the death of every red Indian that crosses my path." He turned and walked back toward the fire where the Indians were preparing to cook some of the deer meat they had stolen from the Hershbergers. He stood over the brave who was unpacking the bundles of meat. Then he spoke loudly so the other Indians could hear. "That's my deer meat, give it to me." The Indian looked up in surprise and then grunted and laughed. He turned away. Swiftly, Jonathan kicked him into the fire. The brave howled and rolled out of the coals, slapping flames off his leggings. Then he leaped up and grabbed his knife, lunging at Jonathan. Before any of the other Indians could make a move, Jonathan sidestepped the Indian's rush and smashed his powerful fist down on the back of the brave's head. The Indian sank down without a sound. Jonathan grabbed the knife and was about to leap on the fallen brave when Scar grabbed him and knocked the knife from Jonathan's hand. The big warrior held Jonathan in a grip of steel. "Good, you strong, make great warrior, but no kill. I say when kill. Then you kill all the enemies of the Lenape." The other Indians crowded around and grunted signs of approval at Jonathan's prowess. The fallen Indian groaned and someone threw a gourd of water on him. The man stood shakily to his feet and then took a step toward Jonathan. Scar stepped between them.

"This one is mine. If you are so stupid as to let a white man knock you down, it is not his fault but yours. Go!"

The Indian looked at Jonathan with dark hatred and then turned back to his tasks. Scar laughed. "You have made big enemy. Stalking Bear not forget you shame him. One day he will challenge you."

Jonathan shrugged. "Good, then I can kill him without fear." Scar grinned and then said something in his own language to the rest of the braves. "*Temetet!*" The braves laughed and repeated the word. "*Temetet, Temetet.*"

Jonathan frowned and looked at Scar. "What are they saying?"

Scar looked at Jonathan's fierce face. "*Temetet.* It means wolf cub. You are a cub, but the heart of the wolf is in you. I think these will know you now as Temetet, until you become *Xinkwtemew*, the big wolf."

Jonathan nodded. "Yes, I will become like the wolf, and every man's hand will be against me. But they will fear me as no other." He turned and stalked away from Scar. The other Indians called after him. "Temetet! Temetet!"

Joshua stood by the tree, watching. His father had not even noticed the commotion but was lost in a daze, muttering the name of his wife over and over. Joshua looked up toward the heavens. He cried out, *Ach Mein lieber Gott. Was taten wir, um das zu verdienen?*

The next day, the Indians were up before dawn breaking camp. Their activities awakened Joshua and he stirred. He had slept on the cold ground next to his father all night and his body was stiff. He turned to his father to awaken him and gasped. The morning sun brought a startling revelation. Jonas had aged. His hair had turned white and his face was seamed with creases of grief and pain. Joshua could not believe the change in his father. As Joshua watched in shock, Jonas sat up and looked around. He saw his son. "Ah, Joshua, time to milk the cows. Where is your mother? I would like a bite to eat before we go to the fields." Jonas stood up and began to look around. "Where are Martha and the girls? Have they gone for berries in the woods?"

Joshua put his arm around his father's shoulder. "Yes, Papa, they have gone looking for berries. *Maam* said to eat breakfast without her." He led his father to the fire where Jonathan sat eating with the braves. He reached down to take some food. Scar leaped up and smashed him to the ground. "You slave. You no eat with warriors. You eat what is left." Scar pointed toward Jonathan. "You are not like him. He will be a warrior. You are a woman."

Joshua looked at Jonathan. For a moment he could see remorse in his brother's face and then Jonathan turned away. Joshua led his father back to the tree. He remembered that he had some jerky in the pocket of his shirt, so he led Jonas out of sight of the Indians and fed him a piece of the dried meat. After a while Jonathan came and found them. "Hurry, we are leaving soon."

"Where are we going, Jonathan?"

Jonathan pointed down the river. "We are going to Shawnee Town."

Chapter Eleven

The Princess

The prisoners and their captors floated down the river all the next day. The Indians did not seem to be in any hurry since they had passed well beyond the last of the white settlements. The second night, they camped on a long island in the middle of the river. Jonathan had been kept apart from his father and brother by Scar. After his initial rage, his heart had softened somewhat toward Jonas and Joshua, and he vowed to himself to do his best to see that they weren't treated too harshly. So at dinner he managed to hide a chunk of venison in his pocket. Later, when the Indians were resting by the fire, Jonathan took the meat to his father. He was startled to see how far his father had sunk into mindlessness. When he walked up to them, he found Jonas sitting on the ground holding a conversation with his dead wife. He saw Joshua watching as he approached and there was sadness in his eyes as Jonathan offered him the meat.

"Are you convicted then, Jonathan, for your harsh treatment of your own father?"

"Just take the meat, brother, and do not question my motives."

Joshua took the provision and handed it all to his father who began to chew it noisily. Then he offered some to Martha. Jonathan watched sadly.

"Will you not eat, Joshua?"

Joshua looked up at Jonathan. "I have made my choice, brother, and I will accept the consequences. If the savages do not choose to give me meat then that is my lot, and I will bear it. But I will take nothing from your hand ever again. As for Papa, you can see the poor man has lost his mind and cannot make these choices for himself. So if your conscience demands that you help, then help him, for no matter what, he is still your father."

Jonathan felt the heat rise in his face. "Yes, a father that stood by in craven cowardice while his own wife and daughters were slaughtered."

Joshua smiled sadly. "Someday, Jonathan, you may learn the difference between cowardice and conviction. I, for one, see how much it took for father to stand for his faith, and I will always love him for it. *Maam* and the girls are in a far better place, and their trials are over. You, however, will face a lifetime of regret. I think that your hardest tests are still before you." With that, Joshua rolled over and laid his head on the coat that served him as a pillow.

Jonathan stared at his brother's back for a long while, and then he strode off into the darkness. He looked for a place to quiet the conflicting emotions of his heart. At the end of the island, he found a great fallen tree that extended out into the water. On this he climbed and sat silently in the streaming moonlight. The scenes of the massacre rolled through his mind in grim procession. He saw his *maam's* fear as the brutal Scar forced the meat into her mouth. He heard the shrieks of his sisters. Tears ran down his cheeks as the terrified face of Aaron flashed before his eyes.

But as he sat in the stillness, broken only by the soft sound of the dark water flowing by, a remarkable transition came over Jonathan. Gradually, the bitterness died out from his face, as he pushed the pain into the dark recesses of his heart, and he became engrossed in the silver sheen on the water, the lapping of the waves on the pebbly beach, and in the overpowering, mysterious silence of the forest.

In that moment Jonathan realized that some force greater than he had brought him to this place. He did not understand it, but he accepted it. His heart was torn by the tragedy behind him, but even in his sorrow, the call of the wilderness beckoned his heart.

On the third day, the Indians reached a small river flowing into the Ohio from the north. They turned their canoes up and paddled against the current for another hour. Then as they labored around a bend in the stream a great sight opened before Jonathan's eyes. A huge village lay along the banks of the river, the wigwams and huts stretching along the bank as far as he could see. Hundreds of Indians were moving among the dwellings. The braves gave signals to the village, by firing their guns and giving a hideous yell that they had returned with prisoners, plunder, and scalps. Dark-eyed children ran along the bank shouting to the warriors in the canoes as Scar directed his craft to a broad shelving bank where hundreds of craft lay along the shore. The Indians beached their canoes, and Scar directed his men to unload. He motioned for Jonathan to get out while Joshua and Jonas were dragged roughly from their canoe.

A crowd of excited villagers gathered around the men as Scar strutted before them, talking in his own language. The braves of Scar's band held up the scalps of the Hershberger women and the excited murmuring of the crowd turned to howls of delight. Scar pushed Jonas and Joshua to their knees in the sand and pointed at them. Although Jonathan could not understand the words, the contempt in Scar's voice was plain. Scar said something to a group of women standing near and they rushed over to the two men and began switching them with willow branches as they pushed them toward a clearing in the middle of the camp, all the while laughing and shouting.

Jonathan watched as his father and brother were led into the clearing. Then many of the squaws and young boys formed two lines. Joshua and Jonas were pushed to the head of the line, and by motions, they were shown that they must run through the two lines. Jonathan knew this was the dreaded gauntlet that all prisoners must submit to. The squaws were armed with clubs and switches, and their shrieks and cries filled the air with a terrible sound.

Joshua grabbed his father and, shielding him as best as he could, darted swiftly down the rows. He took the blows intended for his father and ran straight toward the finish. One lad stepped out to try and block them, but Joshua lowered his shoulder and bowled the lad over, much to the delight of the watching braves. Joshua reached the end, still dragging his father and the Indians crowded around him, very impressed by his prowess. One even took a cloth and wiped the blood from Joshua's face. Then they were led away.

Jonathan watched the whole proceeding and, surprisingly, a feeling of pride rose up in him as he watched his brother win through to the end. He was wondering if he was going to have to undergo the same torment when Scar pushed him forward and began to speak. This time Scar's voice carried both a boastful arrogance and a hint of warmth as he pointed to Jonathan. The rest of the braves crowded around and gave Jonathan friendly pushes as Scar bragged. Jonathan noticed that Stalking Bear stayed apart with a look of pure venom in his eyes, but he merely looked straight back at the brave he had bested until Stalking Bear lowered his eyes and strode away.

Suddenly, there was silence. A tall warrior pushed through the crowd. He carried himself with a regal composure that denoted power and authority. Behind him came an Indian maiden, fair of skin and with astounding lovely eyes. With a shock, Jonathan realized that this was Wingenund, the great chief, and his daughter, White Deer, the ones he and Joshua had seen at Fort Pitt years ago. Only now, the little girl had grown into the loveliest woman Jonathan had ever seen. She was tall and slim, dressed in white buckskin. Her long black hair fell softly about her shoulders, and a white beaded band around her forehead held her tresses in place. Her movements were sure and graceful, and she looked every bit the daughter of the great man she walked beside.

Jonathan stared at the girl and her father. They walked up to him and Wingenund began to question Scar. He did not look happy with the answers so he turned to Jonathan and said something in his tongue. Jonathan must have had a puzzled look on his face, for the girl stepped forward and spoke to him in very clear English. "My father asks what you did to provoke this man to murder your family?"

Jonathan drew himself up. "We did nothing. This man demanded we give him meat that we had just hunted. My mother refused and it angered him."

The girl spoke to her father. He spoke to Scar again. Scar shrugged and pointed to Jonathan. A torrent of words flowed out as he addressed Wingenund. Wingenund nodded and grunted an affirmative to Scar's words. Jonathan looked at them and then at the girl.

"Scar claims you as his adopted son. It is our way. The British killed his own sons, and he has no family. Now he says the Great Spirit has sent you to take their place. He will raise you as he would have raised his sons. My father says yes. You will be adopted by Scar."

The girl turned to go but Jonathan stepped forward. "Wait!"

White Deer turned back. "What?"

Jonathan began to speak swiftly. "I know you. You are White Deer. I saw you at Fort Pitt seven years ago. I have a brother who looks like me. You smiled at us."

White Deer moved closer and looked at Jonathan. "*Kahpèsàk!*"

"What does that mean?"

The girl smiled. "It means twins. Yes, I remember you now. Your brother has yellow hair. Where is he?"

"He has been made a slave along with my father because he refused to learn the warrior way. But he sure gave them a warrior's turn when he ran the gauntlet."

White Deer shrugged. "That is his choice then." She started to leave.

Jonathan took a chance. "Where did you learn English?"

White Deer turned. She had an impatient look on her face. "My grandmother was French. My father says that I am the one who will show the Lenape who the white men really are–good or evil. So he made me learn your talk from my grandmother. Now I speak English and *Francais*."

Jonathan stared at the girl. Joshua's words came back to him from that day long ago.

"She's the most beautiful girl I've ever seen."

Jonathan shook his head and held out his hands in a pleading gesture. "What do I do now?"

White Deer pointed to Scar. "You will go with him and become his son. He will teach you the warrior way. If you do well, you will become one of us. Then you will no longer be a prisoner but a Lenape warrior." She spoke some words to Scar who beamed and motioned to Jonathan to come. Jonathan followed Scar as they walked away toward another part of the village. But he kept glancing back at the young maiden. He remembered his own words from that day.

"Aw, she's just a kid and besides she's a reddy."

Then his face hardened and his eyes narrowed as he turned and walked away.

Don't even think about her, Jonathan. For one day you may have to kill her too!

White Deer stood and watched as Jonathan strode away with Scar. She had always felt pity for the white prisoners. She had rescued many from the fires of the Delaware. As she watched him go, a feeling she had never experienced before swept over her. Many braves had come to her to tell her of their love, many suitors had begged her to love them in return. But she was Opahtuhwe, the White Deer, princess of her people. Her life had been set aside as a servant and a leader. She had no time or inclination for the foolishness of love. And yet, when she looked into the eyes of this young giant, with his handsome face and superb build, she knew that she had met the man who would possess her heart.

Chapter Twelve

Desperate Days

Jonas and Joshua's captors dragged the two men through the village until they reached a dilapidated hut. The two brawny braves that held Joshua's bound arms shoved him inside, and he fell heavily to the ground. He could hear his father talking to the Indians outside the hut.

"Have you seen my wife? I haven't been able to find her. And my daughters are gone."

Joshua could hear the grunts of the captors and then the sound of a blow. His father fell through the door backwards and lay as one dead. Joshua crawled over to the inert form. His arms were tied in front of him so he was able to lift Jonas onto his lap. He sat that way for a long time until Jonas finally opened his eyes.

His voice was a hoarse whisper. "Joshua, are you still with me, lad?"

Joshua was surprised at the clarity of his father's question. He looked at Jonas' eyes, and for the first time since the massacre, Jonas appeared almost to be himself. Joshua held his father closer. "Father! I thought I had lost you."

Jonas smiled at his son. "Despite the clout from that big one, I do feel better today. I must admit, though, that I have felt my mind slipping away from me these past few days."

Then Joshua had an idea. "Listen, Father. I've heard that the natives fear and respect insane people and treat them less harshly. Maybe it would be best if they continue to believe that about you. Then they might treat you less harshly. Perhaps you will even find an opportunity to help us escape."

Jonas nodded in agreement. "But I fear for you, son."

Joshua smiled down at his father. "I will manage, Father. Though I will not strike back at them, I think I am strong enough to keep them from bothering me too much. They seemed to be impressed when I bowled that stout lad over in the gauntlet, though I tried my best not to hurt him."

Jonas sat up and looked around. "Where is your brother?"

"Jonathan has submitted to adoption, but I think that he, too, is deceiving these savages. The only thing in his heart is revenge, and he means to bide his time and find a way to slaughter as many of the Indians that killed Mother as he can."

Jonas shook his head sadly. "My son has renounced the ways of his people. I am afraid for his immortal soul."

"I'm not sure, Father. We follow the *ordnung* because it is what we believe Christ truly taught. But there are many settlers, God-fearing Christians, who are in the militia and the army and take up arms in the defense of others. So I wonder if it is the *ordnung* that ensure us a place in heaven. Rather, would it not be believing in the work of the Lord Jesus on our behalf, as the Bible tells us?"

Jonas stared at his son as he considered the unorthodox idea Joshua proposed. "I do not know if you are right, my son. It is something that only God knows for sure. But I do know this. I believe with all my heart that Jesus commands us to harm no man. And He said, 'If you love me, keep my commandments.' So that is how I will live my life."

Just then two Indians entered the hut and, with signs and grunts, demanded that the two stand up. One pulled out a knife and threatened Jonas with it. Jonas jumped back and the two savages laughed. Then the one with the knife cut the thongs binding their wrists and motioned for them to come outside. Scar was standing there waiting for them.

"You my slaves now; you do slave's work. You come, my men show you what do."

Jonas looked at Scar. The madness was back on his face. "Have you seen my wife? I haven't seen her for days. I am very worried. She needs to take care of the girls."

Scar turned to the other braves. "*Kepecheonkel!*" He made a motion near his head. Joshua could see that Scar thought his father was insane. The other Indians nodded. "*Kepecheonkel!*"

Scar pushed Jonas back toward the hut. "You stay; this one work." He grabbed Joshua's arm.

Joshua pulled away. He pointed toward his father. "You give him food. He is weak. You would not want to harm him for he has lost his mind. *Kepecheonkel!*"

Scar looked at Jonas who was staring off into the woods as though he were waiting for someone. He nodded and said something to the others. One left and returned in a moment with a bag. Joshua took it and looked inside. There was some dried meat and fish as well as some vegetables and other food. Joshua handed it to his father and pointed to the hut. "Go inside, Father, and eat. Do not wait for Mother for she has gone to visit friends at Fort Pitt and will not return for many days."

Jonas nodded in agreement and went inside the hut. Scar motioned to Joshua and started away. Joshua followed. Soon they came to a clearing in the forest. Indian men were cutting trees and clearing the land. Scar handed Joshua an axe. As Joshua took it, Scar held on to it. He pulled Joshua close and smiled an evil smile. "You want kill me?"

Joshua felt a rush of anger as the savage leered at him. He wanted to pull the axe away from the brawny savage and strike Scar's head from his shoulders. Instead, he released the axe and pointed to the trees. "I will not lift my hand against you. Show me what I must do."

Scar grunted and said something to the other Indians. "*Xkwewtët!* Little woman." The Indians laughed. Scar pointed to where the trees and brush were the thickest on the edge of the clearing and handed the tool to Joshua. "You clear land for garden. Not try run away, me kill father."

"I won't run." Joshua took the axe and headed toward the brush.

At least not today…

The weeks that passed were both a curse and a blessing for Joshua. If he did not do exactly what the Indians wanted, they would try to strike him or knock him down, but he was too big and strong. Often he would catch their arm in mid-swing, and his powerful grip would force them to drop the stick or the club they were aiming at him. One day while he was working in the garden, an Indian tried to sneak up from behind him to assault him. Before he could strike, Joshua leaped quickly to the side and tripped the brave so that he fell heavily to the ground. The man leaped up and rushed at Joshua, but Joshua grabbed him by both wrists and held him. He shook his head at the Indian. "Leave off! I do not wish to hurt you, brother."

Joshua's grip was like a vise. The man pulled with all his strength, but he could not free himself. All the while Joshua kept asking the Indian to stop, but the brave did not understand. He tried to kick at Joshua, but Joshua blocked him with his legs, doing everything he could to neutralize the man's attack. Suddenly, the brave jerked convulsively trying to free himself. The bone in the man's arm snapped with a crack, the Indian's face contorted hideously and he passed out.

Several other Indians had gathered around, grunting and pointing at Joshua in admiration. Joshua could see the horrible bend in the man's arm where the bone had broken. He knelt down and took the man's arm in his hands. Just then, the man's eyes opened and he saw Joshua bending over him. He tried to pull away but groaned again as the bones ground together. Joshua put both hands on the man's chest and shook his head to tell him not to move. Then he took the arm in gentle hands.

Carefully, he moved the arm until he felt the bones slip back together. The Indian groaned and passed out again. There was a pile of branches lying nearby that were being prepared to patch the roofs of the long houses. Joshua selected two that were straight. An Indian standing by had a leather thong tied around his head, and Joshua motioned to the man to give it to him. Then he placed the two sticks on either side of the broken arm and wrapped them tightly with the thong so that the bone would set. He pulled a large handkerchief from out of his pocket and improvised a sling for the man's arm. Slowly the man came to. He looked at his bandaged arm and then up at Joshua. He nodded his head and spoke in his own language. "Wanishi."

"He say, thank you," a voice behind Joshua said. Joshua turned to see Scar looking at him with a strange look. "Why you help him? He try kill you."

Joshua nodded. "Yes, he did, but my God tells me that all men are brothers, and we should help each other, not hurt."

Scar shook his head. "Me not understand. We kill your mother. You strong, brave, but you do not fight. Why?"

"Our God says that love is more powerful than hate."

"Your brother hate. He have big hate for Scar."

"Yes, but Jonathan has turned his back on the words of my God. He will be unhappy all his life unless he repents."

"Repents?"

"Yes, Scar, repents. It means to turn from bad things and do only good for others."

Scar stared at Joshua. "You strange, me no understand this God. Our god tell us kill enemies, protect family."

Joshua shrugged. "Yes, and your face is set in hatred toward all white men because of it. But if you followed the words of my God and helped others to find the way of peace, you would not have to fight many wars. All Indians would live in peace."

Scar scowled. "Never will Indians live in peace—with white man or other Indians. We must be strong, fierce. Hate keeps us strong."

"Yes, Scar, but you are not free."

Scar grunted and turned away. Joshua had an inspiration. "Scar?"

The big man turned.

"Would you ask this brave if I can say words and ask my God to heal his arm quickly?"

Scar paused and then said something in Lenape to the brave. The man looked at Joshua and then to his arm and nodded.

Joshua placed both hands on the man's arm. "*Lieber Vater im Himmel, bitte dieses Mannes Arm zu heilen. Bitte machen Sie es, als ob es nie gebrochen hatte.*"

Scar stared at Joshua with a puzzled look on his face. "What you say?"

"I asked my God to heal this man's arm quickly and to make it like new."

"We see if your God answer." Scar turned and stalked away.

The man with the broken arm got up carefully. He looked at Joshua. "Wanishi." Then he turned and left, holding his arm gingerly. A group of his friends walked with him pointing to the man's arm and talking excitedly.

Joshua turned to pick up his hoe and stopped. Standing a few feet away was the lovely princess, White Deer. She had a very strange look on her face. Her eyes met Joshua's for a moment and then she looked away. Without a word she turned and walked back to the village.

White Deer sat alone in her tent. She did not know what to make of the events she had witnessed. The yellow-haired twin had tried to keep from fighting and after he hurt the brave, he had helped him. A Lenape warrior would have killed his fallen foe so there would never be a question about who was the greater man. It puzzled her. She remembered her father telling her the words he had spoken over her on the day of her birth:

"It is said that the men with pale skin will offer two paths to the Lenape—the way of peace and great prosperity, or the way of death. If the Lenape will not listen to the way of life, then the

Lenape will be uprooted and sent to a far land by the pale skinned people. It is your daughter who will see both faces of the white man—the way of life and the way of death, and it is she who will offer this choice to our people."

White Deer had often thought about these words and what they could mean to her people. From time to time she had asked her father but he only smiled as he looked at his beloved daughter. "You will know the meaning of the words on the day appointed."

Now, with the coming of the *Kahpèsàk* to her village the answer was made clear. For in the face of the dark-haired twin was only hate and death, and in the face of the yellow-haired one was peace and life. A terrible anguish came into her heart and White Deer collapsed weeping on her bed; for she had given her heart to the way of death.

Chapter Thirteen

The Light of the World

It was the longest day in White Deer's life. When her weeping was over, she left her father's lodge and wandered into the forest. Her heart was filled with terrible and unknowable emotions as she walked the familiar paths, searching for something that seemed lost to her forever. She looked for that contentment which had always been hers in the deep, hidden places of the forest, but instead of the sweet song of the forest birds or the chirrup of the black squirrels, she heard only the words of her father:

> *"It is said that the men with pale skin will offer two paths to the Lenape—the way of peace and great prosperity, or the way of death."*

The hours slipped by as she sought the fastness of dark, shaded hollows where the light of day did not reach; she walked the open, grassy hillsides and roamed far over her beloved meadows. But always before her were the faces of the *Kahpèsàk;* the twin brothers. The dark-haired one with hate in his heart and the yellow-haired one who walked the way of peace. Up until the day that Scar brought them to their village, she had been content. Love had not touched her, and the young men of the village sought her favor in vain, for she was the princess of her people and no warrior great enough to win her hand had approached her. Wingenund often smiled as he watched the hopeless faces of those braves who brought unanswered suit to the lodge of his beautiful daughter. Unaccepted gifts and fresh game lay unnoticed at her door or were sent to the lodges of widows.

And then in one day her whole world had changed, for when she looked into the face of the dark one, she knew she was lost beyond hope. Now she wandered, seeking something to block the turmoil in her heart but that sought-for peace eluded her. The beautiful life of the forest sang no more in her heart. The soft moss, the shaking leaf of the aspen tree, the deep mysterious pools where the great trout lay in his kingdom, all these no longer spoke to her soul, but seemed empty and meaningless in the face of the burning in her heart.

Finally, she came to a glen in the green and golden woods where a rugged, giant rock, moss-stained and gleaming with trickling water, rose before her. A wall of intertwined ferns dressed in autumn's auburn hue hid the base of the gray-green cliff and circled a dark, deep pool, dotted with yellow leaves floating on the mirrored surface. Here she cast herself down on the soft forest bed and wept. The golden rays of the afternoon sun filtered down and bathed her in their warm embrace, but she did not feel their touch. Muffled sobs came from deep within. "I love him and yet I do not know him. His heart is filled with bitterness toward all of my people, but the Great Spirit has given me to him, and I know not why. I cannot love him, for he is the way of death, but my heart tells me he is the one."

Thus the maiden lay while the hours crept by. The golden rays softened and the white clouds above her were softly brushed with blushing rose as the day began its age-long surrender to the night. On a branch of a small-flowered agrimony near her, a counting katydid began its raspy inquiry— two notes, then three, then four. A black squirrel chattered away a gray invader that dared to seek food in the same tree. Around her the forest began to come alive with the voices of the night. At last, as the pale pink of the clouds succumbed to the gray of twilight, White Deer rose from the bower where she had fought the greatest struggle of her life. Her face was pale but her heart was set in its path.

I will follow my heart as the Great Spirit guides. Whatever may come to me is not for me to know, but my trail has always been laid before me, and I must go where it leads me.

When White Deer returned to her lodge, her father saw the pale but composed face of his daughter, and he instinctively knew that something of great import had happened before she even spoke. She came and knelt at her father's feet, and Wingenund's heart was troubled. A great sadness stole over him as he listened to the whispered words of the Indian princess.

"Father, I am troubled. My eyes tell me that I have looked upon the face of death in the eyes of the white brother with the black hair, but my heart says I have looked upon love. What am I to do? Why cannot I find happiness with one of our own people?"

Wingenund looked at his beautiful daughter. "The white blood that runs in your veins speaks louder than the Lenape blood. You are drawn to the whiteskins, and your heart has no control of the matter."

White Deer shook her head. "You once told me that at the appointed time I would understand the words spoken over me when I was born. Today I know. The white twin with the dark hair can only show me the way of death. In his brother's hand is the way of peace and prosperity. Yet before I knew this, I had already made my choice. Now I come to you for counsel."

Wingenund arose and paced the center of the lodge as he thought. Then he turned to White Deer. "My heart is heavy when I say this because I think in the end, when you discover the path of peace, it means that you will forsake the ways of our people. But you must learn from the yellow hair. He is a good man and the words of his God have power. Elk Running came to me and showed me where his arm had been broken. In only one half of a moon it has healed completely and he has full use of it again. The yellow-haired one asked his God to do this, and it has been done. Even Scar wonders at the power in this man's words."

"I will do as you ask, Father. But what about the other?"

"I do not know, my daughter. His heart is filled with hate, and because of that, he will not see the love you offer him. I am sad for you. I had hoped to live out my days with Lenape grandchildren on my knee and a great warrior for a son. Now I think that will never be, and I see our people diminishing and going to a far land."

"I am sorry, my father."

The girl bowed her head, but her father came quickly and lifted her into an embrace. "We do not decide our destiny. You must follow the guidance of the Great Spirit. The end we do not know, but I fear it will come with a sad parting."

That night in her bed, her father's words rang in her spirit and she wept, for bitter would be such a day.

From the moment he saw the Indian princess watching him, Joshua Hershberger was entranced. He remembered White Deer from that day long ago when his family had arrived at Fort Pitt. He thought she was beautiful then and now that she was a young maiden, her loveliness had captured him. The look in her eyes after she saw him pray for the man with the broken arm had been strange—full of wonder and fear at the same time. And as she looked at him that day, it was as though he had dived into a deep, dark mysterious pool and had gone down and down, never to come back to the surface. Since then, he could think of nothing else but her beautiful face, the grace of her form and the hidden strength of her as she walked through the village. So it was a great surprise one morning, a few months after he arrived in Shawnee Town, to see her coming toward him through the fields where he was working. She approached him shyly and when she looked up into his eyes, he felt that same rush— something overwhelming and powerful—go through his whole body.

She smiled. "You have the way of peace. I see it in your eyes. Elk Running has told the whole village how his arm has been healed quickly, like new, the thing you asked your God to do for him."

Joshua smiled. "Ah, Princess, that is good news. I am glad to hear he has recovered."

"Does your God always answer you in this way?"

Joshua leaned on his hoe. "Well, sometimes He says yes to our prayer and gives us the answer we want, and sometimes He says no. But He always answers."

The girl was puzzled. "Why did he say yes to your prayer for Elk Running?"

Joshua pointed to a nearby elm that spread its branches over a grassy spot at the edge of the wood. "Will you sit with me for a moment? I cannot be too long, for I have my duties."

White Deer smiled. "I have told Scar that I need to talk to you, so he will not interrupt us."

The two sat together and Joshua looked at the girl. He could not still the beating of his heart, but he did his best. "Now, to answer your question, my God always works in ways that will make people want to know more about Him. It is so they may come to know Him as the greatest of all spirits."

The girl nodded. "Yes, I believe that. When I was born it was foretold that I would discover who the whiteskins really are. I will see both the way of peace and the way of death and I will be the one who tells this truth to my people, so they can decide which path they will choose. I believe the Great Spirit has sent you to tell me the way of peace."

The thought came as a shock to Joshua. In a blinding revelation it all became clear to him why the events of the last months had happened. Grief and joy swept over him and he put his face in his hands and began to weep. The girl drew closer. "Why do you weep?"

Joshua struggled to regain his composure. "Princess, for many months I have struggled with the death of my mother, sisters, and brother at the hands of Scar. I cried out to my God for an answer to my question: why would he allow such a terrible thing to happen? And now I see."

The girl nodded. "Yes?"

Joshua continued. "Your people do not know of my God. So He has sent someone to tell you. I am that one. I see now that my mother and my sisters and my brother suffered only a little while so that Scar would bring me to this place. My heart is glad for they are with God now in heaven, and I am here to tell you of Him."

"And will you tell me?"

"Yes, Princess, I will tell you. I will meet with you if Scar will allow it. There is much to say."

White Deer tossed her head. "I am Wingenund's daughter, a princess of my people. What I wish, Scar will do." Then she looked around to see if anyone was listening and said quietly, "We will meet tomorrow at dawn, here in this place. And you will tell me of this God. What is his name?"

Joshua looked into the eyes of the lovely girl and knew that he had been chosen to give her a great gift, the gift of life. "His name is Jesus. He is the way and the truth and he is life itself and no one can find heaven without him."

The girl looked sad as she stood. "I want to learn of this God, but I am also afraid."

"Afraid of what, Princess?"

"I am afraid that once I know Him I will have to make a choice that will be very hard. And I do not know if I am strong enough to make that choice." White Deer turned and slowly walked away.

Joshua stared after her. The feelings in his heart were so strong that he wanted to leap to his feet and run after her. But he did not.

Chapter Fourteen

The God of This World

The ensuing days flew swiftly for Jonathan Hershberger. At first the Indians watched him closely but after a few months, when he had made no effort to escape, their vigilance began to relax and soon Jonathan was accepted among them with friendly greetings and camaraderie. His great strength and athletic skill soon made him a favorite among the younger braves, but it was his marksmanship that excited the attention of the seasoned warriors. Most of the Indians never learned the finer skills of shooting with the long rifle. Some of them could shoot well, but for the large part, they were poor marksmen. Jonathan, on the other hand, was one of the most skilled shots the braves had ever seen, and in shooting contests he was unrivaled. Because of his unerring aim, the braves began to call him Black Eagle, for they swore that Jonathan had the eyes of the king of birds.

When the village men were not out on hunting expeditions or raids against the settlements, the greatest part of their day was spent in shooting and running competitions. They loved wrestling contests and canoeing. One of their favorite pastimes was the game of lacrosse. The men of the village would form teams consisting of fifty to one hundred men each and play on a field half a mile long. They used a wooden ball, about three inches in diameter, and moved it up and down the field using a strong staff with a hoop net on the end of it. These games lasted from sunup to sundown for two to three days straight. Great honor was given to the most skilled scorers, and Jonathan excelled at running through the defenders, bowling over his opponents, and deflecting blows aimed at him while on a scoring rush. His skill soon gained him renown among the braves, and many times the opposing teams almost came to blows when deciding which team Jonathan would play on.

One day when they were in the midst of a particularly ferocious game, Stalking Bear, Jonathan's one enemy in the village, ran up behind him while he was picking up the ball and aimed a powerful blow at the back of Jonathan's head. If Jonathan had not seen the man's shadow behind him, the blow would probably have killed him. But when he saw the attack coming, he spun out of the way. Still, Stalking Bear managed to give Jonathan a glancing stroke that would have finished off a weaker man. It knocked Jonathan to the ground. Furious, Jonathan rolled over and, springing to his feet, swung his stick and delivered a blow to the attacker's head that split Stalking Bear's skull. The Indian dropped without a sound.

Quickly, the braves surrounded Jonathan and the fallen warrior, pointing and gesturing. Scar pushed through the crowd and stared down at the body of Stalking Bear. Then he looked at Jonathan. "Black Eagle kill?"

Jonathan nodded. The blood from where Stalking Bear's staff struck him was pouring down his head and onto his shirt. "He tried to kill me. I only defended myself. If that is a crime, then so be it."

Scar shook his head. "Stalking Bear did not forget you knock him down. Sneak up from behind not the way of warrior. He has paid. Go back to the lodge and let women help your wound. I speak to Wingenund."

Jonathan returned to the lodge. He had kept a stone face during the conversation with Scar, but inside his heart was pounding. He looked up toward heaven.

I have taken revenge on the first of your murderers, Mother, and I will not stop until I see them all dead.

The days did not go by as swiftly for White Deer. The love for Jonathan that had overtaken her heart conflicted greatly with the words that Joshua spoke to her. The yellow-haired twin told her of a God who created all men to live in peace, of the first man and woman who lived in a beautiful garden with everything they needed, and yet it was not enough, for they chose to walk another path, and darkness came into the beautiful garden. After many years the children of the first man and woman spread to all parts of the earth. But hatred and war were everywhere and no man knew peace. Finally, the great God who had created men grew sad for the sorry state of His creation and sent His only Son to pay the price for the evil deeds of men, even though He, Himself, was innocent. The Son had suffered a terrible death but then He rose from the dead and lived again. Joshua told her that anyone who received the death of the Son as payment for their own evil would be forgiven and be granted a place in heaven where they would live with the great God and His Son forever in peace.

These words were almost too hard for White Deer to understand. A God who loved so much that He sent his Son to die for all evil men was beyond her comprehension. She pondered on this for many days, walking alone in the woods or sitting quietly by the river. And when she watched the dark-haired one growing in stature and power among the men of her tribe, she wondered why his God would reward him when he had turned his back and taken the way of death. It did not make sense. So one morning she went to Joshua to speak with him again. She found him outside his hut mending some of his tools. As she approached he looked up and White Deer noticed a red flush pervade his face. He smiled and invited her to sit.

"Good morning, Princess. How is it with you this morning? Are you well?"

White Deer sat down and sighed. "I am well in my body, but my spirit is sad."

"Why is that, Princess?"

"The words that you spoke to me seemed right, and I have given much thought to the idea of men living together in peace. And yet I watch your brother as he grows in renown among my people. He is strong and confident. He excels in the games and in running and shooting."

Joshua nodded. "He was always a good shot."

The princess hung her head. "This morning he killed Stalking Bear."

Joshua's face twisted. "He killed a man?"

"Yes. They were playing lacrosse. Stalking Bear tried to kill him by striking him while he was not looking. Jonathan defended himself. My father could do nothing about it, for Lenape warriors have a strong sense of honor, and for a brave to try and kill someone from his own tribe in that way is considered beneath contempt."

Joshua shook his head. "I see why you are concerned, Princess, for this news brings great sorrow to my heart."

White Deer hesitated and Joshua must have sensed that she had a question. "You are deeply troubled, Princess. What is it you wish to know?"

White Deer took a deep breath. "You told me of a God who loved so much that He gave his son to pay the price for the deeds of evil men. You told me that this God rewards those who love His Son with peace and prosperity. Yet you, who love and follow this God, are a slave, and your brother, who learns the way of death and war, is gaining great honor and prestige among our people. Why?"

White Deer looked very carefully at Joshua as he formulated his answer. She wanted to make sure that there was no deceit in him.

He was silent for many moments and then finally he spoke. "The Lenape call the spirits who live in the world *manitou*. There is an *Aashaa manitou*, *Kitanitowit* the good spirit, who your people say formed the universe, shaped the earth, and created the first people. I believe that when I speak of my God and you speak of *Kitanitowit* we speak of the same spirit. Your people also speak of an *Otshee manitou*, an evil spirit called *Matantu* who created bad creatures, such as flies. Although all was harmonious at first,

Matantu brought unhappiness, sickness, disasters, and death. He appeared as a great snake that attacked the people and drove them from their homes. The snake flooded the land and made monsters in the water, but *Kitanitowit* made a giant turtle, on which the surviving people rode out the flood and prayed for the waters to recede. There is a story much like this in the Bible, which is the book of my God."

White Deer leaned forward. "How did you learn these things?"

"I have spoken with your sachem, Glickhican, for he, too, is drawn to the way of peace."

White Deer could not contain her surprise. "Glickhican?"

Joshua smiled. "Yes, Princess."

White Deer pondered this startling fact for a moment. "But you have not answered my question."

Joshua went on. "*Matantu* is also in the Bible. He appears as the same great serpent, and it was he who caused the first people to forsake the beautiful garden and go the dark way. We call him Satan, and ever since then, he has built a kingdom on this earth, and he rules the hearts of men and women who would do evil."

"But how does that answer me?"

"Satan, *Matantu*, has been granted power by God to offer kingdoms and power to wicked men. God is seeking to learn the true hearts of the men of earth. So He gives them a choice and freewill to choose. Those who want to be righteous and live the way of peace will follow Jesus, the great God's Son, whom you know as *Kitanitowit*. Those who want power and great wealth often follow *Otshee manitou*, Satan, for he can give prosperity and power to men who follow him. But it is only for a time. Eventually, their evil finds them out, and they pay the price— sometimes in this world and sometimes in the next."

The princess was still troubled. "How do they pay the price in this world? You are good, but are you not suffering?"

Joshua nodded. "Those who follow Satan may experience temporary good feelings or wealth, or success, but without the presence of Jesus in their hearts, in the end, they can only know emptiness. Their power does not give them the happiness they seek." He paused. "Yes, I have experienced great sorrow and suffering. But I also have the words and the presence of my God to comfort me." He took a deep breath. "I have also been given the great joy of meeting you and becoming your friend." The red blush flooded his face again.

In that moment, White Deer saw Joshua's heart through his eyes. The revelation came as a bolt of lightning on a hot summer night.

He loves me!

She turned away from those searching eyes and asked another question. "How do evil men suffer in the next life?"

Joshua tried to look into her eyes, but the princess kept them lowered. "Men suffer in the next life, Princess, because if they have not accepted the death of God's Son as payment for their sins, then God puts them away from Him and they dwell forever in darkness. Those who have done great evil even suffer torment."

"So your brother may gain respect and power, but he will be separated from Jesus forever?"

"If he does not turn from his path, yes."

White Deer put her face in her hands. She tried to quiet her heart, but her body betrayed her and she began to cry quietly.

Joshua put his hand on her shoulder. "What is it?"

"I do not wish for Jonathan to suffer. I wish him to know the way of peace again." She looked up. Joshua was staring at her with a great question in his eyes. "Princess, do you… do you…?"

White Deer threw herself down and began to weep. Her heart was breaking. Why could she not love this tender, gentle man, who loved her, instead of his brother, who hated all Indians? Finally, she sat up. She took a deep breath and then looked into Joshua's eyes. "Yes, Joshua, I love Black Eagle. But I wish I did not."

Part Four

Love's Freedom,
Love's Prison

You never know how deep your love is until the hour of parting.

Love's Freedom, Love's Prison
From The Journals of Jenny Hershberger

Chapter Fifteen

A Father's Love

The seasons slipped by and the Hershbergers entered their fourth year of captivity. Jonas kept up his charade of madness, and the Indians treated him kindly but kept their distance. Joshua worked hard at the most menial of tasks and even though the fare given to them as slaves was scanty, he kept up his strength and actually grew stronger and more physically fit. For many months Joshua and Jonas had been trying to find a way to escape, but the nearest settlement was far away, and there were always warriors in the village.

These were days of great activity in Shawnee Town. Word came to Wingenund that settlers were moving into Ohio and Kentucky, taking lands that had been given to the Indians by treaty. Another act by the settlers that angered Wingenund was the construction of Fort Henry downriver from Fort Pitt, near where the Hershbergers had first settled. It had become the focal point for the western invasion by new settlers from Virginia and Pennsylvania. The Delaware, Mingo, and Shawnee tribes had retaliated by attacking settlements all along the border, and Lord Dunsmore, the governor of Virginia, finally declared war on the confederated tribes in the spring of 1774. Because the Lenape were sharing Shawnee Town with the Shawnee and were looked upon as the older brothers of that tribe, Wingenund joined in a series of brutal attacks meant to drive the whites back beyond the Allegheny Mountains.

Early in 1774, Jonathan left with the younger braves on an extended hunting trip. While they were gone, a band of white soldiers on their way to Kentucky came up the Scioto River to attack a Mingo village not far away from Shawnee Town. Scouts came to Shawnee Town to tell of the whiteskins' advance, so the chief gathered all the available braves and rushed to the defense of their Mingo allies, leaving his village almost completely empty of men. It was then that Jonas Hershberger saw his chance. When he realized that the warriors were gone, he gathered some long-prepared supplies and made his way to the field where Joshua was working.

Joshua was tilling the ground for a new corn patch when he heard a soft voice from the woods behind him.

"Kommen Sie Joshua, hier schnell."

Joshua looked around. He saw his father beckoning from the edge of the woods. He made sure he wasn't being watched and then ran to where his father was hiding in the brush. "What is it, *Daati?*"

"The braves have all left the village, Joshua. They have gone on a war party down the river. Now is the chance to escape we have been looking for."

Joshua looked at his father. Jonas had a sack and a rifle. "I have food inside, sun-dried meat and corn meal, enough for a few days."

"Where did you get this, Father?"

Jonas smiled. "They thought I was *veruccht* and left me alone. I've been saving food aside for a long time, waiting for our chance. This rifle I took from the hut of a brave who was killed in one of the raids on the settlements. He was not married and the other braves would not enter to take it, for the hut belonged to a dead man. I also brought your coat and shoes and a water bag."

"But how do we get back to the settlements?"

"I overheard the braves talking. Ebenezer Zane has built a fort downriver from Fort Pitt, near our old farm. If we go due east from here, we'll strike the Ohio in a day or two. Then if we follow the river, we'll find game and fish. I have some cord and hooks. From the river it can only be a matter of a hundred miles or so to Zane's fort. We should make it in four or five days."

Joshua looked long at his father. "Papa, are you strong enough to make the journey?"

Jonas took his son by the shoulder. "With the Lord's help we shall return to our farm. I am not as old as I look."

"But what about Jonathan?"

Jonas shrugged and a look of sorrow passed over his face. "Jonathan has made his choice. He is gone on the hunting trip with the braves, and we may never get a chance like this again. We must go. Jonathan will have to make his own way, as he has done since the day your mother died. *Kumme!* " Jonas motioned to Joshua and started toward the forest.

Joshua looked around. There was no one watching. He started to follow, and then for a moment, something held him and he looked back toward the village. Jonas took his son's arm and began to pull him toward the woods. Joshua hesitated.

"What is it, Joshua?"

"I will never see her again."

Jonas nodded. "The princess. Yes, I have known for a long time that you love her. I can see it in your eyes when she goes by."

"White Deer loves Jonathan."

Jonas stared at his son. "Are you sure, Joshua?"

"Yes, Papa. She told me. And I suppose that is the best reason of all to leave." Joshua straightened up, tall and strong. "Come, Father. Let us put our lives into the hand of our God and pray for a safe journey."

Jonas took a deep breath. "Yes, my son. Let us go."

And together, Jonas and Joshua disappeared into the forest.

That day the two men traveled far into the forest, keeping the sun at their backs and heading due east. Making their way through the trackless forest was extremely difficult. They often came to deep gullies that barred their way, and they would have to go down the steep banks and then try to find a way up the other side. When they could not find a way to climb out, Joshua would lead them south until they found a way up. He knew if they continued south and east, at some point they would strike the river. Finally, it had become so dark they could not see the way and they could travel no more. They crawled beneath the shelter of a stand of pines, shared a little of the dried meat that Jonas had brought, and then lay down on the soft needles and slept as though dead.

Joshua woke as the first rays of the sun pushed through the trees from the east. He stirred his father and the older man sat up and rubbed his eyes. "Are you still with me then, lad?"

Joshua smiled. A short distance away an amber-colored freshet poured down through the trees on its way to the Ohio. The two men drank gratefully and filled their water bag. They had a bite to eat and then talked over their plan for the day.

Joshua pointed to the creek. "If we follow that down, we'll hit the river and it will be easier travel. We won't have as many of these gullies to climb through."

"Yes, Joshua, but we are still very close to the village. It would be unfortunate if we met some of the braves coming down the river from the east. We should continue east through the forest until we strike the Ohio. By then we will be far enough away that we can follow the river in comparative safety. And we will cut off a great loop the river makes."

Joshua pondered that for a moment and then agreed. "Yes, Father, but if we have to climb more of the rough ground we faced yesterday and you weaken, I will take us south to the river."

Jonas nodded. "Agreed. *Lassen Sie uns dann aus sein. Schnell!*" And the two men began the second day of their journey.

They traveled all that day heading east. The forest lay quiet and still and they made better progress than the day before. Often they would see a deer or rabbits, but they dared not use the rifle for fear of attracting any roaming bands of Indians. Toward the end of the day, Jonas weakened and began to lag behind. Joshua put the rifle over his shoulder, and taking hold of his father, he helped the older man make his way over many obstacles and through great thickets of brush. Finally, Jonas could travel no more, and the two chose a campsite in the heart of a manzanita thicket. They shared a meager meal of dried venison and water and then slept again.

Early the next morning, something awakened Jonas just before sunrise, a slight sound, something moving in the forest. He sat up and looked around, trying to see what had disturbed him. Then he looked down at Joshua lying sound asleep. He touched his son's face. Joshua stirred but did not awaken. "Aye, you wore yourself out carrying your father, yesterday. *Du bist ein guter Sohn*, Joshua." Just then he heard the same slight sound. He peered out between the branches of the manzanita. Not more than one hundred yards away, a group of Indians in war paint were silently making their way directly toward the place where Jonas and Joshua lay hidden. Jonas' heart leaped. He looked down at his son and then leaned over and lightly kissed him. He stood up and took a deep breath. He heard his son stir behind him.

"Papa?"

Jonas turned and smiled down at his son. He whispered, "Don't make a sound, Joshua. Remember, I love you and I will see you again beside the throne. As soon as I am gone, get up and run as fast and as far as you can the other way."

Before Joshua could stop him, Jonas turned and burst from the thicket, running as hard as he could. He heard the startled grunts of the Indians behind him and then whoops as they joined the chase.

Jonas prayed as he ran. "Help me, *Vater!* Give me wings that I may fly unto you." He ran with a strength he had not known since his youth. Then he heard the report of a rifle. Jonas felt the ball whistle by his head, and he ran harder, as straight through the woods as he could. He had gained on the Indians, and by now, he was getting farther and farther away from Joshua. But soon the effort told on him, and he began to slow. He heard the sound of the braves closing in. Still he ran.

He cried out, *"Gott, hilf mir jetzt!"* Ahead of him, he saw a break in the trees. The ground began to rise, and he broke out into the open. He was running along a ridge. On one side lay the forest and on the other a great cliff dropped away into a canyon. He stumbled and fell and then picked himself up and ran some more. He heard the Indians coming closer. He raised his arms to the heavens. Behind him, he heard the report of a rifle. Something struck him in the back like a hammer blow, and he stumbled again.

He raised himself up and took a few more steps. He heard another gunshot, and again he felt the hot metal tear through him. He staggered to the edge of the cliff and pulled himself erect. He turned to his pursuers as they came running up. *"Vater, vergib ihnen, denn sie wissen nicht..."* Everything around him faded, and he felt himself falling backward, not into darkness, but into the light.

Joshua lay still. He had awakened to see his father smiling down at him with loving eyes, and had heard his last words. Joshua lifted his hand to stop him, and then Jonas was gone, running like the wind away from where Joshua lay. He saw Jonas disappear into the forest, with the Indians close behind. He heard them whooping as Jonas led them away. He heard a shot, then another. There was absolute stillness and then he heard the exultant whoops of the Indians, ringing through the forest. He knew his father was dead. Joshua grabbed his things and began to run the other way. As he ran he used all his skill to hide his trail. When he came to streams, he was careful to walk in the water. He jumped from rock to rock and looked for tall grass that would spring back after he passed. Finally, he could go no further. Checking his back trail to make sure no one was following him, he looked for a place to rest. Finally, he saw a nearly impenetrable mass of brambles. Ignoring the thorns, he crawled deep into the thicket and lay there sobbing silently. "Papa, Papa."

Joshua lay in the thicket for a long time, but the Indians did not come. The voices of the forest awoke, and he knew that his pursuers had lost his trail. He gathered his things and crawled out or the brambles as quietly as he could. He looked back once and then started east. He traveled until the sun was far down in the west, and then he rested. As he sat he felt a chill in the air, and the light began to fail. He looked up. Clouds were moving in and a cold rain began to fall. He put on his coat and started off. He tried to continue in the easterly direction, but without the sun to guide him, he began to wander. Darkness was fast approaching when he sat by a tree and waited hopefully for the appearance of the North Star. But the dark clouds filled the heavens and no stars appeared. Exhausted and grief-stricken, he dragged himself into the center of some dense undergrowth and lay down to wait for dawn. The dismal hoot of an owl, the furtive steps of some creature of the forest prowling round the thicket, and the mournful keening of the wind in the tops of the pines, kept him awake for hours, but at last, he fell asleep with a sense of deep despair. He was lost.

Chapter Sixteen

In The Wilderness

The morning arrived, dim and gray, and Joshua stirred in his hiding place. Around him, a gray fog drifted slowly through the woods, and the trees were scarcely visible, even a few yards away. The heavy mist damped down every sound and even the birds seemed reluctant to begin their morning melodies. The only noise was the steady drip of moisture from the shrouded trees. The night wind had passed, leaving a cold, stagnant breath lingering in the eaves of the forest, and Joshua shivered in the chill morning air. The heavy dew demanded that he risk a small fire to dry his clothes so he cautiously left the thicket to look for some dry wood. A few yards away, a large pine had fallen and begun the slow return to the soil of the forest. He rolled it over. Reaching underneath, he stripped away pieces of the dry interior and some bark and moss. He carried them back to the thicket and laid them on a clear spot in the middle of his hiding place. He poured a small amount of powder on the kindling and then holding his rifle close to the pile he pulled the trigger. The flint sent a spark into the powder, which ignited the dry moss. As the small flames rose, he added pieces of the pine and bark until he had a nice fire going. The wood was dry and the intertwined branches above him dissipated what little smoke the fire gave off. The fog was so thick around his hiding place that he knew the flames could not be seen unless someone walked right up on the fire.

Joshua ate some of his meager rations and drank some water. Then the recollections came flooding back into his mind—his father's last loving smile, Jonas' sacrificial run through the forest, the shots and the exultant yells of the Indians as they caught up with their quarry, and the grief and sorrow that had flooded his heart when he knew that his father was dead. As he sat quietly before the fire, a scripture came to his mind:

"Greater love hath no man than this, that a man lay down his life for his friends."

The words comforted him and he began to pray. *"Liebster Jesus; erhalten Sie meinen Vater mit offenen Armen heute. Lassen Sie ihn in zu Ihrem Königreich als ein guter und treuer Diener hereingehen.* Lord, receive *mein Vater* into your kingdom today. Let his reunion with *Maam* and the girls be joyous. Let him take delight in his son, Aaron, and, Lord, bless your servant Jonas as a good and faithful servant."

His prayers finished, Joshua tried to decide what to do. Because of the dense fog, the sun was completely hidden so he had no way to find his direction by the heavens. As he sat quietly, he heard the sound of a small stream nearby.

I will follow the stream downhill. It must be flowing south and eventually it will come to the river. Then I can follow the Ohio back to Zane's fort. Or if the sun comes out, I can turn east again.

His decision made, Joshua packed his things into the knapsack, put out the fire, and made his way through the trees until he came to the stream. Turning along the bank, he began to follow the rushing brook downhill toward the river.

A few hours later, Joshua came to an almost insurmountable obstacle. The downhill trend of the land had flattened out, and the swiftly flowing creek lost itself in a dismal swamp. The fog was still thick, and Joshua had to make the choice of trying to find his way around the mire in the mist or pushing ahead. He decided on the latter course and raising his rifle and powder above his head, he waded into the stagnant, foul-smelling water. He tried to make his way across the tufts of dry ground that were interspersed among the still pools, but the going was extremely arduous and many times he found himself in waist-deep water. He felt the sticky mud sucking at his legs and dragging him down. At one point he was in the water up to his armpits. As he was struggling through a particularly dense growth of cattails, he heard a splash and saw a four-foot long water moccasin swimming away through the reeds. An involuntary shudder shook his chilled body. After an hour in the water, he came to an island in the middle of the swamp. He breathed a sigh of relief and crawled gratefully onto the dry land.

After he rested for a good while, he got up and looked around for some dry wood. The island was fairly large and there were several downed trees and lots of dead brush lying about, and within a short time, he had a cheerful blaze going. He had never realized the simple pleasure of a fire on a cold day until then. He spread his clothes to dry and scraped the mud from his trousers and shoes. Then he rested before his fire. As he contemplated the glowing heart of the coals, he heard a rustling in the brush and a curious rabbit poked its head out to see what was happening. Joshua slowly reached for his tomahawk and then with a lightning throw, knocked the rabbit senseless. In a short while, the unfortunate rabbit was turning on a spit over the fire, and Joshua enjoyed his first hot meal in days. He knew that he would find more difficult travel ahead, so he decided to spend the night where he was. The island was hidden in the middle of the swamp, and the probability of anyone stumbling onto his camp was slim. After finishing half of the rabbit meat, he packed the rest into his bag, covered himself with his coat, and lay down to sleep.

In the middle of the night, the flames from his fire died down and the night's chill awakened Joshua. He stirred and arose to stoke the embers with more wood. Once he was awake, he could not go back to sleep, so he sat cross-legged, like an Indian, before his campfire. The blaze was small, but warm. The short pieces of dead wood burned red, like coal. Joshua spread his palms to the heat. As he sat in the silence, a parade of faces began a slow journey through the gold and red embers—his father and mother, his sisters and brothers, but most of all, the wonderful Indian princess. He was very tired but he was afraid to go to sleep because he knew the specters would awaken him during the night, and then he would lie in the loneliness and stillness of the darkest hours before the dawn, tormented by the memories, haunted by the spirits of those who had gone before, and trembling beneath the power of the love that had been born in his heart. The longer he stayed awake, the shorter would be that time he would lie sleepless, with all the events of his past displayed mercilessly before him, like lost ships on the dark surface of some mysterious ocean. So he stayed awake and his fire was his companion. It glowed and sparkled. It was something alive that cheered him as he sat.

But even the fire was a betrayer, for the moment came when White Deer's face appeared like a phantom in the white-hot heart of the fire. It shone there, her beauty crowned by raven hair, her dark, fathomless eyes and firm, sweet lips beckoning to him in the night. Joshua sighed, for he had longed for those lips, but he knew that they would forever belong to Jonathan. He cursed his brother and then, a moment later, repented, for he knew that his times were in the Lord's hands, and Jesus had ordered his steps. Still, his broken heart yearned for the peace that requited love would grant and the fulfillment it would bring. He trembled before those eyes that would haunt him down every path he took, in the embers of every campfire.

"White Deer," he whispered, brokenly.

Joshua mourned to himself while the beautiful face in the fire softened and glowed with imagined sweetness and longed-for understanding, showering him with a revelation that would only be his this one night and then would vanish as the fire burned down to ashes. In that hour Joshua's love for the Indian maiden mounted to sacred heights and then was cast into the abyss, as he put away forever any hope he held to possess the lovely maiden. It was in that hour that he realized the only thing that remained truly his, the only thing that he could hold until his dying breath, was the passion locked in his dreams, and he marveled at the change that had come to his life and manhood simply from knowing her. And so, like his Savior before him, Joshua faced his own Gethsemane, the dark night before an uncertain dawn, when he cried for the cup of his sorrow to be lifted from him. And as he wept, his merciful Lord brought peace and rest before the dawn.

In the morning a single ray of sunlight breaking through the trees fell on his face and awakened him. He stirred. The fire that had sparkled and gleamed with life and visions in the dark night now lay before him, a heap of gray, lifeless ashes. He knew that the Lord was showing him a picture. In the ashes was all that remained of his hopes and dreams for the love of a woman. He remembered the command of the Lord to Abraham when He asked for Isaac as an offering to prove his obedience. And like Abraham, Joshua laid his love on an altar on the mountain and he remembered the Lord's words: *I will provide myself, the lamb.*

In that moment Joshua began to realize that the Lord was setting him apart for some great sacrificial work and that a wife and home were not to be his, at least not now. As this truth broke upon his weary mind, he was comforted to know that a calling had been placed on his life, though he did not yet know what it was to be. He sat for a moment longer, contemplating what the Lord was showing him. Then a verse from Isaiah came to him, unbidden.

"But they that wait upon the LORD shall renew their strength; they shall mount up with wings as eagles; they shall run, and not be weary; and they shall walk, and not faint."

More light began to break through the morning mist. Joshua stood and faced the east. The Lord was showing him the path home.

Quickly, he packed his things and plunged into the swamp following that blazing beacon. East of the island, the land began to rise and the deep waters of the swamp grew shallow under his feet as he forged his way through the tangled brush and heavy reeds. Soon he felt the mud beneath him turn to sand, and ahead of him he saw the edge of the swamp and beyond that, the park-like swales of open forest. With thanksgiving in his heart, he stepped upon the dry land as the sun rose through the trees and led him on.

Hours later, he came to the Ohio. The broad green stream slipped between the silent eaves of the forest like a highway leading Joshua home. He calculated that he was less than one hundred miles from the fort. His spirits rose as hope rose in his heart. He began to follow the deep flowing waters as the river bent its way in a northeasterly direction, back to the place of its birth at Fort Pitt. Salvation lay before him. All the rest of that day he followed the river, putting the place of his captivity farther and farther behind him.

That night he chanced a small fire for warmth, finished the rest of the rabbit, and lay down to an exhausted and blessedly dreamless sleep. Morning brought another day of travel, and Joshua began to recognize some of the landmarks he had passed when Scar carried him down the river as a captive four years earlier. Dusk brought another camp and hope for the morning.

Joshua was awakened by the most glorious sunrise he had seen in many a day. Purple trails of clouds drifted high above the majesty of golden rays rising from the east like ethereal crowns of glory. Pinks and oranges crowded the sky as the ever-changing face of the clouds painted a flowing portrait of

perfection before his astonished eyes. The beloved psalm came
to him as he stood in wonder:

*"Then shall thy light break forth as the morning, and thine
health shall spring forth speedily: and thy righteousness shall go
before thee; the glory of the LORD shall be thy rear guard."*

With a hopeful heart, Joshua stooped to retrieve his bag. As
he did he felt something pass by his head and go ricocheting
away among the trees followed by the bark of a rifle. A musket
ball! Turning, he looked back down the river. Not more than
three hundred yards away was a war party of Lenape. He
recognized the scalp locks and war paint, even from this
distance. They had seen him, and as he turned to run, he saw the
flash of a musket and heard the whistle of another leaden
messenger of death as it zipped past his head. And then a voice
spoke to his heart. *Run, Joshua! I will cover thee with my feathers, and
under my wings shalt thou trust: my truth shall be thy shield and buckler.*

Joshua turned and began to run. But it was not fear that gave
wings to his feet; it was trust in the God who had led him thus
far. Strength from some unknown source flowed into his body,
and he began to fly through the woods. Behind him, the shrill
yells of the braves stirred him to greater effort. On he ran, never
looking back but varying his course from moment to moment to
keep his pursuers from an easy target. His lungs filled with air
and his heart with hope as he put the miles behind him.

Ten, twenty, thirty miles passed beneath his feet, and still, he
ran tirelessly. The cries of the Indians rose, as the strongest
runners stayed close behind, for these were warriors of the
Delaware, renowned for their prowess in the footrace. Late
afternoon was changing the complexion of the day as Joshua
came to a familiar part of the river. He and Jonathan had crossed
over and hunted on this shore often. Fort Henry was just ahead
across the river. Musket balls began to zip around him as he
came to the bank, and without hesitation, he plunged into the
cold waters and began a swim for life. His arms stroked the
water with power; his feet drove him onward through the

stream. His heart filled with joy in his own strength and the power of God surging through him.

There! On the opposite shore, men with muskets pointing to the water, running to the bank! Spurts of flame as they fire their rifles across the river at the opposite shore. Howls of disappointment behind him as the pursuers turn from the withering fusillade coming from the fort and vanish into the forest. Then the bottom of the river under his feet, a few more steps and then out onto dry land. Up the long hill and he was staggering through the gates of Fort Henry and collapsing exhausted amidst the crowd of astonished men and women. Joshua was saved.

Chapter Seventeen

The Escape

When Jonathan returned to Shawnee Town from the hunt, the village was in an uproar. As he was unpacking the horses, Scar came to him and pulled him aside. "Your white father, brother run away. Braves find father in woods and kill."

Jonathan stared at the brave. "Your braves killed my father?"

Scar nodded.

"What about Joshua?

"Braves could not find. He ran away, hid his trail."

Jonathan turned away so Scar would not see the hate in his eyes. He stalked silently into the woods. The fact that his father and brother had left without him was not surprising. What was surprising to Jonathan was that it was so hurtful. And now Papa was dead. The old familiar hate for Scar rose up in his heart like an awful black tide, but above it all was deep sorrow that he had been left behind, and his Papa was gone forever.

He thought of his father, and tears began to run down his face. Memories of the good days in the Northkill settlement flooded his mind. He sat on a log and wept long and bitterly— for his father, his mother, and his lost brothers and sisters. It was there that White Deer found him. He did not hear her approach until he felt a gentle hand on his shoulder. He turned with tear-streaked face to look into the eyes of the lovely princess.

"I am sorry for your loss, Black Eagle. I know you are sad. If I can help you..."

Jonathan pulled roughly away from her. "You're an Indian. You are a savage. You know nothing of what I am feeling so there is nothing you can do. I don't need you or your help. My father was a weakling who let my mother and my brother and sisters die at the hands of Scar and his men. I hated him for it, but I hate Scar more for killing him. If my father had listened to me then, Scar and his band of murderers would be sleeping the long sleep somewhere in the woods by our farm. Some day I will..." He turned away before he could give away his intentions.

White Deer sighed. "I know you hate all Indians. You fool Scar. He thinks you are his white son but you follow the way of death. I see it in your eyes. One day you will kill Scar. Your brother told me of your desire, and he told me of the God you have forsaken."

Jonathan whirled around. "Me! Me! I have forsaken God? Where was God when Scar was cutting the scalp from my mother's head? Where was he when my sisters were being violated and tortured in the woods? No, Princess, I have not forsaken God; God has forsaken me." Jonathan stepped closer and grabbed the girl roughly by the arm. "If you know that I am going to kill Scar, why have you not told him?"

White Deer's face went pale and then turned red. She could not look Jonathan in the eye. She tried to pull away, but Jonathan held her in his powerful grip. He stared at her and then a realization dawned on him and he pulled her closer. "So that's it. You like white men. You like me." He laughed. "Well, well, Princess, maybe you'll like this, too." He dragged her to him and tried to kiss her. She turned away, but his lips found her mouth, and then he was kissing her, his mouth brutal against hers.

Suddenly, White Deer was fighting him with all her strength. She got her arm free and struck him across the mouth. The blow was so powerful that it knocked Jonathan back a step. White Deer reached to her side and then there was a knife in her hand. Her eyes were burning with rage. "I am White Deer, princess of my people. No man has ever touched me like that. I will kill you." She sprang at him like a mountain lioness, but he was too quick for her. He avoided the strike of the blade and then grabbed her arm and twisted it brutally. The girl cried out and the knife dropped from her hand. Jonathan pulled her close. His arms were so powerful that she could not break his grip. Their faces were inches apart. Then Jonathan kissed her again. White Deer struggled at first. But then Jonathan felt her soften and go limp, and then she was kissing him back with all the fire of a woman in love. He pulled away and pushed her down. She fell heavily and did not try to rise, but hid her face in shame. He looked at her with scorn in his eyes. "No white woman would behave like that. You are just a savage." Then Jonathan turned and walked away. White deer's face flushed with rage and humiliation, but she could not push away the memory of his burning kisses. Her heart was still pounding with the love she felt for Jonathan. She lay weeping for a long time and then rose and slowly made her way back to her lodge.

Jonathan's anger against those who had murdered his father burned deep within his heart. He began to lay his plans carefully. Once the furor over his brother's escape died down, he fell back into his familiar ways with the braves. He joined the hunting parties, shooting contests and the Indian games. He made himself invaluable in the part he played provisioning the village for the winter. He seemed happy and content because he wished to win the regard of the Indians, but in his secret hours, he cursed the Indians as he formulated his plan of escape. Finally, when fall's colors were painting the leaves with crimson and gold and the hunting parties were being sent out, Jonathan knew that the time was right. He had laid aside enough supplies for five days journey, and when he joined several braves on a hunt, he was prepared.

The group set out on a bright fall morning. Jonathan carried his long rifle and tomahawk and his bag of supplies. The other Indians were laughing and waving to the maidens as they left the village for they knew that with Jonathan along they would bring back plenty of game and gain great respect among the villagers. They struck out in a westerly direction, heading deep into the wilderness. They were headed for the part of the forest frequented by bears, for bear meat and skins were especially prized among the people.

Bear hunting was dangerous work. When they were preparing to hibernate, the bears crawled into a hole in a tree or a cave in the rocks. It took a skillful tracker to find their signs, but on the second day, the party located a dead, broken-off tree with the scratches of large claws on it and a hole large enough to admit the body of a bear. Gathering around excitedly, the hunters sent the youngest Indian up the tree with a long pole to poke the sleeping bear out of his den. They waited expectantly until they heard the growls of the awakened bear, but the animal refused to come out, so the hunters resorted to fire.

They fastened a dry piece of wood onto the pole, set it on fire, and shoved it down into the den. The maddened beast came out so quickly that one of the braves was unable to get out of the way and fell beneath the sudden onslaught. But before the bear could maul him, the report of a rifle split the air, and the animal fell dead on top of the brave. The Indians looked around in surprise. Jonathan stood calmly reloading his rifle. The Indians whooped and surrounded him, slapping him on the back with approval. Jonathan's shot had gone right into the eye, killing the bear instantly.

The lad under the bear wriggled out and approached Jonathan with respect. "Black Eagle save life. Owe you debt."

Jonathan acted nonchalant and slapped the boy on the shoulder. "Don't worry about it Abhay, you would have done the same. Sometime you save me, eh?" The group began skinning the bear. Once they were done, they decided to camp there and continue the hunt in the morning. The next day, Jonathan got up early and told the hunting party he was going to find some elk. Two of the braves wanted to go with him so he was forced to let them come. They headed off into the woods. Jonathan waited until they were far from the camp and then he suddenly turned and with one powerful blow, knocked one of the braves out. He pulled his tomahawk from his belt and advanced on the other brave. The Indian was so startled that he backed away from Jonathan and tripped over a log behind him. As he fell, his rifle discharged. Jonathan felt the impact and then a hot burning in his flesh and blood began to pour from a wound in his shoulder. Jumping over the log, he looked down into the face of one of the braves who had been with Scar the day his mother was murdered. He raised his weapon. "This is for my mother and sisters, you dog." The tomahawk blade flashed in the sun, the Indian quivered once and then lay still. Then Jonathan turned to the other brave and did the same.

After he scalped the two Indians, Jonathan looked at the wound in his shoulder. The ball had gone clear through him. The place it struck him was high enough on his body that it had not broken any bones or pierced his lung, but it was bleeding heavily. He grabbed up some moss and stuffed it into the hole to staunch the bleeding. Then he tore a piece off the shirt of one of the dead Indians and tied it around his shoulder. When he was bandaged up, he took his bearings from the sun. He was west of the village, a long way from the white settlements and seriously injured.

He pondered his situation for a moment. Then he set off toward the rising sun, heading east.

By the end of the day, Jonathan was weak from loss of blood. He crawled into a thicket and fell fast asleep. All too soon, the rays of the rising sun penetrated his hiding place and woke him. He pulled himself erect and headed east again. For an hour he traveled east, but in his weakened condition, he was not covering as much ground as he had hoped. Around mid-morning, Jonathan heard a noise behind him. Looking back, he saw the rest of the hunting party not more than a quarter of a mile away through the trees. They were on his trail! His heart leaped and then he steeled himself and began to run. Suddenly, he heard a whoop. They had seen him. Jonathan was a swift runner, but he knew that with his wound it would not be long before they would catch him. Looking around, he recognized the part of the forest he was in. Shawnee Town was not far away. He realized he had only one hope. He made his decision and turned toward the village. He ran swiftly but soon he heard the braves close behind. There was a crack from one of the rifles, and he heard a ball whistle past his head.

That has to be Abhay. He's the only one who can shoot on the run, and he's a dead shot. He's deliberately missing!

Then Jonathan saw the main trail that led back to the camp. He ran onto it and headed straight for the heart of the village. He knew right where he was going. Then he saw it—White Deer's lodge. It was his only hope. With the last strength left in him, he burst through the door of the lodge and fainted, falling face first on the floor at White Deer's feet. Startled, she jumped up, her face turning pale. She saw the blood stain on Jonathan's shirt, and her hand flew to her mouth. She grabbed up a gourd of water and splashed some in his face. Jonathan started to come around. White Deer knelt beside him. "What has happened?"

Just then, the braves who were following Jonathan burst into the lodge, followed by Wingenund and Scar. The leader of the hunting party pointed to Jonathan. "He kill Payat and Shotek, take scalps. He must die."

Wingenund stepped forward. He pointed to Jonathan. "Let Scar paint his white son's face black." Jonathan saw White Deer's face go pale when she heard her father's words. Black paint meant torture and death. As Jonathan lay before her, he saw her try to turn her eyes from his face, but she could not. When he had rejected her, he had seen the hatred in her eyes, but from the way she looked at him now, he knew that her love was more powerful. Jonathan looked up at her, his eyes searching hers, his fate in her hands. She made her choice. Her eyes were clear and steadfast as she raised them to her father.

She knelt beside Jonathan and took his hand. When she kissed his hand, she expressed a tender humility. Jonathan knew he was saved. White Deer had claimed the unquestionable right of the princess of her people; what no Indian dared refuse a chief's daughter. She had taken Jonathan for her husband.

Her action was followed by an impressive silence. She remained kneeling. Wingenund shrugged his shoulders and grunted. Scar turned and left the lodge with a gloomy face. The other braves nodded and bowed their heads knowing White Deer's decree was irrevocable. Wingenund stepped to the door and gave a command. The old sachem, Glickhican, entered the lodge. He stood over the couple and mumbled words in the Lenape language. Then he departed, chanting a long song. White Deer arose and pointed to the door. Her father gave her one long, questioning look and then turned without a word and led the others from the lodge. Jonathan and White Deer were married.

Chapter Eighteen

Love's Call

Jonathan lay long in the grip of the illness brought on by his wound. After a few days, infection set in and there followed exhausting days in fever and delirium. White Deer made him as comfortable as she could and nursed him day and night. A week after his attempted escape, Jonathan reached a crisis in the night. Wingenund came with the medicine man and they examined Jonathan with grim faces. Wingenund went aside with White Deer. "He should have died two days ago, and except for your care and his great physical strength, he would have. I will leave the medicine man here for the night. He will call upon the Misinkhalikan, the Mask Spirit, and ask for power to heal Black Eagle. If your husband lives until morning it will be *wapanacheen*, a good morning, because he lived."

White Deer felt a flash of fear as Wingenund left.

Please! He cannot die.

The medicine man knelt by Jonathan's bed and began to chant in a low, indistinct voice. On and on he sang while White Deer sat at Jonathan's side, wiping the sweat from his brow with a damp cloth. Jonathan's face was pale, and his brow was burning with fever. From time to time he cried out.

"*Maam, Maam*, I'll get help; just don't let them in…"

"You coward, you let them die…"

"I will kill you, Scar, you will pay for my family…"

While Jonathan was crying out and writhing on the bed, White Deer felt helpless and alone. His eyes were staring wildly beyond her into the darkness that had filled his soul, and she could not reach in to bring him back. In the darkest hour of the night, she despaired of his life. At one point, the medicine man stopped his chanting, shook his head and left the lodge. White Deer watched him leave. As she looked down at Jonathan in hopeless fear, she suddenly remembered the words of his brother, the yellow-hair, Joshua.

"Well, Princess, sometimes He says yes to our prayer and gives us the answer we want, and sometimes He says no. But He always answers."

White Deer rose, went outside the lodge, and walked into the forest. It was still and gray, the hour before dawn and a solemn silence crushed the world into immobility. Not a sound could be heard among the trees. White Deer looked around to see if any of her people were watching her, but all was silent. She made her way through the dim woods, with just the faintest pre-dawn light to guide her. Finally, in a secluded grove where she often went, she knelt down in the soft grass. She looked up at heaven and hesitantly began. "Oh, Jesus, God of the yellow-hair, the one we know as Kitanitowit; Joshua says that though you may not give the answer we want, You always answer. And so I come to You with a heavy heart and a request. Jonathan, the one I love, lies sick with a terrible wound. Glickhican says he will probably die tonight. But I do not want him to die, I want him to live." Tears began to run down her lovely face. "Oh, Jesus, please show me that You live and that You hear my prayer, for if You let Jonathan live, I will follow You forever."

The girl sat silently, wondering if the white man's God had heard. In a moment of inspiration, she knelt and bowed her head toward the east. As she knelt before this unknown God, she heard a faint sound, as if some great, invisible being had exhaled a boundless breath and then, sudden and magnificent, the sun's broad golden disc showed itself over the horizon facing her; and as she looked up, the first rays took her full in the eyes with a dazzling light. When she was able to see once more, the air was full of the carol of birds that hailed the dawn and the forest had come alive around her.

A great hope rose in her heart, and rising from her worship, she ran toward her lodge. Pushing aside the hanging cloth over the door, she stepped inside. Jonathan was lying like a dead man, and for a moment, a great fear clutched at her heart. Then slowly his eyes opened and he looked up at her.

"Hello, Princess."

She rushed to his side and sank down beside him, staring in wonder at his ashen face. As she watched, the blush of life began to come into his skin, and he smiled weakly up at her.

"I think I'm going to live, White Deer, thanks to you."

"Oh, no, Jonathan, it was..." and she stopped, for she knew that he would never accept the fact that Jesus had answered her prayer.

The days and months that followed were full of wonder for White Deer. Her heart was overflowing with the realization that she had met the real God, and He had answered her prayers. But in that realization came a great fear, for she knew she could never tell her father or Jonathan what had happened to her. So she saved her worship for quiet times when she was alone in the woods with her newfound Savior.

Jonathan improved every day and each moment together brought a softening of his attitude toward White Deer. She could see that her faithfulness and love were winning his heart. Where he had once been rough in his talk toward her, he now was gentle and kind. She could see in his eyes that something was stirring in him, something engendered by more than just her physical beauty. She was patient and kind and expressed her love for him in many small ways—in the things she did for him as he grew well and strong, in the meals that she prepared for him, in the care of his personal things, and Jonathan noticed.

One day, as they were sitting in the woods, in the very grove where she had given her life to Jesus, Jonathan turned to her and spoke quietly.

"Princess, do you remember the day that I kissed you and then insulted you?"

White Deer turned her face to hide the red flush of shame, but Jonathan tenderly turned her face back to his. Surprisingly, she could see tears in his eyes.

"I was wrong. In these last months I have come to see that you are beautiful, inside and out. You did not have to save me from Scar and your father, but you risked everything and did so. You did not have to sit by my side every hour and nurse me through that terrible fever, but you did. And now..." He held her face gently and spoke. "I am sorry for the way I treated you and spoke to you. You are noble, faithful, and true and you have won my heart. If you can forgive me for my actions, perhaps we can..."

White Deer moved into his arms and hid her face against his shoulder. Her voice was a whisper. "My Black Eagle. I have loved you from the day I first saw you at Fort Pitt, so many years ago. I know that you spoke to me in that terrible way because there is bitterness in your heart. But if you can put that aside and just accept me as the woman who loves you with all her heart, we can live and love together for the rest of our days."

Jonathan lifted her face again. "White Deer, with you I have forgotten the things that made my heart bitter. I have never known such a beautiful woman, and now I only desire to be your husband in all ways. Let us forget the people who are around us, white and red. We can live in our own world and know joy."

White Deer's tears began to course down her cheeks. "If we only can, Jonathan, it would be an answer to all my prayers." She felt him stiffen for a moment and then he relaxed, letting the words pass.

"I only have one god, White Deer, and that is life itself. We have been given a gift, to know and love each other, and we need no others to make it real and full."

White Deer felt the strength in his arms and his words, but there was a place in her heart that knew that Jonathan would one day come to a reckoning with his God.

It was winter and the snow lay deep around the lodges of Shawnee Town. White Deer and Jonathan lay together in their bed in front of the lodge fire. There were no words between them in the stillness of winter's deep. The light from the fire danced on the walls, and there was peace in their home. Jonathan unconsciously ran his hands gently over his wife's body and then paused at her belly. He pulled her over on her back and looked into her eyes and smiled. "Is your belly growing or did you just eat too much bear meat last night?"

White Deer blushed. "I did eat much bear meat, but that is not the reason my belly is growing. I am with child."

Jonathan's mouth dropped open. "With child? White Deer…"

White Deer looked up at him apprehensively. "Are you angry with me?"

Jonathan laughed out loud. "No, my dearest, I am delighted. With child!!" He pulled her close to him. "We shall have a son. His name shall be called Matthew."

"How do you know it will be a man-child, husband?"

Jonathan shrugged his shoulders. "I just know, Princess."

In that moment, White Deer felt that her secret God was smiling on her.

Spring came, and with it, the birth of their son. The birth was easy and White Deer was filled with joy as she watched Jonathan with the baby. He was kind and loving, and though the baby was half Indian, it did not seem to matter to Jonathan. It appeared to White Deer that he had put aside his bitterness and had fallen into his carefree life among the Lenape and was enjoying living the life of an Indian brave. But that was to change. One day White Deer found her husband sitting in the lodge alone. The fire had gone out and it was dark, but there was enough light to see that Jonathan's face was twisted in anger.

"What is it, my husband?"

Jonathan looked up at her. In his hand he held a fresh scalp. The hair was long and blonde. "I took this from a Shawnee today. The braves have been attacking the settlements again and they massacred a family downriver from Fort Henry. This scalp came from a girl who was about the age of my sisters. Before they killed her, they violated her. The brave was bragging about his conquest, and when I appeared, he began taunting me, telling me that he had killed some of my white sisters. Anger rose up in me, and I told him that he was no man if the only ones he could kill were women. I took the scalp away and challenged him. I said he could take it back if he was man enough to kill me. He backed down and walked away, but I shamed him and he is now my enemy."

White Deer felt her heart constrict. "Jonathan, I…"

"Do not speak, wife. I have been lying to myself. I cannot live here. I must return to my people. You must come with me to my home and live there."

White Deer drew herself up. "Go with you to the village of the whiteskins, where White Deer would be scorned and pitied? No! No!"

Jonathan rose and faced his wife. "It is the only way. You would not be scorned. You would be my wife. My people will love you. Come, White Deer, save me from this place where my dreams are filled with the blood of my mother and the screams of my sisters; come home with me or I will go alone."

White Deer was silent for a long while. Then she sighed sadly. "It can never be. How would we reach Zane's fort by the river? Wingenund loves his daughter and will not give her up. If we try to get away, the braves will hunt us down and then even

White Deer could not save your life. You would be killed. I love you too much to let that happen."

"If you really loved me you would come with me."

White Deer grabbed her husband by the arm. Pain and scorn were in her eyes. "Love you! Can an Indian princess who has the blood of great chiefs in her veins prove her love any more than I? Some day you will know that you wrong me. I am Wingenund's daughter. A Lenape does not lie."

Chapter Nineteen

The Dark Trail

Over the next few weeks, Jonathan's moods grew blacker, as reports of bloody reprisals against the white settlers grew in number, and raiding parties began bringing captives back to the village. Finally one day, when White Deer was caring for Matthew, Jonathan came into the lodge in a great state of agitation. He knelt down beside her and took her hands in his. "White Deer, I must go. Today the warriors brought prisoners back to the village and tortured them before they killed them. One of them was a man I knew back in the settlement at Fort Pitt. He didn't recognize me. I watched as they scalped and mutilated his children before him and then tied him to a stake by a leash and piled a ring of wood around it. They set the wood on fire and he ran around and around the stake while his skin burned and peeled off his body. After a while, the poor wretch collapsed onto the pile of wood and burned to death."

Jonathan looked at White Deer with anger in his eyes. "I beg you, Princess, once more, to come with me. If you do not, I will go anyway. I cannot stay one more day with the murderers of my family and my people. I have a horse for you and the baby, and I plan to leave tonight. Please, you must come."

White Deer's heart was torn. That which she feared the most had come upon her. "But I am a Lenape, daughter of Wingenund, the most feared of your people's enemies. They will hate me and hate you for bringing me. Our son will be despised as a half-breed, and we will never know peace. At least here we know how the people will treat us."

"You mean you know how the people will treat you, White Deer. Even those that scorn you for your love for me will not dare to speak it, for your father and his braves would repay such insult in blood. Your people tolerate me because you are Wingenund's daughter, and I am your husband. But still, I see in their eyes that I will never truly be one of them. You are my wife. In the white man's world, the wife does as her husband desires. I know you fear my people, but I will protect you. If we must, I will take you far away, back to Pennsylvania or even New York. There the name of Wingenund is not feared, and you will become as one of us. Please, White Deer, you must come with me. I love you and our son."

Jonathan's words of love wrung the last bit of resistance from White Deer. With a deep sigh, she laid the baby into his cradle and began to pack her things. Jonathan cautioned her. "We must travel light. Take only what you need. I have food and water hidden outside the village. Our horse is waiting in the woods."

As she gazed about her home for the last time, tears began to flow down White Deer's cheeks. Each familiar item spoke to her of the peaceful days she had spent with Jonathan as they grew in their love—but no more. White Deer instinctively knew that the days of peace were behind her, but the overpowering depth of her love for Jonathan made her willing to sacrifice all.

Jonathan felt it would be better to leave under cover of darkness since he knew the trails and did not need the sun to guide him east. They waited until the sun was disappearing behind the western hills and then slipped out of the lodge and made their way to where Jonathan had tied the horse. Jonathan had a travois hidden in the brush, and he tied it to the horse and set the bundles of food and clothing into it. Then, putting White Deer and the baby on the horse, he led them quietly into the deep woods surrounding the village. As they pushed deeper into the forest, a sense of doom filled White Deer's heart. She had never been away from her people, and she knew that her father would pursue her until she was returned to him or dead. The moon rose, but it was only a slender sliver in the sky, and the woods were dark and foreboding. The baby woke and began to fuss, but she held him close and comforted him until he fell asleep again. They went on and on through the woods, following a trail that Jonathan, even with his sharp eyes, could only see dimly reflected in the faint light of the moon. The lonesome mourning of a wolf, far away on a hilltop, drifted through the dark night. The soft sounds of the horse's hooves on the path were like a heartbeat. The questioning voice of an owl broke the stillness over her head, and she could hear the rustle of some unseen animals in the brush beside the trail as they made their nocturnal rounds.

Soon, White Deer fell into a trance-like state, and her thoughts wandered into dreams as she fell into deep sleep on the back of the horse. Visions of her husband bound at a stake with burning stacks of wood around him began to torment her. She saw her father and Scar standing with grim looks as Jonathan defiantly faced his torturers. The face of Scar loomed out of the mists in her mind, but she could not shake herself awake. They went on and on with White Deer passing from waking to dreaming as the hours wore on. Finally, Jonathan stopped and lifted White Deer and the baby down.

"We will camp here, Princess, though we dare not light a fire. I have blankets on the travois, and you and the child will be warm. I will stand guard."

White Deer lay down on the blankets and Jonathan wrapped them snugly around her. The baby awoke and White Deer fed him. Then, as Jonathan stood watching over them, she fell asleep again.

As the dawn slipped through the last vestiges of night and sent the first rays of the sun over the eastern hills, White Deer awoke with a start. She looked up from her bed. Standing not ten feet from Jonathan was the warrior, Scar. Jonathan held his rifle at the ready. Scar appeared to be alone.

A puzzled look was on his face. He walked slowly toward his adopted son, his eyes taking in the horse and the princess lying in the blankets with the baby.

"Where does my white son go?"

Jonathan stepped between Scar and his wife. "We are leaving forever, Scar. I can no longer stay with those who murdered my family."

Scar's face twisted in sorrow. "You never forget. Scar make you his son, love you, give you honor, you still hate."

Jonathan laughed. "You thought you could change me, make me an Indian. But I will always be white, and I will always hate you."

Scar held out his hand in a gesture of peace. He spoke to Jonathan in the Lenape tongue. "Come, Black Eagle. Return to the lodges of your people. You lived with us, learned our ways. Do you not love the path of the Lenape? Would you return to the lodges of the lying, stealing whites—those that take our land and kill our people? Before the saltwater people came, the Lenape lived in peace. We were rich in lands, our hunting grounds were full of deer and buffalo and we were a great nation. Now we are pressed ever to the west, leaving our beloved *Lenapehoking* behind in the hands of greedy settlers who take what is not theirs and kill us for defending our homes. Will you return to them or come home with me? All will be forgiven and we will make no further mention of this."

White Deer watched as a look of uncertainty came over Jonathan's face. He hesitated and the barrel of his rifle started to lower toward the ground. Scar smiled and stepped forward, his hands still outstretched. A thrill of hope rose up in White Deer's heart. Jonathan was going to forget his rage and return to her people!

But it was not to be. As she watched, Jonathan's face hardened, and his eyes became gimlets of steely blue. His rifle came back up and he motioned for Scar to stop. "You speak of peace and the way of the Lenape, Scar. Yet is it the way of a Lenape to murder innocent women and girls and kill a young boy because he cannot keep up? Is it the way of a warrior to murder innocent people in blood lust? When you stabbed my mother to death and then scalped her, when you raped my innocent sisters and then tortured them until they begged for death, then you showed that you were not a warrior but a dog, a dog that deserves only death. Yes, I have been your son but only to learn about the Lenape way so that I could become your worst fear. I am no longer Black Eagle, son of Scar. No, now you will call me *Nènhìlëwès*, the murderer of the Lenape. I will come like a destroying angel upon your lodges and your women will weep for the braves who do not return. Your scalps will dangle from my lodge pole. No Lenape, no Indian will be safe from my knife and my tomahawk. And you will be the first."

The barrel of Jonathan's rifle rose up to point directly at the warrior. Without a moment's hesitation, Scar sprang to the side as Jonathan pulled the trigger. The ball whistled past, cutting the fringe from his deerskin shirt. Instantly, Scar was dashing for his life through the trees, dodging and running at full speed. Jonathan reloaded quickly, stepped forward, and raised the rifle. He waited until Scar appeared for a moment between two trees and then fired. He saw Scar stagger and then regain his stride and quickly disappear among the trees. "I hit him, but it was hard to tell if I got a killing shot." He turned to White Deer. "Quickly, woman, we must go. If he's not dead, he'll bring the others. And even if I killed him, Wingenund is on our trail."

White Deer looked toward the woods where Scar had disappeared. The baby had been frightened by the sound of the rifle and was crying. Sadly, she turned and Jonathan lifted her and Matthew onto the horse. He cut the straps holding the travois and let it fall. He quickly rolled the supplies into a bundle and tied it with thongs. He threw it over his shoulder, handed the rifle to White Deer, and led the horse toward the woods. Jonathan pointed in an easterly direction. "When we were on the last hunting trip this spring, we left canoes hidden on the river.

If we can make it to that place before they catch us, we have a good chance of getting away safely."

Suddenly, far off in the distance, they heard a long, piercing yell in the quiet morning air. The strong, sudden, startling sound broke that almost-perfect calm like a club, and for a moment, Jonathan and White Deer stood in the death-like silence that followed. Their eyes turned to the faraway ridge where the call had come from.

White Deer felt the blood drain from her face. "It is my father. He is coming to find me. When he catches us, he will kill you. You will not escape the fires this time. I will not be able to save you."

Jonathan's face set in a sardonic smile. "Then, my dear wife, we must go as quickly as we can, for I do not intend to be sport for anyone, your father included." He turned and led the horse into the woods at a run.

Scar staggered along the trail. Jonathan's ball had struck him high up on the shoulder and torn a terrible wound in his back where it entered and his chest where it exited. A bloody froth had formed on his lips and he knew the ball had probably nicked his lung. He felt a great weakness coming over him, and he staggered a few feet farther and fell to the ground. As he lay there in agony, he heard the sound of running feet. He struggled to turn over, and when he did, he saw three men coming toward him. They were white! Scar collapsed backward, awaiting death. The men came up and knelt down by the wounded brave. One man turned to another. "Brother David, it is an Indian and he is terribly wounded."

The second man placed his hand on Scar's shoulder and spoke in Lenape. "Do not fear, my brother. I am Zeisberger, the Moravian missionary. I will do all I can to save you."

Scar looked up at the kindly face and then the light faded and all was dark.

Chapter Twenty

In the Heart of the Storm

Wingenund stared hard at the trail before him. His warriors stood silently around him. For many miles they had closely followed Black Eagle and White Deer. Their tracks now led along the bottom of a rocky ridge. The hoof prints of the horse were plainly visible in the loamy soil, and they were headed due south. Wingenund determined by the direction of the tracks that Jonathan and White Deer were trying to make it to the river. He nodded and the pursuers took off at a trot, following the tracks. After about two miles, they came to a clearing in the woods. The horse was standing quietly, foraging in the lush grass. The animal tossed its head at the sight of the warriors and then went back to grazing. Jonathan and White Deer were nowhere to be seen.

Wingenund and his braves searched the area near the horse, but there were no tracks to be found. Wingenund smiled grimly and nodded to his men. "Black Eagle has learned well. I did not think he had the skill of a Lenape warrior to hide his trail, but he does. He has made the horse run ahead and took to the rocks somewhere back along the trail. He has gained time, for we must search along the ridge to find where he left the trail."

Wingenund looked around him and studied the lay of the land, trying to understand what the fugitives had done and the direction the pursuers might take to pick up Jonathan's trail. At last he nodded and pointed in an easterly direction. "Black Eagle thinks to lose us by crossing over the ridge where his trail does not show. We will go over to the other side and then we will find his trail coming down off the hill."

His warriors grunted their agreement and they broke into a run as they headed up and over the ridge.

When they arrived on the other side, they began walking along the bottom of the ridge, looking for tracks. But to his surprise, Wingenund found not the slightest indication of a trail coming down out of the rocks. The warriors searched long but found nothing. Wingenund smiled again. "Black Eagle has fooled us. He did not cross the ridge but only made us think he did." Wingenund paused and stood still, thinking. Then he spoke. "The Black Eagle knows that he must go to the new fort. That is his only hope. So he made us think that he was headed east. But he did not cross directly over. I think he has turned south and used the rocky ground along the top of the hill to fool us. He has come down south of where we crossed." He pointed back the way they had come, and the Indians turned and headed back.

After two hours, the rocky ridgeline descended and petered out in the soft grass of a meadow. Here, the warriors began a patient search. One of the braves gave an exclamation and knelt down. Wingenund came over to see what had been found. The brave pointed to a small fern, with the drops of dew brushed off. Wingenund examined the grass but there were no marks. The brave lifted the fern and pointed to a plant with dark green leaves, growing beneath. Breaking off one of these leaves, Wingenund exposed its lower side to the light. The fine, silvery hair of fuzz that grew upon the leaf had been crushed. Light steps had bruised the leaf.

Wingenund nodded and pointed east. "Scar has taught his adopted son well. Black Eagle knows that the grass will spring back up and not show where a man has passed. But this plant does not lie. A mocassined foot has marked it. My daughter and Black Eagle have come this way. They are going to the river. He will find the canoes our warriors have hidden then go upstream to the fort. They have gained much time. Come, we will cut straight across and catch them as they come past the bend of the river."

It was just before dawn when Jonathan and White Deer stumbled down to the broad Ohio. Far away to the east, the first light of the day was being born, and golden halos of light formed around the tops of the trees. High clouds drifted through the slowly brightening sky, and as the sun rose, the billows above were touched with a beautiful orange that faded into a dusky pink as it reached toward heaven. The rising sun touched the tops of the hills across the river, marking them with beautiful panoramas of gold and rose. The air along the river was fresh and invigorating, but White Deer felt only darkness in her heart.

All through the exhausting night Jonathan had never faltered from his course, and he led them unerringly to the place where the canoes were hidden. When they arrived at the river, he walked along the bank until he came to a brushy overhang. He set his rifle down, waded into the water, and pulled a long canoe from under the bushes. He pushed it to the bank and nodded to White Deer. She put the baby's blanket in the bottom of the canoe and laid Matthew on it while Jonathan knocked holes in the rest of the canoes with his tomahawk. Then she climbed in.

Jonathan followed. He handed her a paddle. "We are about thirty miles from Fort Henry. The river is deep here and the flow is not strong going downstream, but when we are going upriver, we must hide from the current. I will look ahead and find spots where it is slower. If we are lucky, there will be eddies that are circling upstream along the shore. Follow my lead and I will maneuver the canoe so we will be in favorable current much of the time. If we do that, we should make good upstream progress without getting too tired. It should take about twelve hours to get there."

White Deer nodded. "What about my father?"

Jonathan smiled. "Hopefully my little trick on the ridge fooled him, and we gained some time, but not much. Your father will be determined to get you back, so we must do all we can to stay ahead of him." He pointed upstream along the bank. "We will go on the inside of that bend and look for big rocks or trees that break the current. I will try to stay very close to the shore, but it will be hard work. Can you make it?"

White Deer nodded. "I am a Lenape princess. I am strong. The river is my mother. I will do my part."

Jonathan shoved the canoe out into the river, and the couple set off up river toward Fort Henry.

Fifteen miles away, Wingenund and his band of warriors ran at a steady pace through the slowly awakening forest. They had been running all night but they were not tired. They were Lenape warriors and they were pursuing the man who had taken their princess. They would not rest until they found Black Eagle, and then there would be no mercy for him.

At midday Jonathan pulled the canoe ashore on the southern bank. The fugitives had been paddling for seven hours, and the sun was sliding into a rampart of storm clouds that was rolling in from the west on a bitter wind. As they rested on the bank, the wind picked up. All along the storm front, Jonathan could see veils of rain sweeping down like curtains. In the heart of the monstrous grey billows, weird bursts of pale light illuminated the frothing, churning mass. Jonathan pulled a blanket out of his pack and put it over White Deer's shoulders. "That's a real *mordskerl.* We must get back on the river and go as far as we can before the storm catches us. When it does, we must abandon the canoe for we cannot be out on the river in the lightning. We will have to run through the woods to the fort. Can you do it?"

White deer grabbed her oar and began to push the canoe off the bank. "Come, Black Eagle, what are you waiting for, then?" They scrambled into the canoe and pushed off into the current to begin the final leg of their journey. As they paddled upstream against the current, the wind began to blow harder, but it was coming from behind, and the canoe began to sail over the water.

A few drops of rain began to fall and suddenly it was coming down in torrents. The towering bank of clouds swept out of the western sky—tossed in the heavens like the crashing wild waves along some fog-bound, rock-strewn coast. The front of the mass was dead black and blood red, with gray in between, a bulging, mushrooming, vast monster devouring all before it. All of heaven's breath pushed and piled the clouds until they were roiling in an ungovernable mass of destruction.

A bright explosion in the heart of the storm burned out like cannon fire, flashed from the west to east, and died. Then from the depths of the deepest black burst an explosion of sound. It was like mighty cannons firing in a deafening volley along the crags and parapets of the clouds, and the crushing sound seemed to roll on and on and then fall down upon the fugitives with malice and vengeance. Another flash rent the darkness, and the rain began to blow sideways before the howling wind. Soon the canoe began to fill with water as mighty wind-driven waves ran down upon them like stampeding buffalo. Jonathan pointed to the shore and shouted above the storm. "We must go ashore. We are only a few miles from the fort, but if we stay on the river, we will capsize!"

Together, they pulled for the shore and ran the canoe up on the bank at the foot of a huge oak. Jonathan lifted the baby out and then bent down to grab his rifle. As he did, he felt something sting his face and then strangely he was pinned to the tree. He jerked his head and felt a sharp pain in his earlobe. He turned to look and saw a black arrow sticking out of the trunk of the tree. There was something stuck to it and Jonathan put his hand to his face. It came away bloody. An arrow had come flying across the river, guided by the stern eye of the mightiest of Lenape chiefs and had just missed skewering him to the oak. It had cut his cheek open, hit his ear, and pinned him to the tree. When he pulled away, he had torn a piece out of his ear and now the blood was pouring down his face.

Jonathan pushed White Deer behind the tree just as another volley of arrows filled the air around them. There was a war whoop from the opposite shore, and Jonathan looked around the trunk. Wingenund and his warriors were gathered on the opposite bank, but they could not get across because of the raging waters. Quick as a flash, Jonathan lifted his rifle and fired across the river. Wingenund saw the weapon rising and, with marvelous instinct, ducked behind a tree. But the warrior behind him was not so fortunate, and he fell with a shriek as Jonathan's bullet tore through him. A terrifying yell pealed above the storm. It was Jonathan and a blood lust was on him. Quickly, he reloaded and fired his rifle. Another Indian fell and again came the terrible cry from Jonathan.

Once more, the deadly barrel of the rifle slowly lifted. Wingenund had jumped behind a tree that was too small to hide him. Jonathan drew a bead on the chief's exposed shoulder, but just as he pulled the trigger, a hand reached in and pushed the barrel up. There was a flash. The bullet went wide over Wingenund and careened off through the trees. Jonathan turned, but his words of rage died on his lips. White Deer stood with burning eyes, the baby in her arms and a knife within inches of Jonathan's heart. She screamed at him over the storm.

"I will go anywhere with you and do anything you ask, but you will not kill my father. If you ever try again, I will kill you."

Jonathan looked at his wife. A taste of bile was in his mouth, and he was shaking with rage. And then, for just a moment, he saw his wife clearly, and the fury that had possessed him drained away. He looked back across the river, then shrugged and shouldered his rifle. Blood covered his face.

He was a chilling sight, and he smiled a ghastly smile as he pointed to his torn face. "Ah, Princess, you will always be Indian at heart. Your father has marked me for life, and I only wished a chance to repay the favor. But come then, we must go before the baby catches a chill." He took his wife by the hand and led her away through the trees. In a few moments they came to a well-worn trail. It was the road to Fort Henry.

Chapter Twenty-One

Choices

Joshua Hershberger closed the gate behind the recalcitrant cow and leaned against the corral fence. He had chased the wretched animal through the woods for two hours before he got her back to the farm and into her pen. He smiled as he turned and walked back toward the new log cabin that stood where the first farmhouse had burned down. Since his escape and return home, the old Hershberger farm had prospered under his willing hands. As he walked through the barnyard, he looked around at the changes he had wrought in two years. Besides the rebuilt main house, he had added a new barn and several out buildings, and he had cleared another acre of forest for fields. He went up on the porch and dipped a drink of water out of the barrel standing by the door. Then he sat down on the bench under the window and surveyed his domain. He thought back to the days when the Hershberger family had worked and toiled together to carve this farm out of the wilderness. He could hear the repaired water wheel turning and splashing in the millrace that he and Jonathan had dug in the riverbank with their *daed*. Joshua smiled. *"Papa, Sie woulde stolz auf mich."*

The sound of a horse racing down the trail disturbed his reverie. He stood as Albert Clark, a boy from the fort, came riding up to the house and pulled his horse up short. Albert was disheveled, as though he had left home in a hurry.

"What is it, Albert? *Was hat, erregten Sie so?*"

Albert looked at him strangely.

Joshua smiled. "Sorry, you don't speak German. What's all the excitement about?"

"Two extraordinary things have happened, Joshua." The boy seemed like he would burst.

Joshua motioned for the boy to get down, but Albert shook his head. "I can't stay, Joshua. I must ride to the other outlying farms and spread the news."

"What news, Albert? Don't keep me waiting all day."

"The colonies have declared independence from England. We have been fighting the Redcoats for a year and now we are going to be our own nation."

Joshua took a step down to stand by the horse. "What? Independence?"

"Yes, Joshua. George Washington forced the British out of Boston in March, and the Continental Congress took courage and signed the declaration two weeks ago in Philadelphia." Albert pulled a sheet of paper out of his saddlebag and handed it to Joshua. "Thomas Jefferson wrote it. Read the second line."

Joshua looked down at the paper and read. "'We hold these truths to be self-evident, that all men are created equal, that they are endowed by their Creator with certain unalienable Rights, that among these are Life, Liberty and the pursuit of Happiness.'" He looked up. "What does that mean for us, Albert?"

Albert shrugged. "I guess they will be raising a militia to join the fight out here, and the reddys certainly aren't going to be happy. After all, it's the British who have been holding back settlers in the north part of the Ohio territory. Now the Virginians will come pouring in here to take more Indian land. I'm afraid we are in for some bad times."

Joshua shook his head.

Why must men always use war to solve their differences?

Then he remembered that Albert had mentioned two bits of news. "What's the other news, Albert?"

"It's about your brother."

"Jonathan?"

"Yes, he's escaped and returned to the fort. He brought a squaw wife and a baby with him."

"Jonathan is back? Can you tell me more?"

"He's up at Colonel Zane's cabin. That's all I know. I can't stay, Joshua." Albert pulled his horse back from the rail, waved his hat, and spurred into a gallop. Joshua watched as he rode away.

Jonathan has returned! And White Deer is with him...

Jonathan and White Deer sat in the front room of Colonel Ebenezer Zane's spacious cabin a few hundred yards up the hill from Fort Henry. The formidable blockhouse commanded the hilltop and, in times of siege, could provide sweeping crossfire down upon anyone trying to reach the fort. Colonel Zane, the founder of Fort Henry, a tall, broad-shouldered man of middle years, sat in a chair by the fireplace smoking his pipe. With them were Jack Zane, the colonel's younger brother, and Lewis Wetzel, two of the bordermen that helped defend the fort. Wetzel seemed particularly interested in Jonathan and White Deer's story. Jonathan spoke quietly of all that had happened since the murder of his family while Wetzel listened with a grim look on his face. Finally, he spoke. "Well, don't that beat all." He looked at White Deer with an appraising eye. "Ye say ye are Wingenund's daughter, eh? Many's the time I've had that old fox in my sights only to have him sense me drawin' a bead on him and then disappear in a flash."

White Deer nodded and answered. "Yes, I am Opahtuhwe. Jonathan and I were married almost two years ago. We were happy together at Shawnee Town until my people began raiding the settlements and killing Jonathan's people. Then Jonathan could no longer live as a Lenape warrior. When we ran away, Jonathan's Indian father, Scar, found us, but Jonathan shot him.

My father trailed us, but if it had not been for the storm, we would not have escaped, for my father almost caught us. He is the one who shot Jonathan."

Wetzel nodded in approval. "So ye shot old Scar. He's one of the trickiest, most murderous of all the Delaware on the border. Glad to hear the old buzzard is gone." He pointed at Jonathan's face. "And your husband will carry Wingenund's mark for the rest of his life. I haven't heard a story like this since McCullough's ride for life."

Jack Zane spoke up. "You may not know that my brother Isaac married a Wyandot woman. The two of them visit here often, but then we are at peace with their tribe. Myeerah has made a place among the white people and is much loved by the settlers." He looked at White Deer. "You may find life here a little more difficult than she did, since you are the daughter of one of our most implacable enemies. But your skin is light, and if you change your name and wear settler's clothes, you might pass for white and avoid any trouble with some of our more unpleasant citizens."

White Deer lifted her head. "My great-grandparents on my mother's side were French aristocrats. That is why my skin is white. My grandmother was stolen from them when she was a child. It was she who taught me to speak and read the white man's tongue. I love my husband and I will do my best to fit in here."

Colonel Zane took a long pull on the pipe he was smoking. "Your brother, Joshua, has been back for two years. He went back to your old place and has been doing a wonderful job bringing it back to life."

Jonathan looked away. "I do not wish to speak of Joshua. He and my father abandoned me when they escaped. If they had taken me with them, my father might still be alive. As it was, the bloody reddys killed him too."

Wetzel shook his head. "Ye seem to be in a fix here, young man. Your hatred of the Indians almost matches mine, yet ye married an Indian woman."

Jonathan took a long look at Wetzel. The borderman was dressed completely in buckskin and his long black hair hung nearly to his waist. The tall hunter's reputation was well known on the border. Wetzel, like Jonathan, had survived a massacre of his family when he was young. Since that day, he had been the most terrible enemy of the tribes on the border. His name among them was *Le Vent de la Mort*, the wind of death.

There was not an Indian brave who did not quail in fear when they heard the name, and Indian mothers made their children behave by simply mentioning Wetzel.

Jonathan spoke. "White Deer saved my life. She did not have to marry me, but she did and her father could not refuse her. I was dying from a horrible wound that got infected and had it not been for her care day and night, I would not be here today. I owe her a great deal, and I love her. She has promised to follow my ways and let my people become her people. As you say, she is light enough to pass for white. She has sacrificed much to follow me."

Colonel Zane knocked the ashes out of his pipe and refilled it from a pouch. "What will you do now, young man?"

Jonathan shrugged. "I haven't given it much thought, Colonel. I've been six years among the Indians and have not been thinking much of my future."

The colonel pointed to White Deer. "Well, lad, you have a wife and a son to take care of. Will you not go back to your father's farm and help your brother? There's plenty of land to support you both."

"As I said, Colonel, I do not wish to speak of Joshua. And I do not think I am made much for farming. I was hoping that I might find a place among the scouts here at the fort and also serve as a hunter. I know the ways of the Indians and our personal needs are few. A cabin and a bit of land to grow some vegetables would serve us, and we could be very helpful in defending the fort and providing fresh meat."

Wetzel and the younger Zane looked at Jonathan with interest. Finally, Wetzel spoke. "It might be a good idea, Colonel. We're shorthanded as it is, and this young man's record speaks for itself. I'd be willing to take him in hand. What about you, Jack?"

Jack Zane shook his head. "I don't know, Lew. If we raised up another Injun hater as fierce as you, why the reddys would just pack up and head west, and there'd be no more excitement around here." He chuckled. "Shore, Lew, we'll give the young man a try. From what I hear from his brother, he's almost as good a shot as you."

White Deer could tell that Jonathan was pleased, for she knew her husband. To be allowed to roam the woods with Wetzel and Jack Zane was more than he could have hoped for. He started to thank the two men, but Wetzel shook his head and offered his hand. "Jonathan, I think you have the makin's of a real borderman." Wetzel and Zane got up and walked out the door.

Mrs. Zane came in carrying Matthew. "Your boy's a quiet one. He's been wide awake but he just stares at me with those big eyes and never makes a sound."

Colonel Zane spoke to his wife and then turned to Jonathan and White Deer. "You'll stay and have dinner with us, and then after dinner I'll show you a cabin with a piece of land just over the bluff from the fort. It will take a bit of fixin' up, but that shouldn't be too hard for young folks. Wetzel and Jack are leaving on a scouting trip soon, but there should be enough time to get you settled in. I'd like you to go with them if you are up to it."

Jonathan put his hand on his face. "If you mean this, it's nothing. I will be ready to travel after a few days' rest."

Colonel Zane rose. "Fine then, it's settled." He took White Deer by the arm. "Come, my dear, and sit at table with us. My wife likes you very much, and we will do our best to make you feel at home."

White Deer went out with Mrs. Zane. The colonel motioned to Jonathan. "There's a place to wash up outside. My wife will see to Opahtuhwe and the baby. Dinner will be ready soon so don't dawdle.

Jonathan went outside to clean up. When he walked around the corner of the cabin, he saw his brother, Joshua, walking up the path to the house. The two brothers stopped and stared silently at each other. Finally, Joshua spoke. "Well, brother, I see you have returned safely. It's good to see you."

Jonathan scowled. "Well, if it isn't Joshua, the good brother. Glad to see me, are you? Feeling guilty because you left me behind while you and Father ran like dogs and left me to the mercy of those savages?"

Jonathan could see Joshua stiffen.

"We had no choice, Jonathan. All the braves were away, and you were gone on a hunting trip. It was the only chance we had. Besides, you seemed to be living the good life among your red brothers." He put his hand on Jonathan's shoulder. "Can't we leave the past behind? Once we were good brothers who loved one another, as Christ commands."

"Still clinging to your foolish religion, I see." Jonathan struck his brother's hand away. "Let me tell you this once and we'll never speak of it again: Our father was a weakling who let our family die. You stood with him and his cowardly religion. I will never forgive you for that or for our mother's death. If we had fired upon Scar and his braves when they were gathered outside the house, they would have run away, and mother and the girls would still be alive. But he's dead now and that's one score settled. As for you, I want nothing to do with you, ever, so stay away from me and mine."

"You mean White Deer, don't you?"

Jonathan nodded. "Yes, I married White Deer after you left. I brought her and our son, Matthew, when I escaped." Jonathan put his finger in Joshua's face. "I know you cared for my wife and talked to her about Jesus, but I am warning you—stay away from my family. I do not want you bothering them with your useless religion."

Joshua stepped closer. "But White Deer is already a Christian."

Jonathan's body jerked in shock. "What do you mean?"

"Yes, I shared the Lord with her many times while I was still a captive, and she was very receptive."

Jonathan balled his fists and glared at Joshua, who lifted his hands in a peaceful gesture.

"Did she tell you she was a Christian?"

Joshua shook his head. "No, but I could see on her face that she believed. And she brought Glickhican to me and I believe his heart was changed, also."

Jonathan's face began to twist with rage. Suddenly, he leaped at Joshua and knocked him down. He stood over his brother, but Joshua rolled away and sprang to his feet, his hands outstretched in a gesture of peace.

"Jonathan! Joshua! What are you doing?" White Deer stood on the porch with the Zanes.

Jonathan took a step towards her. "He says you're a Christian. Is that true?"

White Deer turned pale. She looked at the faces of the two brothers, one twisted in rage and one sorrowful. Finally, she nodded and spoke quietly. "Yes, husband, I am a Christian. Who do you think I prayed to when you had no chance to live? Who answered when we were running in the woods from my father? It was Jesus."

Jonathan raised his hands to silence her. "In my house there will be no mention of this weak God who lets innocent women be butchered while powerless men stand by and watch. You can follow him if you want, but do not mention him to me. And stay away from this coward. That is my last word." He brushed past his wife and the Zanes, leaving White Deer staring down into Joshua's stricken face.

Chapter Twenty-Two

A Divided Heart

White Deer stood on a hillside above the cabin Colonel Zane had given them. From the east, faint rays of light brushed an overhanging bank of gray clouds, painting them with tinges of coral and pink. The air was fresh and songbirds lifted their melodious choruses to the light filtering through the forest from the east. A faint breeze, redolent with the smell of pine and cedar, danced softly around her, but it did not soothe the girl's troubled heart.

It had been five months since they arrived at Fort Henry. Jonathan had given himself totally to his new life as a scout. Wetzel's implacable hatred for every Indian had infected Jonathan and brought the fires of revenge boiling to the surface, and now he was leaving everything behind to follow the reclusive borderman. White Deer had done everything she could to abandon her Indian ways and please Jonathan. She had discarded her buckskin dress and now wore the linsey and wool of a frontier settler's wife. She had changed her name to Ruth and tried hard to fit in with the white man's life. But mostly, she found the white settlers ignorant and crude. And sometimes she would catch Jonathan looking at her with contempt in his eyes.

That morning, Jonathan had gone with Wetzel and Zane on another scouting expedition to the north. He left her standing at the door of their cabin with a feeling of great emptiness in her heart, and as she watched the golden top of the sun rise over the hills of Ohio, she wondered if she had made the right choice in leaving her home. For a moment the rising sun's rays blinded her and when she recovered she was startled to see a tall figure standing before her. It was Wingenund, her father!

Wingenund looked at his daughter for a long time. The sadness in his eyes reached out to her, and she wanted to run to him and feel his strong arms around her. Instead, she spoke. "Why have you come, Father? You are in great danger if you stay here. The white men must not see you."

Wingenund did not answer her. He looked at her as if seeing her for the first time. Then he spoke to her in Lenape. "You have become a Christian." His simple statement struck her like a blow.

White Deer started in surprise. "How did you know, Father?"

"When the yellow-hair was captive, I watched you talking with him many times, and each time when you came back to the lodge, I could see that your heart was troubled. Then I heard you say it."

"When?"

"Soon after you escaped from me on the river, I came to Zane's cabin. I was hidden in the woods watching when the two brothers fought. I have waited, hoping that you would see the foolishness of your choice, but you have not. So now I have come. I say to you, reject the white man's God and return to your home. You are my daughter and your tribe needs you. Because of you, we have someone we can follow on the path of the Lenape, the path that gives our people hope, the path that the whites would destroy. Give up this strange God and this husband who hates all Indians and come back with me. I am your father. I am real. This Jesus you follow, him you cannot see or touch or feel. But you can touch the trees, the animals, the solid ground of our earth mother. You can touch me. And the day will come when the hatred in Black Eagle's heart will overpower his love for you."

White Deer's heart twisted within her. Her father stood before her, his face impassive, but she could feel his love for her in his words. For just one moment, her faith wavered and nearly broke. But she had given her heart to Jesus, and because of that, she was bound to her husband. Slowly, she lifted her head and looked into her father's eyes. "I cannot leave Jesus and He tells me I cannot leave Jonathan. You may be right about Jonathan, but it is too late to do anything about it. He is my husband and the father of my child. I think that you speak wisdom and there are times when my heart trembles in fear for me and for my son, but no matter. I have changed my name to Ruth, and I have made my choice. I will follow the white man's God and remain with Jonathan."

Wingenund stood silent for a moment. Then he put his hand on his daughter's shoulder and looked into her eyes. "Then I say that Opahtuhwe is no more. The princess of her people is dead to us, and we will sing the song of mourning in our lodges. You will not see me again in this life."

With that, Wingenund turned and walked into the woods. White Deer called after him. "Father! Father!"

But he did not answer her or look back. A great sadness came over her as she watched her old life vanish into the woods with her father. The Indian princess was gone forever, and the woman, now known as Ruth, put her face in her hands and wept bitterly.

Hours later, she sat alone on the front step of her cabin. She held a mirror in her hand, staring at her reflection.

I am no longer Opahtuhwe, the White Deer. I am Ruth. I am a follower of the white man's Jesus. My father has renounced me and says I am no longer Lenape. My husband loves me but part of him hates me, for no matter what name I take, to him I will always be an Indian. The hatred is too strong. One day he will forget his love for me. Lord Jesus, why did you lead me on such a trail of bitterness?

Her heart was gripped with deep sorrow, and she realized that resentment against her husband was growing within her. From the day he became a scout, Jonathan had volunteered for the most dangerous missions, ones that took him far to the north into British territory and gave him opportunity to wreak vengeance on the Indians. At first he was gone for days at a time, then the days became weeks. He was never at home to help her, and Ruth spent most of her time alone. When he did come home, Jonathan was sullen and distant, his mind fixed on his terrible vendetta against the Lenape and all the tribes. He would bring supplies enough to feed her and the baby, but there was no joy at his return. Jonathan was only happy when he was in the woods, hunting Indians. A dark rumor was spreading among the tribes of a man who was called *Nènhìlëwès*—the Murderer—a man who came silently like the night mist into their very villages and towns, bringing death and terror into the heart of the Indian lands. She knew Jonathan was that man.

Now her father had disowned her, and it seemed as though she were lost in a very dark place with no one to guide her. As she sat with tears running down her face, she heard a light step on the path. She looked up to find Joshua Hershberger standing before her, a haunch of deer meat and a basket of vegetables in his hands. She looked around in fear. "Joshua, what are you doing here? If my husband finds out..."

Joshua smiled. "Do not worry, Ruth, no one saw me come. I have brought supplies, for I know my brother has been remiss in his care for you."

Ruth stepped down off the porch and took the food. She stared at Joshua.

Why did I not choose this one, Lord? He is as kindly as his brother is hateful.

She saw the love in his eyes, but she kept silent and turned to go into the house.

"Ruth?"

The unspoken question in his voice stopped her, and she stood for a moment looking down at the boards in the porch.

Then she turned to Joshua. "I know what you would ask. I cannot tell you what is in my heart, for that would be a betrayal. I say too much already. Jonathan is my husband and my heart is his, no matter what he does."

"But you are unhappy, Princess."

Ruth felt the pent-up resentment rise in her. "Do not call me that again. I have forsaken that trail to follow your God. I have put those ways behind me, and even though I did not know the sorrow my choice would bring, I must go on and not look back. Jonathan loves me and one day he will remember that. He is my husband and the laws of my new faith bind me to him. I want to be a good follower of Jesus, even though I do not understand his ways."

"Then at least let me help you to do just that. Let me teach you from the Bible."

Her heart leaped at the thought of having someone to help her to know God's word better. She hesitated, for there were many things she did not understand when she read the Bible, but the thought of going against her husband's command did not sit well with her. Ruth looked into Joshua's eyes. She knew that Joshua loved her, but she also knew that he was true in his walk with God, and he would never compromise her. Finally, she nodded. "Yes, you may help me, but we must not meet. My husband has forbidden it."

Joshua nodded. "I understand. I will write lessons for you to read. I will leave them at the mill under the steps. Has Jonathan forbidden you to have a Bible?"

She shook her head. "No, but he does not want me to speak of it to him."

Joshua smiled. "Do you even have one?"

"Yes. Mrs. Zane gave me one, but Jonathan never even looks at it."

"Then that would be a good place to hide my lessons and go over them until you really understand them."

Ruth smiled too. The kindness and compassion she felt from him was almost too much. "You are a good man, Joshua. Sometimes I wish…" She stopped herself and turned away. "But those choices have been made. Now you must go before someone sees you here. Thank you for the venison, and I will look forward to your lessons." She turned and walked into the house. She could almost feel his love burning her, enfolding her as she walked away.

More weeks went by and still Jonathan did not return. Ruth went eagerly every few days to the mill and retrieved Joshua's lessons. And some mornings she would arise and find a turkey or some deer or bear meet hanging from the tree in front of her cabin. She knew that Joshua was watching over her, and it comforted her deeply. Often she would find herself thinking about what it would be like to be married to Joshua instead of his brother. She would envision herself living at Joshua's prosperous farm, working with a strong man beside her, having…having his children. But she would stop her thoughts before they got too far. Then she would feel shame and weep before the Lord.

The only happiness she knew was in studying the Bible. Each morning she rose before the sun while Matthew slept and read by the light of the morning fire. Joshua's notes helped her to grasp the truth. Joshua also taught her the words of Menno Simmons and Jakob Amanm, the founders of Joshua's faith. The words of peace and love toward her fellow man captured her heart until she knew that the way of peace was the true way. One day she went to the mill and waited until Joshua came. He was surprised to see her.

"You shouldn't be seen here, Ruth. What if Jonathan hears of it?"

Without thinking Ruth took Joshua's hand. "I have come to tell you that I wish to follow the Amish way."

Joshua smiled. "Well, Ruth, I don't think there has ever been an Amish princess before."

As she looked into his eyes, Ruth realized that she wanted Joshua to take her in his arms and hold her, forever. She pulled her hand away in confusion. "I'm sorry, Joshua, I just wanted to tell you…" She turned and ran into the woods. Behind her, she heard him calling after her.

One morning before dawn, Ruth awoke to the sound of footsteps on the porch and a knock on the door. She threw on her robe and peeked out. Wetzel and Zane were standing on the porch. Her heart sank, for they had never come to the cabin before without Jonathan. She opened the door. The two men nodded and then Wetzel spoke.

"I've bad news for you, ma'am. The Mohawks have taken Jonathan captive. He was spying out the strength of Fort Niagara when he ran into a band led by the traitor Joseph Brant. He was taken to the fort and turned over to the British Colonel Butler before the Indians realized who he was. We tried to arrange for his release, but because of Jonathan's deeds against the reddys, the tribes allied with the British are insisting that either Jonathan be hung or turned over to them for torture. So far, Butler has not decided. That's all we know. Sorry to be the bearer of bad tidings."

Ruth held onto the doorframe to keep from collapsing. "What will I do?"

Zane shrugged. "Jonathan's brother is a good man. He will help you and surely others at the fort…"

Ruth shook her head. "I am an Indian princess, daughter of the greatest foe of all the white men on this frontier. My child is taunted as a half-breed. No, I do not think the other settlers will be eager to help me."

Wetzel stared at her for a long time. Then he spoke. "You made your choice by marryin' a white man. Now you'll have to live with it." Wetzel's words chilled her.

The two men turned and left. Ruth watched them go, her heart held fast with an icy fear.

Chapter Twenty-Three

The Sword of Sorrow

Joshua was in the barn when he heard a noise behind him. Turning, he saw Ruth in the doorway. She was trembling and her face was streaked with tears. "Ruth, what is it?"

"Jonathan has been taken by the British. He is being held at Fort Niagara. The Indian allies of the British are demanding that he be turned over for torture. Oh, Joshua, what am I to do?"

Ruth took a few steps toward him and began to fall. Joshua leaped to her side and caught her. He pulled her close in his powerful arms. He felt her heart beating against his chest and then suddenly her arms were around his neck and she was kissing him fiercely, unashamedly. Joshua's head began to whirl, and then he was kissing her back. All the love in his heart poured out to her as they lost themselves in each other.

Suddenly Joshua pulled away. "No! Ruth, this is wrong! You are married."

She stood before him, a vision of loveliness, her breast heaving with passion and emotion. "I am married in the Indian way, not the white man way. I never promised before God."

"But what about Jonathan?"

Tears were running down her face. "Jonathan has abandoned me and our son. He would rather kill Indians than stay at home and be a good husband. My father is right! One day his hatred for all Indians will overcome his love, and he will kill me too! I can't live this way anymore. You must take me away, Joshua. You love me, you care for me, I can feel it and it keeps me safe. Please, Joshua, please!"

Joshua looked at the woman before him, and his heart was torn. He loved her. He had loved her since the first day he saw her at Fort Pitt so many years ago. He had dreamed that she would be his and now the door had opened. A million thoughts rushed through his head.

We could sell the farm and go far away. I could find work as a miller anywhere in the colonies. Jonathan is going to be killed anyway. What would it hurt? No one would know us—

"You cannot!"

The word's came into his mind as clearly as if a voice had spoken them out loud. He stared at Ruth silently and fought a great battle in his heart and his mind. Finally, he spoke. "I cannot take you away, Ruth, even though it is what I desire most in all this world. It would be a great sin against our Lord. Yes, it is true that I love you. I have always loved you. But that does not change the way things are. You belong to Jonathan until death do you part. I can only be your friend and your brother, though I long with every fiber of my being to have you for my wife. Once you loved Jonathan, I know that."

Ruth looked down. "Jonathan has killed my love. An Indian princess gives her love to the warrior who loves her most and is willing to die for her. He shows her in many ways his undying devotion. She chooses him so that she will be provided for and protected. I thought Jonathan was that one, but he is not. I see now that he loved me for his own selfish reasons. He was going to die, and I saved him and nursed him back to health. He felt obligated and thought that was love. But he will never love me as you do. I know it now and I am sorry for my choice."

"But do you love me?"

Ruth came to him and stood before him. She looked straight into his eyes. "You are good and kind. You love me and you love Matthew. You care for me and protect me. I have fought my feelings, but as my love for Jonathan grew cold, a new one has taken its place in my heart. I know the truth now. The love I have for you is a different kind of love, because when I am with you, I fear nothing. It is an eternal love, not a momentary passion. If you would let me, I would love you with a love so strong it would crush you if you were a lesser man."

Joshua turned away and raised his arms to heaven. His mind was in turmoil.

Oh Lord, this is a great bitterness to my soul. How often have I longed to hear these words from these precious lips? Is there no way that this can be?

He stood silently for a long time and then lowered his arms and turned back to Ruth. He placed his hands on her shoulders and spoke gently to her. "Ruth, we cannot. You are not free unless Jonathan dies and we do not wish that. It it is in the Lord's hands. Until we know the outcome, we must do our best to return to the way things were. We should not meet. I will provide for you and watch over you, but it must be from a distance. I cannot betray my Lord or my brother, and I would have you to be a virtuous woman all your days."

Ruth looked at him for a long, silent moment. Tears began to trace their way down her lovely face again. She nodded. "You are right, Joshua. Every part of me, body and soul, would have it otherwise, but you are right. Somehow I knew that in the end you would be a man of honor. It makes me love you all the more, but my heart is breaking." She started to go, hesitated, and then rushed back to his arms. "Hold me once more, before I go, please, Joshua. Give me strength."

His arms went around her and they stood together in a deep embrace. He felt his very being flowing into her and the warmth of her body pressed against him was almost too much to bear. He wanted to push her away but he could not. He bent again to kiss her.

"Joshua Hershberger."

This time the voice was very real. Joshua jerked away and put his finger to his lips. He pointed to an empty stall and whispered in her ear. "Hide in there while I see who this is."

He watched as she ducked into the hiding place and then he walked through the door out into the barnyard. Three men were standing there. Two were armed.

"Joshua Hershberger?"

He looked at them. "Yes, I am Joshua Hershberger. How can I help you?"

The man without the rifle stepped forward. "I am Captain David Williamson of the Colonial Militia. We are taking enlistments among the men to form a chapter here and your name came to our attention as one of the men of age to fight. I am here to give you your orders and tell you the date you are to report."

Joshua stepped forward. "You must have the wrong man, Captain. Surely Colonel Zane told you why I cannot join the militia."

"Yes, the colonel mentioned something, but I wanted to hear it from your own lips. This is a time of great peril for the frontier and every able-bodied man is required to take up arms in defense of his country, by order of the Colonial Government."

"But I cannot fight; it is against my faith."

"Are you saying that you refuse to take up arms to defend this country?"

"I will do whatever is necessary to help my country except take up arms to kill other men. The Bible forbids it."

"That's what Zane said you would say. I'm afraid you will have to come with us until this can be sorted out. Men!" Williamson nodded to the two men, and they pointed their rifles at Joshua. "Come with us and do not resist or it will go ill with thee."

Joshua turned to the barn. "But I…"

"Never mind your chores, Hershberger. You will come with us now!"

Joshua stared at the wall that Ruth was hiding behind. His heart pounded in his chest. Then he felt the prod of the rifles in his back. "Let's go, coward."

He turned and walked slowly away from the farm.

This cannot be happening! Lord, where are You?

As the men escorted Joshua away, they did not see Ruth come to the door, her great sorrowful eyes watching as they took Joshua away.

Joshua Hershberger stood before a group of three men in a meeting room at the fort. One of them was Williamson. They were looking over some documents. Finally, Williamson looked up. "So, Mr. Hershberger, you still refuse to join the militia and fight for your country?"

"Yes, sir, that is correct."

The man glanced at the document in front of him. "It says here that you are a member of a religious sect that holds that non-violence is the command of Jesus and you cannot violate the Lord's word. Is that true?"

"Yes, sir. I am Amish by faith and by birth. My father was Amish before me and his grandfather was a Mennonite. We have been non-violent for many generations. I cannot change what I am."

One of the other men spoke up. "Yes, we heard about your father. Wasn't he the coward who let your family be butchered by the savages and didn't lift a finger to help them?"

Joshua lifted his eyes to the man. "My father was an honest man who did not deviate from what he believed. When the savages were burning our home he told us, 'A man does not give up what he believes, simply because the test is too hard.' He was not a coward; he had principles which rose above the demands of men who only live to kill each other."

The first man spoke again. "Pretty highfalutin words from a man who will not take up arms for his country or even to defend those who protect the land you farm. I don't think you are principled. I think you are a coward and a traitor to our cause, and I'm going to recommend that the local magistrates clap you in irons until you change your mind. Guards!"

The door opened and two armed men walked into the room.

Williamson pointed to Joshua. "Take this traitor to the lockup until we decide where to send him."

Joshua looked at the men. "But my farm, my mill. I do all the grinding for the fort, and I supply grain and vegetables for the settlers. Would you cut off these services?"

Williamson growled. "You should have thought of that when you refused to serve your country. Take him!"

The two guards seized Joshua and hauled him from the room.

Ruth sat weeping in her cabin when another knock came on the door.

Who can this be? It has already been a day of sorrow.

She went to the door. A man dressed in plain clothes and wearing a clergyman's collar stood at the door.

"I am Zeisberger, the Moravian missionary. I am a friend of Joshua. I have come to tell you that Joshua has been taken to prison for refusing to take up arms against the British."

The man's words came crushing down on Ruth like an avalanche, her head began to spin and she fainted.

When Ruth awoke, she had been carried to the bed. Zeisberger was cooling her brow with a damp cloth. She started to sit up, but he gently held her.

"You must rest. You have had a hard day, what with Jonathan being held by the British and Joshua in prison."

"You know about Jonathan?"

The missionary put down the cloth. "The word spread quickly at the fort. There was even talk of a rescue party, but Colonel Zane would not allow it. The Fort at Niagara is defended by British regulars and a large force of Indians and Tories."

Ruth put her face in her hands. "What am I to do? Joshua has been caring for me while Jonathan has been gone. Now I have no one." She began to sob.

The clergyman put a gentle hand on her shoulder. "I have established a village at Gnadenhutten. We call it the Village of Peace. Many of your people who follow our Savior have come there. It is a place of safety and joy. Will you not join us?"

"How would I get there?"

"I am leaving tomorrow, Ruth, before daybreak. You and the child should gather your things. You will travel with me. It is only two days' journey. And I think it best that you not speak of this to anyone. You are the daughter of Wingenund and there is already much anger against your father's bloody raids on the border. With Jonathan as good as dead and without Joshua's help, that anger will soon be directed toward you. It is no longer safe for you to be here alone."

Ruth looked into the kindly eyes and hope was reborn in her heart. The events of the day came crashing down, and her heart cried out for a place of refuge. She nodded. "I will come."

Part Five

The Village of Peace

And so, in 1777, White Deer became Ruth, the woman our family calls the Amish Princess, and after being abandoned by her husband, went with her son to Gnadenhutten, the Village of Peace. Ruth faced many trials in her life. But her faith in her Lord and His plan for her life never wavered, even when He seemed far away and she could not see the path before her.

The Village of Peace
From The Journals of Jenny Hershberger

Chapter Twenty-Four

A New Season

Ruth knelt in the bow of a birch bark canoe while the missionaries, David Zeisberger and John Heckewelder, paddled up the small stream. Each hour of travel had taken them deeper into the Ohio wilderness. Tall, majestic pines and oaks rose in solemn cathedral splendor while the lesser citizens of the leafy bower, cedars and basswood trees, stood below them in silent, worshipful ranks. The stillness of the forest was broken only by the small splashes of the paddles and the occasional chatter of black squirrels watching the unwanted visitors and venting their displeasure from the safety of a lofty branch.

Six-year-old Matthew sat quietly in front of his mother as the canoe slipped softly through the crystal waters, but his eyes watched everything. He pointed to a deer along the bank as it lifted its head at the sight of the travellers and then went peacefully back to browsing. A half-grown fawn peeked warily from behind its mother's flank and then followed her quietly into the shelter of the laurel and hawthorn thickets that filled the ground between the larger trees. Ruth touched her son and nodded.

He will be a great hunter like his father and grandfather...

As they swept around a bend in the stream, signs that the village was near became evident. Dozens of birch bark canoes lay in orderly ranks along a shelving beach. Ahead of them, a small bridge spanned the stream, and Ruth saw the roofs of Indian lodges above the slight rise of ground along the shore.

Along the bank, groups of men and women began to gather to greet the newcomers. Ruth turned to Zeisberger. "Tell me the story of this place."

Zeisberger smiled. "Six years ago we came with sixteen canoes filled with our new brothers and sisters. We had drifted down the Allegheny to Fort Pitt looking for a site, but our guides led us farther down the Ohio to the Big Beaver River. We traveled up that stream almost twenty miles into the forest. From there we paddled up the Tuscarawas River until we came to this spot. When we saw it, we understood how Moses felt when he stood on Mount Pisgah and looked down into the land of Canaan. We founded our settlement here."

As the missionaries beached the canoe, excited shouts began to ring out. Dark-eyed children peeked shyly from behind their mother's skirts. The scalp locks and other adornments of Indian warriors were conspicuously absent, and the men all wore their hair long or tied back with thongs. Zeisberger and Heckewelder clambered from the canoe and lifted Ruth's things out. Ruth came behind them. As she scanned the group of happy faces, she stopped in amazement. A tall warrior with a prominent scar on his face stepped out of the crowd. Ruth ran to the man. "Scar! What are you doing here?"

Scar frowned at the memory of his old name. Then he pointed to Zeisberger. "When my son, Black Eagle, shot me, I lost my strength and fell beside a tree. Brother David and Brother John found me. They stayed with me and cared for me until I was well enough to travel. Their kindness was new to me, and I asked them why white men would care for a dying Indian. They told me the story of the Good Samaritan, how a man hated by the Jews cared for a beaten man when all others passed him by. I was persuaded." He smiled again. "Now I am no longer *Ehèntawisèk*, the scarred one. I am Jeremiah. My life is new and I have forsaken the trail of war. And others have come, too." He pointed.

Ruth followed his hand and stared again as the sachem, Glickhican pushed his way through the throng. He greeted her with joy. "My princess. To see you here brings gladness to an old man's heart. Come, let me show you where you can stay."

Ruth was comforted at the sight of these familiar faces. She took a deep breath and, taking Matthew's hand, she followed Glickhican and Jeremiah into the village.

Later, the three Lenape sat in front of a glowing fire in the center of the village. Ruth listened while Glickhican, now called Isaac, told the story of the village. The old man stirred the glowing embers with a stick as he spoke in the Lenape language. "After Brother David founded this place, it was as if the Creator sent his blessings upon it. The crops prospered, the children were healthy, and the Word was preached. People from all of the tribes came to the village. The speaking of Brother David and Brother John persuaded chiefs and warriors, squaws and maidens, from the lowest to the highest. When they heard the words of peace, they laid down their arms and joined us. While all the lands around were gripped in the flames of war, the Village of Peace lay quietly prospering, an island of hope in the midst of a growing storm."

Ruth watched the old man, and when he paused, she asked him the question that was on her heart. "When did you find the way, Glickhican?"

The old man looked up at the stars. "For many moons my heart had been troubled by the bloodshed among the tribes and the hatred toward the whites. But I did not have the words to speak to the chiefs to lead them from the warpath. When the yellow-haired brother spoke to you in our village, I heard the truth. He had nothing to gain by guiding you from the old ways.

His heart was true and he was of a generous spirit. So I listened also."

Ruth thought of Joshua.

Why did not I love him from the beginning? He is the gentle one and truth is in him.

A tear ran down her cheek as she thought of the sad turn her heart had taken when she gave it to Jonathan.

Glickhican went on. "I came here to the village to see if what I heard was true, and I found *Ehèntawisèk*. He had been changed from a merciless killer of whites into a true person. I knew in my heart that the power to change hearts in this way was from the Creator, so I embraced the truth I heard here." Isaac Glickhican laughed. "I can tell you that there was great excitement when Glickhican, one of the great chiefs of the Turtle Clan of the Lenape, became a follower of the white man's faith. More came, and in just a few years, this beautiful Village of Peace arose, a place of refuge from the terrors of war.

Jeremiah spoke. "It was the Indians of the warring tribes that gave this village its name. The vast forests surrounding us are teeming with game; the rivers are filled with fish. We have meat and grain in abundance, buckskin for clothing, and soft furs for winter garments. While they see their villages decimated and burned, we live in peace and plenty. We do not side with either the British or the colonists in this war. All are welcome here."

Glickhican looked around and pointed out different areas as he spoke. "At first there were only a few lodges, but we worked together and put up our church. After that we built a school, a mill, and a workshop. The fields are overflowing with crops. Our horses and cattle graze with the timid deer on the grassy hillsides. The Village of Peace has blossomed as a rose."

They heard a quiet step on the path and turned to see Zeisberger approaching. They stood to greet him, but he motioned them down and sat with them. "I have heard you speaking of the village and, yes, it is wonderful to me how the Lord has blessed us here. It is exactly as Jesus said it would be when men love one another. When they hear of the love and happiness existing in this community, warriors from every tribe journey to visit us. All who come are amazed at the change they see in the hearts of these people. Some warriors look with disdain upon the men who work alongside the women in the fields, but the great stands of waving corn, the hills covered with horses and cattle, these evidences of abundance, make it impossible for them to gainsay the blessings inherent in becoming a Christian. All who visit, whether friendly or otherwise, are treated with hospitality and never sent away empty-handed. And so we share our blessings with the tribes around us and more come because of it."

Ruth listened to the white missionary speak and then shyly she looked at him. "And is there a place here for me to truly find peace, when my husband is known as *Nènhìlëwès*—the Murderer—and my father is the greatest enemy of the whites?"

Zeisberger looked into the fire. "It is a sad thing when a man who knows the truth seeks the path of death. It is especially sad to see the bitterness between brothers who, though they are alike in feature as two peas in a pod, are worlds apart in their hearts. I will leave tomorrow to petition the authorities to release Joshua into my care. I would have him come and assist me in this great work. As for your husband and your father, we will all pray that they will come to a saving knowledge of the truth and renounce their murderous ways."

As they sat in the gathering dusk, the deep, melodious tolling of a bell broke the stillness of the forest. Zeisberger looked up and smiled. "Ah, the bell. If you knew what travails we faced to bring her here. But it has proven to be a great gift to us. The Indians love music and this bell mesmerizes them. On still nights, the bell sings across the forest and even those dwelling in distant towns know that we are summoning worshippers to our evening service. The song of the bell breaks the stillness of our forest home each night and delights the ears of the unconverted as though it were a call from an unknown forest god. Come let us go now and hear the word of our Lord. Brother John has a sweet message for us."

They rose and walked toward the large log building that housed the sanctuary. The quiet stillness, broken only by the melodious tolling of the bell, was a balm to Ruth's battered soul. They filed quietly into the immense building. Benches filled with worshippers covered the hard-packed dirt floor. In the front Heckewelder stood on a raised platform while a group of Indian women began an old hymn. The sweet voices brought a heavenly atmosphere into the room, and as they died away in the last refrain, Heckewelder stepped forward."

Ruth saw many warriors still dressed in their tribal clothing standing impassively against the wall. She whispered to Glickhican, "Are they Christians, too?"

"No, Princess, but they have heard of the village and wish to know if the missionary's words are straight. There is Hepote, a Maumee chief, of whom it was said he had never listened to words of any paleface—yet he has come. Next to him sit Shaushoto and Pipe, enemies of all white men. There stands Half-King, Shingiss, and Kotoxen—all of the Wolf Clan of the Lenape. That these men are here at all, speaks to the power of this work. "

Heckewelder began. "Long ago, the Creator God, the one that the Indian knows as the Great Spirit, made this world. He made the rivers and the streams, the forests and the plains. He filled them with the elk and the beaver, the squirrel and the bear. The rivers were empty so He made the fish to swim in them. The skies were empty so He made the eagle and the raven, the heron and the owl and sent them to fly in the air. But in this entire perfect world there was none to tend it, none made like unto the Creator God. So He reached down and took a handful of the earth and formed a man. Then He breathed his Spirit into the man and the man awoke. The man looked about him and saw that all of the creatures had a mate to be with them. So he spoke to the Creator and told Him of his need for a mate to share his fire and his food. The Creator put the man to sleep and took a rib from his side. From this rib He made a woman to be with the man. He placed them into a beautiful garden, much like the place where we live, and they lived in peace in the garden, eating the food the Creator made for them.

"But the serpent god, whom the Indian knows as *Matantu*, convinced the man and the woman to disobey the Creator. Because of the lie of the serpent, sickness and death came upon the man and the woman and all their descendants. They were cast out of the garden and wandered in darkness for many ages. The serpent god ruled over the beautiful world that the Creator had given to the man and woman.

"This made the Creator unhappy and His heart was broken for the children of the man and the woman. So He sent His Son, Jesus, into the world to restore them from their disobedience, and said if they would listen and believe and teach the other tribes, He would forgive them and welcome them back to the beautiful garden. The Son of the Creator opened the eyes of the children of the man and woman with His truth and gave them all His words written down in this Bible. Then He sent them from across the great salt water to speak to the red man in the forests of this land.

"As you can see, the Indian who hears and believes the words of the Great Spirit's Son put away their war-like ways and are welcomed back into the beautiful garden where they live in peace." Heckewelder's voice filled with strength. His arm swept in a circle taking in the village and the fields. "As you go tonight, look around you, great chiefs of the tribes. Is not this way better than to see your lodges filled with women weeping over their husbands who are slain in war? Is not this better than children lying dead in burned villages, or warriors lying in drunken stupor after drinking the demon firewater? Show me that the way of war is better than what we have at the Village of Peace, and we will tear this village down and depart these shores. But if you cannot, then wipe off the paint of war and join us. Live in peace with every man. Enjoy the blessings of the Great Spirit who desires that all men should be saved and come to the knowledge of the truth."

Heckewelder paused. There was a murmur as one of the chiefs arose and pulled the war bonnet from his head. He turned to the others around him. "I choose the way of peace."

Then another stepped forward and said the same. The Christian Indians smiled and welcomed them as they came to the front. Ruth looked around her. Some of the chiefs just shook their heads and walked away. Ruth's heart was filled with the certainty of her faith. She knew that she had at last found a home. But even as she went to the front to openly proclaim her faith, she did not see her father, Wingenund, who had been standing unseen in deep shadow at the back of the building, turn and walk out the door.

Chapter Twenty-Five

Days of Plenty

And so the days of plenty came to Ruth. From the first morning she awakened in her new home, she heard the birds singing more sweetly than ever before in her life. A silent zephyr stirred the curtains on her window and the smell of lilacs borne on sylvan wings infused her room. In the distance she heard a rooster crow and then the exquisite morning stillness was broken by the sound of a hammer ringing on an anvil. Outside she heard the excited voices of children at play and among them the happy voice of her son. She heard women walking by her hut and laughing as they went.

Peace entered her heart and she rose from her simple bed to wash and prepare herself for the day. Even the water in her pitcher had a sweet, refreshing quality. She turned and saw her Bible on the small stand by her bed. She sat down and picked up the precious book, and as she did, it fell open to the book of Acts, the third chapter. She began to read at verse eighteen.

"But those things, which God before had shewed by the mouth of all his prophets, that Christ should suffer, he hath so fulfilled. Repent ye therefore, and be converted, that your sins may be blotted out, when the times of refreshing shall come from the presence of the

Lord; And he shall send Jesus Christ, which before was preached unto you: Whom the heaven must receive until the times of restitution of all things, which God hath spoken by the mouth of all his holy prophets since the world began."

Ruth knelt by her bed and tears flooded her eyes.

Are these the times of refreshing that you have promised, my God? For I am in need of them.

Ruth stayed long by her bed, praying and weeping with joy as, for the first time, she sensed the Holy Spirit bringing comfort to her soul. Her reverie was broken by a gentle knock on the door. She rose and opened it to find a lovely raven-haired maiden standing on the stoop. The girl held a tray covered by a cloth.

"I am Miriam. I hope I have not awakened you. I know you were tired from your journey."

Ruth smiled and ushered the girl into her room. "No, Miriam, you did not awaken me. The birds and the happy voices of the children did. Please come in."

The girl entered. "Brother David has asked me to help you find out more about our village and to show you the things we do here. If you are hungry, the mealtime is over, but I have brought you some food." Miriam set the tray on the table and removed the cloth. It was simple fare—cheese, bread, and a bowl of milk, but to Ruth it tasted like the king's food. Miriam declined to join her. "I have already eaten. Your son also ate with the children this morning. He seems to fit right in here and the other children accepted him right away."

Ruth finished the breakfast and then rose from the table. "Please show me everything, Miriam." She looked at the girl and then a question came unbidden to her mind. "Are you married?"

The maiden blushed and looked down. Her answer was almost inaudible. "I was pledged to a warrior of the Shawnee. We loved each other very much, but when I heard the words of Heckewelder I knew there was to be a greater love in my life. My beloved could not accept my faith and drove me from the village."

Ruth saw a single tear on the girl's cheek. She stepped over and took the girl in her arms. "I, too, have given much to follow Jesus." Ruth felt the girl's arms tighten about her.

Then Miriam stepped away and a smile was on her face. "Come now, Ruth. Let me show you the Village of Peace." Together the two women went out the door.

As they did, Matthew came running up. He took his mother's hand and walked with them. He looked up at Ruth with solemn eyes. "Mama, I like this place. The other children are kind. They do not call me half-breed like the children at the fort. They have already asked me to be in their games and join them in the school. Can I, Mama, can I?"

Ruth bent down and embraced her son. "Yes, son. Go ahead. I will find you in a while." The lad ran off happily and Ruth continued her walk.

Miriam led them to a cabin and stopped at the door. "This is one of our shops. Here we make brooms, harness for the horses, farming implements—everything useful that we can. We have a forge here. Several of the men have learned to blacksmith and keep our horses shod and our tools repaired."

The large shop was filled with bustling people, all active at some task. In one corner, a tall man stood holding a piece of red-hot iron on an anvil, while beating it out with a sledge hammer. The sparks flew and the anvil rang. Miriam pointed to the circle of Indians around the anvil. "We call that the singing stone. Its sound is a source of constant amazement to the people. When the missionaries were bringing it here, the teamsters lost it in the woods. It lay there for two years until it was found again."

At another building a circle of women and men sat around a pile of smooth dried saplings and grapevines. Miriam pointed. "They are making the baskets we use to carry everything."

Ruth was in awe at the industry of the settlement. In her own village, she had grown up watching the men lolling about, smoking or bragging, or indulging in athletic competitions while the women labored day and night. Here the men were industrious and helpful. Young Indian men ran here and there, carrying boards and tools to the carpenters who were engaged in the constant construction. Miriam led her to the stables where she saw beautifully cared-for horses and cattle, many with foals and calves. Chickens flocked under the trees and goats bleated from well-tended pens. Outside the village, the forest had been cleared carefully in different areas and fenced fields set in the midst of the trees were filled with corn, squash, pumpkins, leeks, onions, and melons—a cornucopia of food bursting from the verdant soil. In a sheltered grove, Ruth saw a group of rough structures close to the ground. As she watched she realized that they were beehives.

Miriam laughed at her amazed expression. "Yes, Ruth, even bees. The children do love the honey, and if it were to be told, all of us have a sweet tooth."

Ruth turned and took the girl's hands in hers. "Miriam, I feel in my heart that the Lord has sent you to me to be a comfort. I hope we will be friends who can bless each other when the hard memories come."

Miriam nodded. "I, too, feel that we are to be friends, and I thank the Lord for it."

The two women walked and talked the morning away and soon it was time for lunch. They joined the others in a large open pavilion set with tables. Men and women passed among them serving bread, dried meat, milk, and vegetables. Ruth saw Matthew and beckoned to him.

He came running, tugging another boy with him. "This is Jacob, Mama. He is going to be my best friend."

The boy nodded in agreement.

Matthew pointed to where a group of children were eating. "Can Jacob and I sit with the others?"

Ruth nodded and put her arm around Miriam. "Well, son, it seems we have both found a friend today. *Du lieber Gott* is smiling on us. Run along now." Ruth saw the puzzled expression on Miriam's face. "That is German, Miriam. I heard Joshua use it when he taught me the Amish way. It means 'the loving God.'"

"Who is Joshua?"

Ruth felt herself blush, and for a moment, there was an awkward silence. "He is my husband's brother. He...he taught me what I know about Jesus. It was his words that first brought me to the cross."

Miriam looked at Ruth's face. "I think maybe he is more than a brother to you?"

Ruth looked away for a long moment and then turned back to Miriam. "Joshua is my husband's twin brother. Except for the color of their hair, you can hardly tell them apart. But inside they are very different. Joshua follows the way of peace, and Jonathan is a man of war. I first saw them both on the same day and gave my heart to Jonathan. I do not know why, for Joshua loves me with all his heart, and Jonathan's heart is far from me. But these things are unknowable, and I must accept them as they are."

"But do you regret your choice?"

Ruth felt the heat rise in her face, and she looked down as tears filled her eyes. Her answer was quiet and yet filled with anguish. "Yes, I regret my choice."

She felt Miriam's arm go around her, and the girl whispered in her ear. "Thank you for opening your heart. Your secret is safe with me, and I will pray with you that your husband also finds Jesus and the Lord restores what you once had. Now let us take our fill of God's provision, and we will walk and talk some more."

Ruth sighed and composed herself. An inner turmoil she had battled for months slowly lifted from her mind and departed like the morning mist burning away before the heat of the rising sun. She had confessed her deepest heart and now she felt like a stream of mountain water had washed her clean. But in that moment, she also realized that even though she knew the truth, she could never change the way things were. She lifted a silent prayer for wisdom, for she did not know what to do.

That night she sat with Miriam as Brother David gave the sermon. They had a time of singing and then Zeisberger stepped to the front of the platform. Stillness came over the crowd as he began. "Our greatest testimony to our faith in the Lord Jesus Christ is the way we live out that faith in front of others. Some of the best examples for the younger women are the wives who have served and respected their husbands faithfully for many years, through hard times and good, and even when their love for their husband waned like a new moon. The Apostle Paul tells us in his letter to the Ephesians that husbands must love their wives, but wives must respect their husbands. Even if your husband is unlovable, to respect him in spite of his faults is to deny yourself and take up the cross that Jesus laid before each of us. The man is also supposed to cherish his wife in such a way that all who see them know her value. But even if the husband fails in that duty, the wife must carry out her part."

Ruth felt as though Zeisberger was speaking directly to her.

He continued. "The Apostle Peter tells us to love each other deeply for love covers a multitude of sins. If you love your husband and respect him, it is a testimony to his wayward heart and he can be consecrated by your faithfulness. The security the husband feels from being loved in this way can cause him to make wise choices and draw away from sin. There are many here tonight who are praying for unsaved loved ones, husbands, sons and daughters, brothers and sisters. And I say to you tonight, that He who has begun a good work in you will be faithful to complete it unto that day. Hold fast in your faith. Walk in the way that Jesus tells you, and even in the darkest moments, your faithfulness will bring reward." Zeisberger turned and led the singers in another hymn.

> *Life is the time to serve the Lord,*
> *The time to ensure the great reward;*
> *And while the lamp holds out to burn,*
> *The vilest sinner may return.*
> *Life is the hour which God has given*
> *To escape from hell, and fly to heaven;*
> *The day of grace, when mortals may*
> *Secure the blessings of the day.*

As the words ascended to heaven, Ruth knew that God was speaking to her, and the great conflict in her heart lifted. Like a ray of morning sun, the truth of the word filled her heart and she knew where her duty lay. She was married to Jonathan, and until she knew he was dead, she would pray for him and remain a faithful wife, for by doing so, she might win him back to Jesus. She thought of her love for Joshua, and she knew it could never be as long as Jonathan was alive. A small tear rolled down her cheek as she surrendered to her Savior and gave both brothers to the Lord.

Chapter Twenty-Six

Flight

The room in which Jonathan Hershberger was kept prisoner was on the top story of Fort Niagara's old French castle above the soldier's barracks. The walls were thick stone and the guards were vigilant and ever mindful of the importance of their prisoner—*Nènhìlëwès*, the Murderer. There had been few opportunities for escape and Jonathan had languished in his cell for three months. This morning he stood at the barred window looking out on the parade ground where British regular troops were drilling. Around the perimeters of the parade ground lounged a mixed group of Indians and British loyalists who had fled to the fort, looking for protection from the wrath of the colonial army to the south.

There was a sharp rap on the door, and then it opened peremptorily and the commander of the fort, Colonel John Butler, came in. Jonathan had met with him before and had grown to like the man. John Butler was a warrior and had served the British with distinction in the French and Indian War and his exploits appealed to Jonathan's war-like sensibilities. While second in command of the New York Colony under Sir William Johnson, Butler built a huge estate in the Mohawk Valley, before the outbreak of the revolution. He abandoned his land under pressure from the rebels and fled to Canada. Now he commanded the Indians and those Tories who had joined him when Ethan Allen had pushed the British and their supporters out of New York in the early days of the war.

Butler pulled up the one stool in the room and motioned Jonathan to the bed. "Good morning, Hershberger. Are you being treated well?"

Jonathan glanced through the porthole in the door at the silent guard and then sat down. "I can't complain, Colonel. The food's decent but, present company excluded, the companionship is rather boring."

Butler laughed. "And rightly so, Hershberger. After all, you're not exactly an honored guest." Then Butler turned serious. "I've a problem, Jonathan. As you may know, I was sent here a year ago to keep the local tribes neutral in this conflict between the Crown and the rebels. When Brant captured you, it was of no import to the chiefs until they found out who my prisoner was. Then they became wroth. They are demanding that I turn you over to them for torture. Your reputation as a killer of Indians has preceded you, and I have to face down delegations from the Six Nations every day. I am rather at a loss as to what to do. I like you as a man and would hate to imagine the devilish fate my esteemed allies have in store for you."

Jonathan nodded. "I must say I am of the same mind as you, Colonel. Is there no hope for me then?"

Butler frowned and looked down. "The chiefs held a council yesterday. They wouldn't let me speak. They worked themselves into a frenzy, smashing the war club on the ground and screeching. At the end they demanded your life in no uncertain terms. I've seen men tortured by these savages, and to tell you the truth, I've no stomach for it." Butler glanced up and looked directly at Jonathan. "However, as one white man to another, there may be a way to avoid such, shall we say, unpleasantry."

"And how might that be, Colonel?"

Butler stood and went to the window. "I've noticed the scullery maid making eyes at you from time to time."

Jonathan nodded in silent affirmation.

"She's a brazen wench, and because of her corruptible nature, she might be led into indiscretions whereby you might obtain egress from this charming suite of yours."

"And, of course, the commander of the fort would turn a blind eye to these…these activities?"

"Yes, Jonathan, but only if the commander of the fort received the promise of the prisoner that he would never return to Canada."

Jonathan smiled. "Well, Colonel, since there are plenty of reddys to deal with on the Ohio and south, I believe the prisoner could make that agreement."

Colonel Butler stood up. "Very good, Jonathan, but I promise you that if you ever fall into my hands again, I will not hesitate to hand you over to the savages."

"Understood, Colonel, understood."

Butler turned to go and then he turned back. "I love Britain and I have given much to maintain my loyalty to the king. But the British cannot win this war. There is too much fervor on the side of the Colonials, and the Crown hires mercenaries whose hearts are not in this fight. So, if at the end of this contagion I fall into your hands, perhaps you might remember this conversation and show me the same kindness."

"Agreed, Colonel."

Butler reached out and the two men shook hands. Then he turned and left the room. Jonathan watched him go and hope blazed in his heart.

A few hours later Jonathan was sitting on his bed when he heard the click of a key in the lock and the door opened to admit the scullery maid with his midday meal. The armed soldier stood outside in the hallway. As she set the meal down, the maid ran an approving eye over Jonathan's stalwart frame and pleasing features. It was not the first time she had made known her appreciation of Jonathan's manliness. Jonathan remembered

Butler's words and he winked slyly at the girl. She blushed and Jonathan smiled invitingly. Without speaking aloud his lips framed the words, "Come see me tonight if you can." The girl glanced back at the soldier and then looked down. Her head barely moved as she nodded silently.

The guard pushed the door further open and looked in with a frown. "Come, girl, let's stop dallying. Tis not a royal feast you are preparing for this dog."

The girl placed the bowl of soup and piece of bread on the stool next to Jonathan's bed and then gathered up the tray and turned to go, but not before she gave Jonathan a glance filled with promise. Jonathan smiled back, his mind racing with his plan to escape. All he had to do now was wait.

It was early in the morning before the sun broke the last darkness of the night when Jonathan heard a faint scratching at the door. He roused quickly and walked to the door. Through the barred porthole he could just make out the features of the girl in the darkness. Jonathan barely heard her whisper. "I've come, but you must be quiet. I gave the downstairs guard an extra ration of rum, and he's fast asleep."

Jonathan whispered through the bars. "Will you come in or do we just talk through the porthole?"

There was a faint clank as the girl produced a ring of keys. "I took these from the guard. I can only stay a little while." Jonathan could hear the excitement in her voice, and he waited while she unlocked the door. As the door creaked open, Jonathan reached for the girl as if to pull her into an embrace. Her arms slipped around him and then suddenly his hands were around her neck and he was squeezing with all his strength. Her eyes went wide with terror and then slowly her struggles ceased and she slumped in his arms. Lowering the unconscious girl quietly to the floor, he picked up the keys and slipped through the door. He glanced up and down the hallway and then made his way silently to the stairs.

At the bottom, next to the barracks door, the sleeping guard lay with his face on a table, the empty cup of grog by his hand. Jonathan crept silently down the stairs. The guard's rifle leaned against the wall and a powder horn lay beside it. Jonathan lifted the weapon silently and moved toward the stairs that led to the ground floor. The guard snorted in his sleep and stirred. Jonathan stopped and stayed motionless for a long moment. He waited until he was sure the guard had gone back to his rum-soaked dreams, and then he silently slipped down the stairs to the side door. It was locked. As he lifted the keys, he heard a scream from the upstairs room. It was the maid calling for help. She had awakened! Quickly, he tried the keys. On the third try, the lock clicked and the door swung open.

Across the parade ground, he saw the palisade that guarded the fort along the river. He knew the river would lead him south toward Fort Pitt. Behind him he heard the alarm being raised in the barracks. A group of Indians came running toward him. Quickly, he pointed toward the castle. "Hurry, a prisoner has escaped. I'll go to warn the guards at the river."

As the Indians passed him, Jonathan ran through the open gate toward the water. Dozens of canoes were drawn up on the sandy shore, and he picked one and shoved it out into the current that the river made as it poured into Lake Ontario. Then he turned and ran swiftly south along the river. Behind him he heard the yells of the Indians. The anger in their screeches told him that they had discovered their most hated enemy had escaped.

They'll be after me with a vengeance!

Jonathan kept to the trail along the shoreline and ran as swiftly as he could. Beside him the river flowed smoothly down toward the lake. He knew it was about fifteen miles to the mighty falls on the river, and if he could make it there, he could lose himself in the wilderness above them. Suddenly, a branch beside his head snapped as a musket ball whizzed by. He looked over his shoulder to see that several braves were on his trail, one of them less than one hundred yards behind. In his days in the woods, Jonathan had perfected a skill that he now put to good use. He could load and fire a rifle while on a dead run, and he was a crack shot.

Quickly loading the rifle, he turned and shot the leading brave. The Indian tumbled headfirst into the dust and lay still. Jonathan ran on while the following Indians came up to the body of their comrade. Their shrieks of rage filled the air and then they redoubled their efforts, but Jonathan's prowess as a runner kept him ahead of his pursuers and even gave him a lead of several hundred yards.

Soon the three months of inactivity began to tell on Jonathan. He felt his legs growing tired. With the Indians not far behind, Jonathan knew he would have to use cunning rather than speed to outwit his enemies. Wetzel had taught him many tricks to avoid capture, and now he began to employ them. Plunging off the trail into the deep woods, he began to leap over logs and large stones. He found an area of hard-baked ground where he would leave no track and ran across it. At one point he worked his way up a stony ravine, leaping from rock to rock. He knew that his pursuers would have to go slowly now and look for every sign of his passing. This gave him a great advantage.

After an hour, he came to a long section of moss and sand where his footprints would show plainly, so he slipped off the trail, ran ahead, and then walked backward, leaving a plain trail that pointed the wrong direction. Then he clambered up a hillside until he came to the top, and using branches, he let himself down onto a ledge below the crest; he came to a creek and crossed it by swinging himself into a tree and climbing from one tree to another; he waded brooks where he found hard bottom, and avoided swampy, soft ground.

Soon the forest was silent. The sound of his enemies had faded and vanished. He knew that only the most skilled of Indian trackers could follow him.

The rising sun began to filter through the dense forest. The cries of morning birds and the chatter of black squirrels filled the air. He was alone. Then he turned south with the rising sun on his left and began to travel straight toward Fort Pitt. Once more, Jonathan had escaped.

In the silent time before the dawn, a month after Jonathan's return to Fort Henry, a large group of men crept through the dark, silent forest. Around them the mist hung among the trees like a shroud, dampening all sound. Jonathan Hershberger, now a captain in the militia, signaled to the men following him and pointed through the trees. Ahead, they could see the Shawnee village. Jonathan motioned to the men around him and they spread out, dropped to the ground, and began to crawl through the brush surrounding the village. From the distance came the cry of a nighthawk, but no bird made the call. It was one of Jonathan's men signaling that more of the militia was in place on the far side of the settlement.

The men crept forward, rifles at the ready. No sound came from them, no hesitating; but a silent, slow, forward motion showed their plan. In a huge circle, they surrounded the village of sleeping, unsuspecting Indians. They slipped over the moss and ferns, Jonathan leading the way. Inch by inch they advanced. The slow movement was tedious, difficult and painful. They rustled no leaf, snapped no twig, shook no brush, but moved slowly forward, like the approach of death. The seconds passed as minutes; minutes as hours; an entire hour was spent in advancing twenty feet!

A dog yapped once and was silenced by a swift and silent knife. Then at last, as the faint rays of the eastern sun cut the still darkness with the gray of approaching dawn, Jonathan rose to his feet. The men around him stood, and holding their rifles at the ready, they pushed forward to the edge of the village. Not a person stirred in the quiet lodges, not a sound of warning alerted the villagers to their impending doom. Finally, as the sun edged over the horizon, Jonathan raised his rifle in the long-awaited signal. The men rushed forward into the village, each leader followed by two or three others who burst in on the sleeping natives with rifle and tomahawk in hand. The attack was swift and brutal. Shots and screams filled the air, accompanied by the horrific sound of hatchets striking through bone and sinew.

Crowning it all was the bloodthirsty yell of Jonathan Hershberger—a scream filled with hatred and malice that chilled the blood of those who heard it. Within a few moments, it was all over. Not one of the residents of the village survived.

After the massacre, the militiamen gathered in the center of the village. They looked for their leader, but Jonathan was not to be seen. One of the grizzled bordermen shook his head and spit a chaw of tobacco on the ground. "He's always this way after a fight. Once the bloody work is done, he goes off in the forest to fight his demons. He'll be back soon, and then he'll be ready to kill more of these varmints."

A young man who was new to the troop looked around him at the carnage. His face was pale. "But that awful scream; he sounded insane."

The old veteran nodded. "Well, yung'un, when the blood lust gets on him, he is insane. He came home to find his wife and son gone and his brother in jail. Now he just wants to kill Injuns and when he gets like that, I would advise staying out of the way of his knife and hatchet. He might mistake you for one of the reddys."

"But why?"

Another man spoke up. "The Injuns killed his ma and sisters right in front of him, and he swore eternal vengeance on the whole red race."

The young man pointed to the bodies of a woman and her child that lay where they had been cut down while fleeing the wrath of the militia. "Even on them?"

"This is war, boy, and the reddys have sided with the British. This is our land and them and us can't both live here."

"But they were here first. My father says the Delaware and the Shawnee were peaceful people before the Penn family stole their land. I signed up to defend my home, not to murder innocent women and children. Besides, isn't Jonathan married to an Indian woman?"

"When the captain returned from Niagara, his wife and child had left the fort. No one knows where they went. After that, Jonathan gave himself completely up to his war on the Indians and, truthfully, it's probably better his wife ain't around. She's

Wingenund's daughter and he's the most deadly of our enemies. She probably went back to her people, and she best stay there." The veteran turned the dead Indian boy over with his foot. "See that face? Remember it as long as you live. If we don't kill him today, he's burning your house down around your head a year from now. I know it ain't pretty, but it's the way it is. Whites and Injuns are gonna fight until one of us is gone from Ohio, and if I got anything to say, it ain't gonna be whites. Get that through your head, and you'll live to a ripe old age."

Just then the bushes parted and Jonathan strode into the circle of men. "All dead?"

The veteran shook his head. "Ever' one of 'um, Captain."

"Good! Burn the village to the ground. I don't want anyone to ever live here again."

The young man pointed to the bodies. "Ain't you gonna bury 'em?"

Jonathan shook his head. "Leave them where they lie. The coyotes will take care of them. We got more important business to attend to. Get going."

The men hastily made torches and began to walk among the lodges, setting fire to every dwelling and storehouse. The young man watched the captain as he directed the men. On Jonathan's belt were several new scalps, still red with the blood of his victims. The young man shook his head and then set about to do his duty.

Chapter Twenty-Seven

Separation

In December of 1779, Joshua Hershberger sat in the small cell at Fort Hanna's Town that had been his home for almost a year. The rigors of prison life had not been kind to him. He was pale from being locked up and his clothes hung loosely on his once stalwart frame. The cold winter wind pierced like knives through the bars of his window, and some nights he had to pace the short length of his cell until daylight to keep from freezing.

There was a rattle of keys outside the door and he heard the gruff voice of the guard. "He's in there, though I don't know why anyone would want to visit this traitorous scum." The door opened to admit David Zeisberger.

"Not too long, preacher. We have our rules about visitation." The door slammed shut and the key ground in the lock.

Joshua rose and gripped the hand of his friend. "David, what are you doing here so far from your work?"

Zeisberger looked back at the door and then reached into his coat and pulled out a packet. "It's not much, Joshua, but it's fresh."

Joshua could smell the slight odor of bread through the paper and his mouth began to water. He quickly took the package and slipped it under his mattress. "Thank you, my dear brother. There is a sick man in the cell next to me that will be much strengthened by this provender."

Zeisberger smiled. "You will never change, Joshua. You always think of others first."

Joshua waved aside the compliment. "Now, tell me. Why are you here?"

Zeisberger lowered his voice. "I bring you word of Ruth and of your brother."

Joshua's heart leaped. "Ruth? Where is she? What has happened to her? They took me away before I could even arrange for her care."

Zeisberger laid his hand on Joshua's shoulder. "Do not worry, Joshua. Ruth and the boy are safe with me at Gnadenhutten. She is with her people and has found joy and comfort in the care of her Savior."

Joshua slumped down on his bed. "Bless you, my friend. This good news takes a heavy load from my heart. And what of Jonathan? I thought he was dead."

"Your brother miraculously escaped from Fort Niagara. When he returned he was made a captain and chief scout for the colonial militia. Since then, he has led a number of brutal raids against the Delaware and the Shawnee. His name has gone out across the border as the greatest killer of Indians, a rival only to Wetzel in his blood lust and hatred. Many a stalwart brave has gone to his ancestors with Jonathan's bullet in his heart."

"Does Jonathan know where White Deer...where Ruth is?"

Zeisberger shook his head. "No. I have told no one, not even Colonel Zane. Wingenund has returned Jonathan's depravations stroke for stroke and many settlers have been butchered at the hands of Ruth's father. I think it not wise to let anyone except you know where she is. I fear a great reprisal would come if the militia or Jonathan knew she was at the Village of Peace. Most people think she returned to her father's village."

"You are wise, David, for when the killing lust is on Jonathan, one does not know what he will do. And Matthew? Is he well?"

"The boy has thrived among the Christians. He has found acceptance and respect. Though he is only six years old, he has become a marksman with the rifle. One of our gunsmiths cut down a rifle for him, and his eye is true and his aim steady. He will be a hunter like his father, but not of human game, for he has your heart and is a kind and gentle lad, always helping the weaker boys and esteeming others before himself."

"You bless me more with every word, David. But this is not the only reason you have come."

Zeisberger lowered his head. "Always you see my heart before I speak. Yes, I do have more, and I am afraid it is not good. I have been negotiating with the colonial authorities for your release. I have asked that you would be placed under my supervision and the local magistrates have seemed amenable, but there is a problem. I will continue to work for your release, but you have made an enemy who stands against you."

"Ah, the warden."

"Yes, brother. Why does he hate you so?"

"He took a personal dislike to me after I confronted him about stealing the prisoner's food and selling it to the local inns. When he continued in his scurrilous behavior, I got word to the magistrate and he was severely reprimanded."

"They did not discharge him?"

"The warden is the magistrate's nephew. There is nepotism involved. So the man stays on and, smarting from his rebuke, takes every opportunity to humiliate or otherwise try to break me."

Zeisberger looked at Joshua's thin face. "To the point of starving you?"

Joshua smiled. "Yes, that too. But I do not mind for I reckon that the sufferings of this present time are not worthy to be compared with the glory which shall be revealed in us."

Zeisberger shook his head. "What a fine preacher you would have made in our order. Many more would know the truth of the word if you were among us. In fact, there are some with us that you did bring to Jesus—Glickhican, for one, and Scar, now Jeremiah."

Joshua's eyes opened wide in surprise. "Scar? The man who killed my family? But how…?"

Zeisberger nodded. "The same. Jonathan shot him and I found him dying in the woods. I nursed him back to health. He remembered the words of life that you spoke to Ruth and Glickhican when you were captive, and he saw the love of Jesus in me. His heart was won to the way of peace, and now he is one of our most stalwart Christians."

Joshua slipped from his bed to his knees, tears running down his face. "Great is the Lord, and greatly to be praised; and his greatness is unsearchable." Joshua smiled up at the missionary. "This is wonderful news, for now I see the hidden workings of the Lord in all that has happened since that day so long ago. Had my father allowed us to fire on the Indians, Scar would have died in his sins, never to know the joy of heaven. And when I was fleeing for my life when I escaped the Indians, the Lord showed me that he had a work for me. Back then I did not recognize what it was, but now I see."

Zeisberger stared at Joshua and shook his head in amazement. Then he, too, knelt and began to pray. "Our heavenly Father, we give You praise and glory for Your most marvelous works. For indeed, Your ways are not our ways, and Your thoughts are not our thoughts. You see beyond hatred and strife to the most desperate need of every man, woman and child on this sin-cursed world—the need for a Savior to rescue them and a Lord to lead them. I pray that You would give me the heart of my brother, Joshua—a heart that forgives the sins against him and glories in the revealed will of the father. For it is Your will, not that we hate one another, but that we love each other. For You would have all men to be saved and come to the knowledge of the truth."

As the two men knelt in silent adoration, the clouds outside the prison walls began to open up, and a bright ray of sunlight penetrated the darkness of the cell.

After Zeisberger left, Joshua sat in silence. David had promised that he would continue to do whatever he could to implement his release, but Joshua had little hope for that to happen, not as long as the current warden was in charge. The missionary's words had filled him with amazement. He sat in wonder at the workings of God. His thoughts took him through each of the years from the day he and Jonathan had gone on that fateful hunt—the hunt that changed their lives forever. Had they not had the fresh deer meat that his mother craved, she might have been more accommodating to the Indians. And they might have gone on their way without incident, and Joshua's life and all his family's lives would have been completely different. He and his father and brother would not have been captives. Jonathan would have remained in the church and the Indian, Scar, would never have heard the words of life. Joshua could only sit amazed. A scripture came to his mind.

> *"But without faith it is impossible to please him: for he that cometh to God must believe that he is, and that he is a rewarder of them that diligently seek him."*

Jonathan Hershberger wandered in the deep woods, a black mood upon him. When he escaped from Niagara, Joshua was in prison in New York, and no one knew where Jonathan's wife and child were. He had assumed that they had returned to her father's village and that fact put them out of his reach, for Wingenund's village was far to the west and heavily protected by the fiercest of Lenape warriors. His anger against White Deer grew as his raids against the Indians multiplied until he was filled with hatred for her and her Indian blood.

He came to a part of the forest that he knew well, a dark ravine that led up to a bench from which a lovely waterfall poured down, but Jonathan did not revel in the beauty of the place. He followed the narrow foot trail, which gradually wound toward the top of the ravine. Jonathan's path emerged presently above the falls on the brink of a cliff. The trail ran along the edge of the ravine and then took a course back into densely wooded thickets. Just before stepping out on the open cliff, Jonathan paused. There was no living thing to be seen; the silence was the deep, unbroken calm of the wilderness.

Jonathan stepped to the edge and looked over. The stony wall opposite was only thirty feet away, and somewhat lower. It appeared as if Jonathan would leap the chasm but that was not his intent. Instead, he leaned over and spied a narrow ledge about eight feet below. Jonathan swung himself down to the ledge. At one end of this lower ledge grew a hardy shrub. He grasped a strong root and cautiously slid over the side.

At full length he swung into an opening, a hidden cave that none but he had ever discovered. Here he had lain up many times while pursuing Indians searched in vain in the forest above or stood marveling at the edge of the cliff, thinking Jonathan had leapt across the nearly impassible chasm. Jonathan had outfitted the cave with many necessities and now he set about to build a small fire against one wall. A narrow cleft in the back led out of the main chamber. Jonathan had explored it and found a hidden exit from his lair, far back in the woods at the end. The passage also served to carry away any errant smoke that might arise from his small fire. Once some coals were ready, he laid some strips of dried deer meat on them and waited until they sizzled. Then he stretched out on the bed of spruce boughs and ate silently. His thoughts turned to his family and his mother. At one point, as the dark hatred came over him, he looked up and spoke aloud. "God, I know you exist, but I hate you. I hate you for what you did to my family, and I will always hate you."

The words echoed back to him from the dim recesses of the cave. He thought of his brother, his wife and his son, but the hate was too strong, and so he dismissed them as irrelevant to the great mission of his life—to kill every Indian he could find.

Ruth sat musing before the fire in her small cottage. Zeisberger had brought word to her of both Jonathan and Joshua, and now her heart was conflicted once more. Jonathan was alive, but though she was married to him and committed to her marriage because of what the Word told her, she did not love him as once she had. Instead, her heart turned always to Joshua. Only Miriam and Joshua knew her secret. Zeisberger had warned her about trying to contact Jonathan. "It is best you remain hidden here until the hostilities are over, Ruth, for Jonathan's hatred of all Indians has grown until it is like a sickness that consumes him. You would not be safe in his presence."

And so Ruth sat before the fire. She remembered that Joshua had once called her the Amish Princess, and she smiled to herself. White Deer, the Lenape maiden, had come a long way from her carefree days as the apple of her father's eye. Yet in her heart, she knew that her heavenly Father watched over her and guided her steps and so she was content. She got up and knelt beside her bed to pray. "Heavenly Father, I thank You for all the blessings You have bestowed upon me. I thank You for my son and his heart for You. Tonight I pray for Jonathan and Joshua. You have given me love for both of these men, though the passion for my husband has been replaced by a true love for his brother. I ask that You would speak to Jonathan's heart, take away the blindness of his hatred and bring him back to You. I pray for Joshua, that You would be with him while he is in bondage and walk with him in the cold cell of his prison. Bring him out and bring him back to me. I do not know the end of days, but I know that all things work together for good to them that love God, to them who are the called according to his purpose."

She wept as she thought of the two men whose lives were so deeply entwined with hers.

I give them both to you, my God, and into Your hands I commend my spirit."

Then she rose and, turning down the lamp, went alone to her bed of tears.

Part Six

The Trail of Sorrow

During the Revolution, White Deer's tribe became a divided people. Many Lenape attempted to remain neutral in the conflict, especially those who had adopted Christianity and lived in the Moravian Church missions at Schoenbrunn and Gnadenhutten in what is now eastern Ohio. Wingenund and his tribe supported the British because of the Proclamation of 1763, which prohibited colonists from settling any further west than the Appalachian Mountains. They participated in bloody reprisals, hoping to drive the settlers out of Ohio. They feared that if the Americans were victorious, the Delaware would be driven from their land forever. These reprisals incited the settlers, especially Jonathan Hershberger's militia, to untold acts of savagery against the Indians, culminating in the expedition against the neutral tribes that resulted in one of the bloodiest massacres in American history. Out of this terrible event came the dividing of the Hershberger family, a division that would not be restored until I married my own Jonathan Hershberger almost two hundred years later.

The Trail of Sorrow
From The Journals of Jenny Hershberger

Chapter Twenty-Eight

Captive Town

Wingenund sat alone in his lodge. Summer was slipping away into the slow death of autumn and he had a buffalo robe wrapped around his shoulders, for the days often seemed cold. A great joy had passed from him when Black Eagle had taken his daughter and grandson away. Then Spring of Water had died of white man's fever not long after their daughter left. No more did his beloved wife fill his home with her beauty and gentle ways. He shook his head sadly, for his hope had always been to grow old with his daughter's children gathered about him, but the laughter of little ones did not bless his days and his people suffered at the hands of the settlers. He carried the great burden of protecting his people, but these days the load did not rest as easy on his shoulders as it once had.

He lit his pipe with a small ember from the cheerless fire and slowly drew on it. The smoke drifted like fingers up and away, and the light in the lodge became diffused as he meditated over his pipe. Wingenund closed his eyes and his thoughts drifted far away to the day he sat in the lodge of Owechela, the sachem, and listened to the old man speak about days that were far in the future. He could almost feel the old man's hands on his head and hear the soft voice speak.

"I see the path that lies ahead for this one. He shall be a defender of his people and a force for life and hope. Blood and death shall rage about him, but he shall not be harmed. Strange ones shall come to him. He shall have a child that he will love as his own life, but the child will seem to turn away from the path of the Lenape. But the Great Spirit is guiding all and one shall come to the 'willing one' who shall make all the stories and all the legends of the Lenape become clear at last. The child whom he loves will lead him to the greatest truth, and though all seems dark around him, a great light will shine in his heart. The arrow and bow shall fall from his hand, and his voice shall be the voice of peace, for he shall speak the words of the greatest one who shines through all the darkness. And then this one shall use the truth as a hunter uses the sight on his gun. He shall aim his life by the truth. But before he knows the truth, he will know great pain, sorrow and loss. For he is the 'willing one', and in time, he will learn to be willing to bear the burden of his people with a true heart."

Wingenund sighed. The days had come upon him; the days that were prophesied so long ago. White Deer had forsaken the way of the Lenape and gone after the white man's God. But she had not led him to any truth except the knowledge that Wingenund hated the white man who had stolen his daughter's heart. He longed to see her, but he had disowned her and his word must stand.

And the bow and arrow had not fallen from his hand. Indeed, he was the terror of the settlements from Kentucky to Canada. Many a white man had felt the blow of his tomahawk or the agony of his bullet. The white men were treacherous snakes and liars. They had promised the great chief, White Eyes, a sovereign Lenape Nation when they signed the treaty of Fort Pitt in 1778. Their promises had never been fulfilled and then the American, Daniel Brodhead, had led his troops against the neutral village at Coshocton and massacred the peaceful Turtle Clan. No, Wingenund would never lay down the bow against the white man. He had not seen the great truth prophesied by Owechela, and he would never see White Deer again, so the sachem had been wrong.

Wingenund jumped to his feet, scattering his pipe and blanket as he raised his fist to the sky and shouted into the darkness. "You were wrong, old man, you were wrong. I shall never walk the way of peace with these whites, never! They shall fear me, even after I am dead, for my spirit will haunt their villages until every one is driven from our land!"

It was early morning in the Village of Peace. Fingers of sunlight inserted themselves through the intertwined branches of the stately oaks that ringed the fields around the compound and touched the ground in a dazzling spectacle of diamond facets. In the distance, a dog barked, once, twice, and then stillness settled once more upon the forest. A golden haze filled the meadow where Ruth was walking and praying. Her prayers were for her husband. It had been almost two years since last she saw him. In her heart she knew that he had given himself over to his dark hatred of all Indians, and she expected never to see him again.

And as for the other brother, the gentle Joshua, she only knew that he was still in prison. Brother Zeisberger had visited Joshua once or twice a year since his imprisonment, but there had been no word about a pardon for him, and so he languished. The warden refused to let Joshua send letters, so she only knew what David could tell her.

Ruth had done her best to keep the words of the Bible, but in a secret place in her heart, she knew that if she was ever forced to choose, it would be Joshua that she would follow, and that troubled her deeply. She was caught in a great dilemma, and her future seemed troubled and hopeless. So as she walked, she spoke to her God, for He was her only source of peace. Her prayers sought heaven but there was only silence.

She heard a quiet step on the path behind her. She turned to find Jeremiah coming towards her. She smiled. "Good morning, my brother. And how is it with you?"

The troubled look on his face surprised her. "What is it?"

"The news is not good, Princess. Word has come from some of my friends in the Wyandot village that we are to be taken away. The British believe that Brother David is a spy for the Colonials."

"When will they take us?"

"They are coming today or tomorrow. Brother David and Heckewelder will be arrested and taken to Detroit. We will go to a new village in British territory."

The two walked on together, pondering this news. Finally, Jeremiah spoke. "The trails of our lives are determined by the Great God and most of our days are hidden in a mist. Once I was Scar, a great warrior, killer of white men, and a murderer of women and children, for I did not want the scourge of the settlers to spread to every corner of our land. I saw death for our people and a great hate was in my heart."

"You did not know the truth, Jeremiah, that all men are brothers in the eyes of God."

"No, Princess, I did not, but still I regret those days. My heart is sad for the evil that I did. I murdered the family of Black Eagle and his brother, though they did nothing to harm me, and that day often comes into the eyes of my heart and brings great sorrow with it. Black Eagle's father was a true man of peace. He did not raise his hand against us when we came to destroy him and all he had. He was a servant of the Most High God, and he listened when Jesus told him to love his brother. He offered us that love and we killed his family." Jeremiah shook his head sadly.

Ruth laid her hand on the older man's arm. "But, Jeremiah, if you did not bring Jonathan and Joshua to our village, you and I would not know Jesus, and I would not have my son. For, as the Bible says, all things do work together for good for those who are called to God's purpose, though we may not see it at the time."

Jeremiah was silent for a long while as they walked. Ruth knew he was pondering her words. Finally, he spoke. "I will meditate upon your words, Princess, for they are wise. And what of you? You are a princess of our people, and you have been given great understanding. It was foretold that you would lead the Lenape in the way of peace. Yet you are here, exiled from your people and your father. Your husband and his brother are far away. Does it not trouble you?"

Ruth stopped and looked toward the east. The day rested in quiet splendor upon the meadow in which they walked. Birds sang in the thickets and the bright, luminous haze divided the sunlight into prisms of color. In that moment great peace came into Ruth's heart. She knew that her life belonged to the Lord. She smiled up at her friend. "Since I came here, you have been like a father to me. You have showed me how Jesus can change the most broken hearts and lives and bring His peace. I must trust that He can also change the heart of my father and my husband, though I do not know how that may be. My times are in His hands and I will follow where He leads."

Jonathan Hershberger sat in the tavern at Fort Henry. In the spring he had been a scout for Brodhead in the campaign against the Delaware town of Coshocton. The attack had been a complete surprise, and Jonathan had led the troops in the massacre of the Lenape in the village, men, women, and children. Since then, he had endured a period of forced idleness that galled him. He longed to be out, pursuing the Indians that were the focus of his hatred. He especially longed to find his great enemy, Wingenund, White Deer's father, and face him in battle. Jonathan knew that Wingenund hated him for taking White Deer from his people, and he knew that if they ever met, they would fight to the death.

Jeff Lynn, another scout, came into the room. The dingy place reeked with tobacco smoke, and the smell of rum filled the air. It was crowded with men. This was a place that truly offended Colonel Zane and the other stalwarts of the fort, for liquor ruled the frontiersmen who frequented the foul place. Fights were frequent and many men had been carried out the back door, dead or wounded, and still the black-bearded proprietor dealt out the rum. Jonathan smiled to himself at what his father might have said had he known his oldest son frequented such a place. Lynn slid into the seat beside him at the bar. Jonathan stared moodily into his cup, for he realized that the memory of his father had brought a twinge of guilt with it.

Lynn ordered a drink and then turned to Jonathan. "So have ye heard of the whereabouts of yer reddy wife?"

"Don't speak to me of her, Lynn, for she has deserted me and gone back to her father with my son."

"Well, if you believe that, you would probably pay for my drink to find out what I know different."

"What do you mean, Lynn?"

"I mean she ain't gone back to her father."

Jonathan turned and took Lynn by the front of his buckskin shirt. "Tell me what you know, or you'll have my fist in your face instead of that rum."

"All right, take yer fist away. I'll tell. I was only joshin' you, Jonathan."

"News about my wife and son are not a joking matter. What do you know?"

"That Moravian missionary spirited her out of the settlement after Joshua went to jail. You were still in Fort Niagara, so you couldn't have known."

"Go on."

Lynn took a drink. "She's at the Moravian Mission at Gnadenhutten, the one the Christian Indians call the Village of Peace. She's been there for two years."

Jonathan took Lynn by the shoulder. "How do you know this, man?"

"Abner Johnson took some supplies to the village a few weeks ago. While he was there, he heard the villagers talking about the Amish Princess. Well, when he saw her, he knew right away that it was White Deer, only now she goes by Ruth. He saw Matthew with her."

Jonathan slammed his drink down and rose from his seat.

"Where you headed, hoss? You ain't aimin' to bring her back here? Many's the settler that's felt Wingenund's wrath, and she would not find this a hospitable place."

"She can go to blazes, but I want my son, and I'll have him with me." Jonathan picked up his rifle and walked out.

Two days later, Jonathan stood in the midst of the deserted village. The inhabitants were gone and the place was silent. He heard a rustling in the cornfield and turned. He saw the face of a woman peeking out from between rows. He pointed his rifle at her. "Come out, if you don't want to meet your maker."

The woman crept slowly from the corn. "Do not shoot. I am alone."

"Woman, what has happened here? Where is White Deer?"

The woman looked about her. "Two days ago Captain Pipe, a chief of the Lenape, came with the Wyandots and took all the people away to the north. They took Brother David and Brother John to the British to be tried as spies. They are all gone. I was afraid Captain Pipe would kill us, so I hid in the corn."

Jonathan motioned her away. "Go, if you want to keep your scalp." Jonathan felt frustration rise in him. He knew the area of which the woman spoke. If they were going north to try the missionaries, they would go to Detroit. It was in the heart of British territory, defended by British regulars and the most hostile of the tribes. Ruth and Matthew were as unreachable as if they were in heaven.

Chapter Twenty-Nine

Return to Paradise

Outside, the bitter cold of early February was slowly giving way to the first touch of spring. Through the window Ruth could see a few winter aconites poking through the melting snow and their bright yellow blooms were a welcome relief against the stark dead landscape of Captive Town. She sat in her chair before the small fire, wrapped against the cold of the hut. She was sewing some of Matthew's clothes, old before their time because of the perpetual motion of her young son.

"Mama, I want to go out. I've been inside for a week. I want to go out and hunt some more game. I'm tired of corn meal."

Ruth smiled at her impatient child. He was very much like his father, impetuous, strong-willed and already an excellent hunter. But there was also some of his Uncle Joshua—compassionate and caring, quick to right a wrong, defender of the smaller children. He was a good son, and Ruth delighted in him. "All right, Matthew, you may go. I, too, long for some rabbit stew. Dress warmly and wear your boots."

"But, Mama, I go much more softly in my moccasins. The animals can't hear me coming."

Ruth looked at her boy. He was almost nine years old and growing tall and strong. He had his father's face and his mother's coloring. But amongst the Christians, his heritage had never been a problem for Matthew. She nodded. Matthew slipped on his moccasins, grabbed his bow and flung open the door of the hut to leave. There was someone standing on the step. Ruth looked up in surprise. "Brother David! You have returned." She motioned the missionary in and closed the door.

Zeisberger sat on a stool that stood by the corner of the hearth and warmed his hands at the small fire. "Are you well, Ruth?"

"It has been a hard winter, Brother David. It is much colder here in the north, and the British gave us very little food. Matthew hunts game for us and that helps. But how are you here? The British arrested you."

"Yes, they took us to Detroit. Our main accuser was the Delaware, Captain Pipe. It was he who was authorized by the British to take us from the Village of Peace. Pipe knew that after he went on the warpath, Heckewelder had been sending reports of their movements to Brodhead at Fort Pitt. Pipe was no fool. He knew the information sent to Brodhead was causing the death of his warriors, even though John was only trying to prevent more bloodshed. Pipe and the British wanted us out of the way. That is why they took us."

Ruth was puzzled. "But why, then, did they release you?"

Zeisberger smiled. "After we were there a few days, the British Commandant summoned us to be examined before the tribunal. But in the days before our trial, Captain Pipe had been observing the demeanor of you and the rest of the Indian Christians, and I think he knew in his heart that our influence had been good for you. I believe he remembered the dying words of his own chief, Netawatwees, when he implored Pipe to follow the teachings of the Moravians. When the British Commandant called on Captain Pipe to present his charges against us, the chief declined to make any. 'These are good men,' he said. 'I would be sorry to see them ill-treated.' The major, accordingly, dropped the case and set us free—with a gentle admonition henceforth to leave war matters alone. So now we have come to be with our flock."

"The Lord works in wonderful ways, David. Your story gives me hope, for if Jesus can change the heart of one such as Captain Pipe, he can change the hearts of my husband and my father."

"Yes, Ruth, he can. And now, what of you and the rest of the villagers?"

Ruth took a cast iron pot from a hook over the fire. "There has been much hunger and disease among us. The winter was long, and once we were here, the British and the Lenape put us in these old cabins and left us to our own ends. They give us cornmeal and some meat from time to time. Many have been sick and all are suffering from lack of food."

"I have good news, then, Sister Ruth. The British have given us permission to return to the Village of Peace and collect the supplies and the stored food we were forced to leave behind. You may leave tomorrow."

"Will you and Brother John go with us?"

"If there are many sick, as you say, then John and I will stay and tend them. Isaac Glickhican and Jeremiah will lead you back."

Ruth went to the fire, spooned some mush into a bowl and placed it in front of Zeisberger. "Since we are able to return to our village, let us rid ourselves of the last of this terrible cornmeal mush."

The two laughed together. As they did, the sun finally pierced the grey clouds and streamed in through the window. Ruth looked up.

It is a sign from heaven. All will be well.

Wingenund lay on the ground, his warriors gathered around him. The chief's face was pale and blood streamed from a terrible wound high on his chest. Militiamen had ambushed the war party, and during the ensuing battle, a musket ball had found the seemingly invincible warrior. His warriors had carried him away into the deep forest and now they were deciding what to do with their fallen chief. Wingenund could hear his warriors speaking in low voices.

"It did not pierce his lung, for there is no blood on his lips, but he has lost much blood. We cannot carry him all the way back to the village. He will die before we get there."

Another voice was heard. "The Village of Peace is nearby. Our scouts have reported that some have returned from Captive Town and are in the village. We can take him there. They will help him."

Wingenund tried to lift his hand to dismiss the warrior, for he did not trust the Christians, but a wave of darkness swept over him and he could not move. As the light faded, he heard his men agreeing. Then he was lifted up and borne away.

◇◇◇

In the early hours of the morning, a light knock on her door awakened Ruth. She rose and threw on her robe. She went to the door. "Who is there?"

"It is Jeremiah, Princess. You must come quickly. Your father is here."

Ruth's heart leaped. "My father?"

"Yes. He is badly hurt and is calling for you."

"Give me a moment and I will come. Where is he?"

"In the chapel, Princess."

Ruth heard Jeremiah's steps fading away. She began to dress. In the corner, Matthew stirred. "What is it, Mama?"

"It is your grandfather. He has been hurt and I must go to him."

"My grandfather, Wingenund?"

"Yes, Matthew."

"Can I see him, too?"

Ruth leaned down and kissed her boy. "Not now, Matthew, but when he is better. Now go back to sleep." Ruth pulled the blankets up around Matthew and then ran out the door.

Wingenund lay on a table in the chapel, a blood stained sheet beneath him. His shoulder was bandaged skillfully, but Ruth could see that blood had already seeped through. Many of the Indians were gathered around him. She rushed to his side. "Father, I am here."

Wingenund's eyes opened. His face was very pale and his voice was weak. "Opahtuhwe, my daughter…"

Ruth looked at Isaac Glickhican. "How is he?"

The old man shook his head. "He has lost much blood. The wound itself is clean, and the ball did not hit his lung, but I fear for infection. We have done what we can. Now we should move him to a bed where he can sleep."

Ruth nodded. "Take him to my cabin and put him in my bed. I will care for him."

Isaac Glickhican motioned to the other men. Jeremiah and several others took the edges of the sheet and lifted Wingenund. Ruth led the way to her cabin and pulled back the blankets on her bed. The men laid her father down. Ruth pulled the blankets around him.

Matthew slipped out of his bed and stood behind the men, looking at his grandfather. "Will he live, Mama?"

"I do not know, Matthew. He is badly hurt. But we will care for him and pray for him. He is in God's hands now."

Throughout the night, Ruth sat by her father's bed. He moaned occasionally, but for the most part he was silent. Ruth bathed his face with damp cloths and prayed. "Oh, Lord Jesus, You have brought my father here. It is Your work and I do not think You brought him here to die, but to show him Your face. Heal him, Lord, and bring him to Your side."

Wingenund moaned again and then cried out. "Opahtuhwe, Opahtuhwe!"

"I am here, Father, I am here."

Wingenund was unconscious for two days. During that time, infection set in and the Christians prayed fervently. On the morning of the third day, the fever broke. The sun was shining brightly through the window when he opened his eyes. The first thing he saw was a young boy kneeling at his bedside. The boy's head was bowed, and he was talking to someone. "Please let my grandfather live, Lord. Do not let him die before we get to know each other."

Wingenund reached out with his good hand and touched the boy. The boy looked up. "Grandfather, you are awake."

"Who were you speaking to, boy?"

The boy swallowed hard but he was not afraid of the great warrior. "I was asking Jesus to heal you. I have always wanted to speak with you, and I did not want you to die before I could."

"Who are you, boy?"

"I am Matthew."

Wingenund was silent. Then he motioned to the boy. "Stand up then, and let me see you better."

Matthew stood and came close to the bed. Wingenund looked upon his grandson for the first time in many years. The boy was tall for his age and already looked strong. He was the son of Black Eagle, for that was written on his face, but Wingenund could also see the softness of White Deer in his features.

"Why do you want to talk to me? Am I not the enemy of all Christians?"

The boy did not hesitate. "You are my grandfather. My mother has told me of you all my life. I am not afraid of you."

Wingenund smiled. "No. I can see in your eyes that you are not afraid."

Just then the door opened and Ruth came in. "Father, you are awake. I thank God for it. Matthew, are you bothering your grandfather?"

Wingenund looked at his daughter. She was radiant and lovely. The settler's dress she wore did not hide her Lenape heritage. "He is not troubling me, daughter. I would learn more of him. Have him sit beside me. I am hungry and he can feed me." He motioned to a stool beside the bed. "Sit there...grandson."

Ruth went to the stove where a pot was simmering. "There is broth made from venison. Matthew can help you." She filled a wooden bowl and brought it to Matthew. Then she started to leave.

"Do not go, Opahtuhwe. I would have you both here with me. I would learn of you, for I never thought to see either of you again."

And so Wingenund ate broth at the hand of his grandson, while his daughter and grandson chattered about their life in the Village of Peace. The sound of their voices was like the sweet rushing of a mountain stream on a soft spring morning to the ears of the chief.

Many days later, Wingenund stood with his daughter and grandson at the edge of the forest. "My heart is full and I do not go in sorrow. You have found the way of peace. The people of this village have shown me kindness and mercy and it is good you are here. I will think long on what I have seen and heard. The words of the past come back to me and I hear wisdom in them. May our trails cross again." He turned to Matthew and laid his hand on the boy's shoulder. "Grow in strength and wisdom. Learn the way of peace, but do not forget the way of your people. When we are not at war, there is much wisdom in the path of the Lenape."

Mathew smiled. "I will not forget, Grandfather."

Wingenund turned to go.

"Father!"

The chief looked back. Ruth ran to him. He took her in his arms. They were silent for a long time. Finally, Ruth let her father go. Wingenund stepped into the forest and then, like a cool breeze, he was gone.

Chapter Thirty

Lament – March 1782

It was a bright, sunny day at Gnadenhutten. The hearts of the people of the village were glad. They had returned from Captive Town to find their corn still standing and eagerly set about the work of bringing in the harvest. Isaac Glickhican was directing the villagers, and Ruth worked side by side with Jeremiah. The ugly scar on his face reminded her of the days when he had been known as *Ehèntawisèk*, the Scarred One, a fierce and violent warrior. Now he was like a father to her, and the gentlest of men. She stopped to rest and spoke to Jeremiah. "Do you remember, my friend, the day that you brought Jonathan and Joshua to our village?"

The older man frowned. "Yes, Princess. It was a day I boasted in, but now I have only sorrow for the ways of my youth."

Ruth laid her hand on Jeremiah's shoulder. "No, Jeremiah, do not sorrow. Each of our paths is laid before us from our mother's womb. We have all done evil in our lives, but now we are free."

Jeremiah looked up toward heaven. "Yes, and we praise Him who gives us life."

At that moment they became aware of a commotion on the far side of the village. As they watched, a group of armed men began marching into the village. They looked like settlers, dressed in the buckskins and linsey-woolsey of the backwoodsman. Ruth's heart beat faster as she realized that the men had surrounded the village and were coming in from every side. The people of the village huddled together as a tall man stepped out from among the armed group and spoke.

"We are the American militia. We come in peace and friendship to help you. Your village is in a dangerous place. You are between the armies of the British and the Americans. We have come to take you to Fort Pitt for your own safety. Bring your arms and stack them here for you will not need them."

Ruth heard her friend, Miriam, heave a sigh of relief. Glickhican stepped forward. "We are glad for your offer of protection. There is another of our villages at Salem. Will you not break bread with us, while we send for the people at Salem to join us?"

The tall man nodded. Glickhican turned to one of the young men. "Go to Salem and give the good news. Bring the people back. Tell them to bring only what they need for personal comfort while we are away."

The lad raced off down the trail toward Salem, while Glickhican instructed the men to bring the few arms they possessed. He turned to the tall man. "We only use these arms for hunting. You have no need to fear us for we will harm no man. We are the people of the Village of Peace."

The tall man ordered his men to stack the rifles. Then they waited while the villagers prepared a simple meal of corn mush, fresh-baked bread, and dried venison. After they ate, the group walked together toward the village. Suddenly, the tall man gave an order and the armed men gathered around the villagers with their guns leveled. The tall man called out several soldiers who proceeded to bind the hands of the villagers. Then they were pushed at rifle point into the two largest buildings in the village: the men in the dining hall, the women and children in the chapel. Ruth heard Isaac Glickhican questioning the tall man and assuring him that his people posed no danger, but the man said nothing. He pointed to the building where the men were being imprisoned and his men led Glickhican away.

Ruth sat with her hands on Matthew's head, brushing his hair softly. Her wrists were bound, so her motions were clumsy, but she needed to comfort him. She tried to still the beating of her heart, but she could not dispel the fear that gripped her.

The boy looked up at his mother. His face darkened as he moved closer. "I won't let the bad men hurt you, Mother."

Ruth smiled at her son, even as her courage failed.

He is so much like his father.

Miriam began to weep. Ruth stirred and spoke to her. "Miriam, you must not weep. You will frighten the children. Remember what the word of truth says: 'Thou wilt keep him in perfect peace, whose mind is stayed on thee: because he trusteth in thee.' Do not fear, Miriam, for our God is with us."

Just then a door opened and one of the soldiers came in. "Which one of you is the one they call the Amish Princess, Wingenund's daughter?"

The others looked at Ruth and she stood up. "I am Wingenund's daughter."

The soldier nodded. "Come with me."

Ruth pulled Matthew up. "May I bring my son? He might be frightened without me."

Matthew stood up and pushed between his mother and the soldier. "I'm not afraid, Mother."

The soldier smiled. "Bring your son. He's a bold one."

As they walked together, the soldier looked Matthew over. "Say, he doesn't look like a reddy."

Ruth gazed at her son.

No, he looks like his father.

"His father is white. His name is Jonathan Hershberger."

The soldier stared at Ruth. "You must be lying, lady. Jonathan Hershberger hates all Indians."

A sharp pain shot through Ruth's heart. "Yes, I know, but I am his wife, and this is his son."

The soldier said nothing but brought Ruth to a group of armed men standing under a tree. The tall man was speaking to Glickhican. "I am David Williamson, the commander of this militia. We are here because we know that you have been harboring the Delaware warriors who fight for the British. They have perpetrated bloody massacres on our settlements, and we have come to destroy this village."

Glickhican nodded. "I am Isaac, once known to you as Glickhican. I was a great war chief of the Lenape, but when I met Zeisberger and he told me the way of peace, I believed. I have been a friend to all people since then. We give food and shelter to all who come here, for we do not fight on the side of any army."

Williamson pointed to Ruth. "It is said that recently you gave help and comfort to Wingenund, our greatest enemy, and that this woman, who is his daughter, lives among you. Is this true?"

Glickhican nodded. "We turn none away who need help. His daughter lives with us because she has renounced the ways of war and is a Christian, as are you, Colonel."

The men around Williamson stared at Glickhican with dark looks. One of them stepped in front of the old man and waved a bloodstained rag in Glickhican's face. "You see this! This is all that's left of my wife!" The man turned to Williamson. "The dirty redskin confesses with his own mouth that they have given aid to the murderer that slaughtered Constance and my children. I say kill them all."

A chorus of angry voices rose, demanding death. Ruth felt a chill of fear sweep over her. She knelt before the colonel. "Please, sir. Do not harm us but give us protection. We are peaceful Christians. We are non-violent. We harm no one and fight on neither side. We follow the gentle Savior who is your God also. Show mercy, sir. And if you cannot, do not hurt the children. They are innocent. My father may be your enemy, but I am not."

Williamson pulled Ruth roughly to her feet. "It is not for me to decide. I will put the matter to a vote. If my men decide for mercy, then we will grant it. If they do not, then you will all die." He turned to his men. "Men, I put the question to you. Should these Moravian Indians be taken prisoners to Fort Pitt or put to death? Whoever is for mercy, step to that side and form a second rank."

Ruth watched in horror as only a few men stepped out. The colonel waited for a few minutes until the men had gathered. "Is that all? I count eighteen men and we are almost two hundred." He turned back to Glickhican. "The vote has been taken. You see the count. Now accept your fate."

Glickhican's face was impassive. "If it is the will of our God, we accept it. I only ask that you allow us to prepare our hearts to meet our Creator."

Williamson looked at his men who nodded in agreement. "You have until the morning. Take them back and when the Indians from Salem arrive, put them in with the prisoners."

Some of the men who had stood for mercy confronted the colonel. One man spoke angrily to Williamson. "You call yourself a Christian and yet you would massacre these innocents? Where is your soul, man? You may have the support of these others now, but at the end of your life, you will look back on this day and beg God to forgive you. I cannot be part of this. I am going back to the settlement."

The man put his rifle on his shoulder and walked away. Those who had voted for mercy followed. Williamson shouted after them. "Go then, cowards! The blood of our dead cries out from the ground. And no one will listen to you in the settlements, for they all have lost loved ones to these butchers." He turned to his aide. "Take these redskins back and put them in with the others. In the morning we will deal with them."

Rough hands pushed Ruth and Matthew back to their prison. When they stepped inside, the women and children were gathered together, praying. They had heard the words of Williamson and fear was on all their faces. Then, from the other building where the men were being held, they heard a strange sound. It began quietly and then as voice after voice joined in, the old Moravian hymn lifted up and began to echo from the woods and hills around the village.

*Morning Star, O cheering sight! Ere thou cam'st, how dark
   earth's night!*
*Morning Star, O cheering sight! Ere thou cam'st, how dark
   earth's night!*
Jesus mine, in me shine; in me shine, Jesus mine;
Fill my heart with light divine.

Morning Star, thy glory bright far excels the sun's clear light.
Morning Star, thy glory bright far excels the sun's clear light.
Jesus be, constantly; constantly, Jesus be
More than thousand suns to me.

The men were singing! Ruth looked around. One by one, the women joined in. Peace flowed into the room and began to fill every heart.

It was the time of the darkness that reigns just before the dawn. Ruth sat on a bench in the chapel with Matthew and the rest of the women and children. Through the windows by the altar, Ruth could see just the faintest gray light through the trees to the east. She had been praying for hours, and Matthew had finally fallen asleep. The room was silent. She heard a soft noise and then the door slowly opened. It was the man who had taken her out to the council. He motioned for her to be silent as he slipped up to her and whispered. "I do not agree with the decision of the men. I know Jonathan, and if this is his son, I want to save him. Will you let me take him?"

Without a moment's hesitation, Ruth nodded. Then she thought of something. "Do you also know his brother, Joshua?"

The man nodded. "Yes, he's the one that's in prison because he won't fight."

"Yes, that is Joshua. Will you take a letter to him for me?"

The man shook his head. "I can't promise anything, but give me the letter, and I'll see what I can do."

"Can you untie me for a few minutes?"

"Yes, but hurry. I don't want the men to see me." The man untied her hands.

There was a small table with pen, ink and paper that Brother John used to write his sermons near Ruth. She sat at it and wrote quickly. When she was finished, she patted the ink dry, put the letter in an envelope, and addressed it to Joshua Hershberger. She handed it to the soldier who retied her hands. Then she leaned down and kissed Matthew. "Good bye, my son."

The man picked up the sleeping child. Matthew groaned in his sleep. "I will see that he gets to Jonathan." Then he slipped out as silently as he had come.

Morning came softly on the wings of angels. Ruth sat at an open window and looked out. Around her the women were praying or weeping softly. Ruth's heart was touched by the loveliness of the world outside. A warm breeze stirred and filled the room with a heavenly perfume. She could hear the birds singing in the trees. Her heart looked back over the trail of her life.

There was a sound and then the door opened. Somber men with hatchets and knifes entered the room slowly, silently. The women stood and faced their executioners. Ruth looked upon the face of death, but she was not afraid. She raised her eyes toward heaven. "Father, into thy hands we commend our spirits."

Someone screamed and the men ran toward them...

Chapter Thirty-One

Wind of Death

Jonathan Hershberger awoke from the ruins of a three-day drunken revel. His head ached and his mouth tasted like a parade of mules had marched through it. His buckskin shirt was dirty and stank of sweat and rum. He tried to lift himself from the bed but he could not. He tried again and finally got his body upright. He swung his feet over the side of the bed as a wave of nausea passed over him and he almost fell. He had to close his eyes for a minute and then slowly opened them against the dim light filtering into the cabin.

He lifted his head and looked around the cold room. There was nothing there that reminded him of the time he had shared this home with White Deer and Matthew. The curtains that used to freshen the window with a lovely white border now hung in tattered gray shreds.

Curse her for taking my son.

The once well-kept house was filled with trash, and empty rum bottles littered the floor. Jonathan groaned and felt under his pillow. The rum bottle that he had hidden from his drunken friends was still there. He pulled out the cork and took a long drink. The rum tasted horrible and burned all the way down, but in a minute the swirling in his head began to fade. He struggled to his feet and staggered to the pitcher and basin. There was no water left in it, so he stumbled outside to the rain barrel and plunged his face into it. The icy shock of the freezing water cleared his mind somewhat.

As he leaned over the barrel with the water dripping off his face, he smiled at his unkempt reflection in the slowly quieting water. His usually shaven face was covered with a three-day growth of beard and his hair hung down over his eyes. He spoke out loud. "Not looking so bright this morning, Jonathan lad. Looked upon red likker again? What would your papa say?"

He didn't like the answer that came into his mind, so he went back inside, picked up the bottle from the bed, and swigged down some more rum. The nagging thought that there was something he had to do kept pushing at his mind. He took another long drink and then he remembered.

Williamson and the militia—a raid against the Delaware tribe!

I am supposed to be with the men!

His rifle was leaning against the wall. He grabbed it up and looked around for his tomahawk and knife. They were both sticking in the wall where he and his drunken friends had thrown them during some sort of contest the night before. He pulled them down and stuck them into his belt. He glanced around once more, then went out the door and headed for the fort.

"Aye, Jonathan, they left yesterday morning." Metzger, the owner of the tavern, leaned on the bar and tried to wipe away a stain with a filthy rag. "Colonel Williamson was mad as a Carolina gator when you didn't show, but he didn't have time to go hunting for you, so off they went. Will you have a drink?"

Jonathan hesitated and then nodded. Metzger reached under the bar and found a bottle.

"The good bottle, Metzger."

Metzger smiled and changed bottles under the bar. Jonathan waited while Metzger poured a tall glass of rum and then took it down in one gulp.

"Clearing away the fog, eh, lad?"

"Which way did they go?"

"They are going after Wingenund. They heard that them Christian Indians at the Village of Peace took him in and nursed him back to health. A lot of the boys are pretty hot about that."

"The Village of Peace? But I thought the British cleaned them out."

"Aye, but some of 'em straggled back and t'was them as gave Wingenund shelter. Our boys are ready to burn the place down. Well, you best be off if you wants to catch 'em. Would ye like a bottle to warm your journey? I'll just add it to what you owe me."

Jonathan nodded and Metzger handed over a bottle. Jonathan stuck it in his pack and headed out the door.

Jonathan arrived at the village just before dawn. He found the militia gathered about several campfires in the center of the village. They were passing bottles from hand to hand. Jeff Lynn saw Jonathan and pulled him aside and handed him a bottle.

"Yer just in time, lad. The reddys have been singin' and prayin' in them buildings over there and the boys have been gettin' likker'd up to do the deed."

Jonathan took a long pull on the bottle. "What deed, Jeff?"

"Why, the boys voted to kill 'em all. They been helpin' the Delewares, and they even had old Wingenund here after some of the boys ambushed him a while back."

Jonathan took another pull. He could feel the rum building the fire that was already in his veins. "Well, if that's what we're about, let's get to it." Jonathan stood up on a stump. "You men, what are you waiting for?"

One of the men shouted back. "They said they wanted to pray and get ready to meet their maker." A chorus of guffaws and shouts followed the remark.

Jonathan lifted his hand and silence fell. "These Indians claim to be Christians. If they really are, then they are ready and they don't need to pray anymore. Let's get the job done."

Jonathan waved his hat and the men grabbed up their knives and hatchets. He turned to Lynn. "Where are they?"

Jeff pointed to two buildings set back from the campfires. "The men are in that one and the women over there."

"Come then, let's finish it." Jonathan led the way to the first building. The rum coursed through him and a red haze was before his eyes. He threw open the door. "Come out and meet your maker, you reddys."

The first man through the door was a tall warrior with an unmistakable scar on his face. Jonathan halted. "You!"

Jeremiah nodded. "So, Black Eagle, my son, the broken circle closes." The fires lit his face and cast a horrifying light on the militiamen gathered before him.

Jonathan reeled. A scene came back to him, from years before. The fire leaping from the roof of the burning cabin, the savages crowded around his family, brandishing their tomahawks and screaming for blood, the cries of his sisters as they were tormented in the woods, the fear in his mother's eyes before Scar killed her. Hate filled his heart. He lifted his tomahawk. "Now, Scar, at last I will have my revenge."

No fear showed in the old man's face. Scar bowed his head. Jonathan's hatchet flashed in the light and the tall Indian sank down without a sound. The men stared at Jonathan. A horrible, blood-curdling cry burst from his lips. The madness was upon him. "Kill them, kill them all!"

The men took up the chant and burst into the buildings. Jonathan could hear screaming from inside the women's building, but the fever was on him and he heeded it not. His knife and his hatchet swung and swung as the Indians fell before his awful wrath. Around him, the men joined in, their minds and hearts gripped in a frenzied blood lust.

In the midst of the carnage, he felt someone pulling on his arm. It was Jeff Lynn. "Jonathan, Jonathan!"

Jonathan's senses cleared for a moment. "What do ye want, Jeff?"

Jeff pointed at the women's building. "Yer wife, Jonathan. I was going to tell you, but you didn't give me time. She's in there. Yer boy was with her."

Jonathan tore loose from Lynn's grasp, raced to the building and rushed through the door. The inside of the building was like a scene from hell. Blood spattered the walls, women and children lay everywhere, cut to pieces by the hatchets and knifes of the crazed militiamen. Jonathan went from body to body, but he could not find her. Then he heard a groan. A woman lay at the front of the room, face turned toward the wall. Many women and children lay close around her as though they had sought final comfort with her. He ran to her and gently rolled her over. It was White Deer! Her shoulder was laid open with a horrible gash and she had been struck on the side of her head. Her clothes and hair were soaked in blood. She moaned and her eyes opened.

"Jonathan, you have finally come."

Jonathan's heart twisted in his chest. As he stared down at the beautiful face, he remembered the unconditional love that she had given him, the son she had borne for him, the moments of peace and love they had spent together. He remembered the life she had given back to him when he was marked for death, the sweet surrender of the greatest of Indian princesses. And then, finally, Jonathan Hershberger's eyes were opened, and he saw at last the depth of his madness. "White Deer, White Deer! What have I done?"

She smiled at him and slowly lifted a bloody hand to his cheek. Her touch was gentle and loving. "It will be all right, Jonathan. I go to my Lord. I know the way of peace. Always remember that I loved you." Her eyes closed and her hand fell back, lifeless.

A great cry burst from Jonathan. "Noooooo!" He grabbed her to his breast, her blood staining his buckskin shirt. "White Deer, no, no, please, no." But she was gone. And with her went all the hate that had filled his heart. He stared down at the face of the only woman he had ever loved. The folly of his ways was laid bare and something inside him broke. Gently, he wiped the blood from her face and closed her eyes. Then he laid her down, and rose to his feet. He began to search frantically among the bodies. "Matthew, Matthew!" After a few minutes, he realized that everyone in the room was dead. Ceasing from his search, he went to the door and stumbled out of the building. Jeff Lynn grabbed his arm.

"Jonathan, what's happened?"

"They're dead, Jeff, they're both dead…" Jonathan's eyes were glazed. He shook off Jeff's hand and started away.

"Jonathan, where are you going?"

Jonathan ignored him as he staggered toward the woods. He came to the edge of the forest and, as Jeff Lynn watched, he looked back once and then disappeared into the trees.

Chapter Thirty-Two

Many Tears

In the spring of 1783, Joshua Hershberger walked out of prison into the sunlight. The heavy oaken door creaked shut behind him and he stood in the courtyard, blinking against the light. David Zeisberger was waiting. Beside him stood the new warden of the prison. Zeisberger's face broke into a broad smile. "Joshua, my brother. Welcome back to life."

Joshua smiled too. He had lost much weight and his face was pale and drawn. The strong, straight shoulders now were bowed and the arms and hands that once could lift great weight trembled weakly. The warden approached him. "I wish to apologize for the corrupt behavior of the past warden. His dishonesty became apparent when his uncle, the magistrate, died. It could not be overlooked any longer. That is why he was discharged. But in the meantime, you have suffered unjustly through eight long years in this prison. I am truly sorry."

Joshua took the man's hand. "I hold no bitterness toward you or even toward him. This prison has been a fertile field for the gospel and many have come to Christ as they heard the Word."

The warden nodded. "Yes. And the prison is better for it. I thank you."

Zeisberger led Joshua toward the wagon that was waiting. "And now that I have you out, I must give you terrible news."

Joshua turned to him. "What is it, David?"

The missionary hesitated and then turned to Joshua. "Did you hear about what transpired at Gnadenhutten?"

"No. The warden kept me confined in my cell with no news of the outside. What has happened?"

Zeisberger put his arm on Joshua's shoulder. "I will make it short. The British thought we were spies for the Colonials and took us all to Detroit. When Captain Pipe would not testify against us, John and I were released. The British commander let some of the Christian Indians return to the Village of Peace to harvest the corn and gather the supplies that we left behind when they took us. While they were there, Wingenund was brought to the village by his braves. He had been severely wounded in an ambush. The villagers took him in and nursed him back to health. When the colonial militia found out, they came and massacred all of the villagers."

A sharp pain shot through Joshua's heart. "And Ruth? Matthew?"

"I am sorry, Joshua. Ruth was among those who were killed. Of Matthew, I do not know."

Joshua staggered and nearly fell. Zeisberger held him up and led him to a bench that was by the prison gate. Joshua sank down on the seat, and the two men sat together. Joshua was silent for a long time. When he looked up, tears were running down his face. "I loved her, David. Though she was Jonathan's wife, I loved her. From the moment I first saw her at Fort Pitt, I could look upon no other woman with favor. But she loved Jonathan and married him. So I became her brother and cared for her when Jonathan was in prison. I...I..." Joshua could not go on.

They sat for a long while. Finally, Zeisberger took Joshua's arm. "We must go, Joshua. The day grows short and we have many miles to travel before we reach the place of our rest. You need care and we will give it to you. I would see you strong and straight once more."

Joshua nodded and David helped him to stand. A carriage was waiting by the gate. They climbed in and the missionary took the reins. Joshua sat with his head down. "You said you do not know what happened to Matthew. What does that mean, David?"

Zeisberger chucked the reins and the horses started. "You must talk to John Heckewelder. He is at Gnadenhutten now. He can tell you what he found, for he was one of the first to arrive after the terrible events. It was John who gathered the bodies and buried them. And there is one more thing I must tell you."

Joshua looked up.

"It is about your brother, Jonathan. He was one of the men who instigated the massacre. Some of the men who were there have spread the tale of his butchery in the taverns."

A rage rose in Joshua's heart. "Jonathan! White Deer always said that Jonathan would murder her one day, that his hatred for Indians would overcome his love." Joshua's fists clenched in anger. He sat for a long time as the wagon bumped along and then turned to Zeisberger. "For the first time in my life, David, I wish to kill someone, and it is my own brother. This is too hard to endure." Joshua put his face in his hands and sobs shook his body. After a while, the sobs ceased and Joshua sat like a dead man.

Zeisberger drove on in silence.

Wingenund sat silently in his lodge. No fire burned in the pit to cheer the darkness. Nor could any fire ever again cheer the empty place in Wingenund's heart. A great battle raged within him, for when he had last been with White Deer, he had finally understood the way of peace. He had seen it lived out in the lives of the Lenape who followed the white man's God. Now the hatred for the white man that had raged within him all his life warred against the truth that he had seen in his daughter's life and the words he had heard from her lips. He thought of

Owechela and that day so long ago and a small smile came to his lips. "So, old man, you were right after all. But now that I see the way, my daughter is gone to the Great Spirit in the sky. I know that it was God who spoke through you so long ago, and that He was always leading me to his Son. But without White Deer, there is deep bitterness in this truth."

In the heart of the Ohio wilderness, a man moved through the shadows among the trees. His hair was filthy and knotted and his face was covered with a long beard. His clothes hung in tatters and his hands trembled. The man came upon a log that a bear had torn apart. He fell to his knees and pulled the rest of log up and turned it over. Several large white grubs lay wriggling on the ground. The man grabbed them up and greedily popped them into his mouth.

When he was finished, he stood and gazed about, his face twitching, his eyes blinking like an owl. Then he wandered down the hillside, laughing, until he came to a stream. There he lay at full length and drank noisily. When he was satisfied, he crawled to a large tree and sat against it. He began to moan softly. "White Deer, White Deer…" Then he slowly got to his feet. He looked up into the sky and raised his fist. "You! You who claim to love your children, and then laugh while they suffer torment and pain. I hate you. I will always hate you. You are no god, you are a devil." The man fell on his knees. "White Deer, White Deer, I am sorry, please forgive me…" Then the darkness of the night slowly closed down around him as he sat, eyes glazed and spittle running from the corner of his mouth.

A few weeks after he was released from prison, Joshua stood with John Heckewelder by a mound on the south side of the Village of Peace. The once thriving village lay in ruins, the buildings burned, the fields stripped.

Heckewelder's voice was soft as he began to tell Joshua what had happened. "The militia rounded up the Christian Lenape and accused them of aiding Wingenund on his raids into Pennsylvania. Although the Lenape denied the charges, the militia held a council and voted to kill them.

"The next morning the militia killed them with knives and hatchets. In all, the militia murdered twenty-eight men, twenty-nine women and thirty-nine children. The militia piled the bodies in the mission buildings and then they burned the rest of the village down. I collected the remains and buried them here. I know all this because there were two Indian boys who hid under a bed and survived to tell me of the massacre."

Joshua looked around at the ghost town that had been one of the most beautiful places in all of Ohio. "What can you tell me of Ruth?"

"I found her in the women's building. The other women were gathered around her and lay where they had fallen. Knowing Ruth, they were most likely looking to her for comfort when they died."

"Matthew?"

"I never found his body. The rest of the children were with their mothers, but not him. He may have escaped. Some of the men that were with Williamson might know if you can track them down. Or if you can find Williamson, he should be able to tell you what happened."

"Williamson? Captain David Williamson?"

"A colonel now, but yes, the same. Do you know him?"

"He was the man that sent me to prison. What strange paths our lives go down."

Joshua stood silent for a moment.

"And what of Jonathan?"

"He was there, but it is said that when he found Ruth in the women's building he went mad with grief and disappeared into the forest. He has not been seen since." Heckewelder went on.

"The militia looted the village before they burned it. The plunder required eighty horses to carry. They took everything left in the village: the food, furs for trade, pewter, tea sets, and clothing."

"Was there no revulsion against this horrible deed? What of the settlers? What did the regular army do?"

Heckewelder shook his head. "Although many were outraged, most of the settlers generally supported the militia's actions. The authorities talked of bringing the murderers to justice, but because Wingenund has waged such a long and bloody war, the feelings against him ran high and most people believed the Christian Indians got what they deserved. So no criminal charges have ever been filed."

"And the Delaware?"

"Wingenund's people were furious and immediately sought revenge for the murder of their princess. When General Washington heard about what happened here, he ordered his troops to take great care in battle. He feared what the hostile Lenape would do to the captured Colonials. Washington's close friend, William Crawford, was taken by the Indians while leading an expedition against the Lenape. His men were murdered and he was tortured unmercifully, scalped alive and burned at the stake. One of his men witnessed the terrible acts and then escaped. He said that the Indians were so angry that even the women and children helped to kill the soldiers."

Joshua sighed. "And men wonder why the Amish have forsworn violence. Cannot they see that hatred of your fellow man only leads to horrors like this? Will the bloodshed never end?"

"An interesting thing was reported by Knight, Crawford's friend who escaped. Many of the most important Lenape chiefs were present when Crawford was killed, and even Simon Girty, the white renegade, was there. But Wingenund was not among them, and he did not participate." He handed an envelope to Joshua. "I thought you might want these. They are Ruth and Matthew's baptism certificates."

Joshua took the envelope and then knelt down by the mound. Heckewelder joined him. "Ruth, I swear to you that I will find Matthew if he is still alive." He paused and then spoke again. "Dearest Lord and Savior, we come to You today with heavy hearts. Our dear brothers and sisters lie here, murdered for Your name's sake. They followed You and would not defend themselves for You truly taught them how to love one another and to give love to their enemies. Though they were Indians, they had become part of the one new man of which You tell us, neither Greek nor Jew nor white nor Indian, but one in the commonwealth of God. I pray now that You will comfort them and give them the promised peace. I pray that You will show them the path of life, and that in Your presence they will find fullness of joy, for in Your right hand there are pleasures forevermore."

Joshua was silent for a time. Then, his voice breaking, he spoke again. "And Lord, I lift up a special prayer for my sister Ruth, *Opahtuhwe*, the White Deer, who by faith, when she had seen the truth, refused to be called the daughter of Wingenund, choosing instead to suffer affliction with her brothers and sisters in Christ. Esteeming the reproach of Christ greater riches than to be a princess of the Lenape, she forsook the old ways, not fearing the wrath of her people, and endured, as seeing You who are invisible."

The two men knelt silently for a long while, each lost in their own thoughts. Finally, as the sun began to go down over the western hills, the breeze which had been stirring the trees stilled, and as the last rays of light lit the mound, a wonderful calm seemed to come over the beautiful valley where lay the people of the Village of Peace. It was as though a great darkness lifted and peace unbidden entered into Joshua's heart as he knelt at the last resting place of the Amish Princess.

Chapter Thirty-Three

Brothers No More

Joshua Hershberger stood at the door of the tavern at Fort Pitt. He hesitated a moment and then stepped into the noisy bar room. The dingy place reeked with the sickening smell of rum and tobacco smoke. It was crowded with half-drunken settlers who reeled across the sawdust floor shouting for more drink. The war was over and the surrender of the British at Yorktown had opened a floodgate of hunters and fur-traders, raftsmen and farmers who were pouring into the Ohio territory. Joshua watched as young men, honest-faced but flushed and wild with drink, hung over the bar. The proprietor dealt out the rum as laughter and coarse banter filled the air. Through a filthy curtain hung over the door to a back room came the rattling of dice, accompanied by the shouts and groans of unseen men. Joshua crossed the room and stepped up to the bar. The proprietor looked up, stared at Joshua, and then put a glass and a bottle in front of him.

"Welcome back, Jonathan. Haven't seen you in a long time."

Joshua waved the liquor away and took off his hat. "I'm not Jonathan. I'm his brother, Joshua."

The bartender stared for a moment and then shook his head. "Well, dang me if you don't look just like him, 'cept for that there yeller hair. He did say he had a brother."

"We're twins. We look alike but that's about as far as it goes."

The bartender took back the bottle. "Well, if ye ain't drinkin' then you're a horse of a different color fer sure. What can I do for you?"

"I'm trying to find Colonel Williamson."

"Williamson of the militia?"

"That's right. I heard he used to come here."

The bartender shook his head. "Well, since Sandusky, we ain't seen much of him."

"Sandusky?"

"You been out of the country, man? Sandusky, where Crawford and his men was massacred."

Joshua nodded. "You could say that I've been out of the country. Yes, I did hear about Crawford. What did Williamson have to do with that?"

"He was there with Crawford. When Crawford was captured, Williamson led the survivors of the attack on a thirty-mile retreat. Saved most of 'em from a horrible death. Since then, we haven't seen him around here. If you want to know more about it, you should ask Knight. He was with Crawford when the reddys tortured the colonel to death."

"Where can I find Knight?"

The bartender pointed. "He's right over there at that table."

Joshua followed the pointing finger. A gaunt, wretched looking man sat at a table in the corner with a flagon of ale before him. Joshua walked over.

"Mr. Knight?"

The man didn't look up, but mumbled into his glass. "Dr. Knight, sir, that's Dr. John Knight, late of the colonial militia."

"Excuse me, Dr. Knight."

The man finally looked up. He was bleary-eyed from too much drink. "What can I do for you?"

"Can I join you?"

"Do what you want."

Joshua slid onto the rough bench opposite from Knight. The man looked back down. Joshua leaned forward. "I'm looking for Colonel Williamson."

"What do you want him for?"

"I want to find out more about what happened at Gnadenhutten. I had a relative there who disappeared after the massacre, and I'm hoping Colonel Williamson can help me find him."

"Gnadenhutten! If that fool Williamson had kept his head and not killed all those innocent Christians, Crawford would still be alive and would never have gone through the tortures of the damned." Knight laid his head on the table and began to weep.

Joshua leaned over and tried to comfort the man. "I'm sorry, man; it must have been terrible."

Knight jerked upright. "Terrible! What do you know? It was hell. We never should have been there, but after Williamson did what he did, the Indians rose all along the border and began killing and torturing as many whites as they could find. We went up to Sandusky thinking to bring the Indians under control, but they were waiting for us with one hundred British rangers and a mixed band of about five hundred Delaware, Shawnee and Wyandots. They surrounded us.

"We tried to escape in the dark, but they attacked and the troops broke and scattered. Colonel Crawford and I and a number of men were captured and taken to Wingenund's camp. Captain Pipe was there and he painted our faces black. That's when we knew we were going to die. Then they took us to the main Delaware village. Four prisoners were killed with tomahawks and scalped along the way. When we arrived there were seven of us left. Crawford and I watched while Delaware women and boys killed the other five with tomahawks, beheading one of them. The little boys scalped the victims and slapped the bloody scalps in our faces. It was horrible."

Knight took another long drink of his rum. Joshua put his hand on his arm. "You don't have to go on, Dr. Knight—"

"But I do, don't you see? I have this in me and it torments me. I can't eat or sleep, even the rum does no good until I pass out." He took another swig and went on. "About one hundred

Indians were at the Delaware village to witness the executions. Dunquat and a few Wyandots were present, as well as Simon Girty and Matthew Elliott. Captain Pipe spoke to the crowd. He accused Crawford of leading the men who had committed the Gnadenhutten murders. Crawford had nothing to do with the massacre, but Williamson sure did, and the Indians were furious.

"After Pipe's speech, they took the colonel, stripped him naked, and beat him until he could hardly stand. They tied his hands behind his back and leashed him to a post with a long rope. Then the devils lit a fire all around him. They shot charges of gunpowder into his body, then cut off his ears. Crawford begged Simon Girty to shoot him, but Girty just laughed. After about two hours of torture, Crawford fell down unconscious. He was scalped but a woman poured hot coals over his head, and he woke up. He began to walk about insensibly as the torture continued. After he finally died, his body was burned.

"The next day, they took me toward the Shawnee towns. Along the way, I struck my guard with a log and managed to escape."

Joshua leaned closer. "What about Williamson?"

"He went back to Pennsylvania. I heard that he died, and I hope he did." Knight fell face down on the table and began to snore. Joshua stared down at the wretched man and then went back to the bar and spoke to the bartender.

"Do you know any of the others that were with Williamson at Gnadenhutten?"

The bartender shook his head. "If any of these men was there, they certainly ain't makin' it public."

"What about my brother; do you know where he is?"

The man looked around. "After the massacre I heard he was in the woods, crazy-like. Then one day about a year after the massacre he came in here. He had gotten himself together and said he was leaving Ohio. He wanted me to arrange the shipping of his goods."

"Where did he go?"

"He told me not to tell no one."

Joshua reached in his pocket and pulled out a gold coin. He slid it across the bar. The man looked around again and then picked it up and bit it.

He leaned over the bar and lowered his voice. "Long Island, he went out to Long Island. Said he wanted to get as far away from here as he could. After he was gone for a month, I got a letter. He had bought some land and wanted his things sent to a place called Oyster Bay."

Joshua nodded and turned away.

The man called after him. "If I was you, I'd leave him alone. He said if he ever saw anyone he knew from here, he'd kill 'em.'"

The wagon bumped along the road that ran along the north shore of Long Island. Ahead was a small hamlet. The teamster who was driving lifted his whip to point. "That there's Oyster Bay. The most important people in town are the Townsends. If anyone has moved into the area they would know about it. You'll find Miss Sally at Townsend Hall." He pulled the wagon to a halt.

Joshua grabbed his bag and clambered down. He tipped his hat to the teamster. "I'm beholden to you, sir."

The wagon driver nodded and then stirred up his team. Joshua watched as they lumbered away and then turned toward the village. He stopped at a market and asked for directions to Townsend Hall. The proprietor pointed down the road. "Goin' out to see Miss Sally; are ye friend of hers?"

Joshua shook his head. "No, I'm looking for my brother, and I was told that Miss Townsend could help me."

"Aye, that's true. Miss Sally knows everything that goes on hereabouts. And she put it to good use during the war."

Joshua paused. "How's that?"

The man smiled. "Why, the British used Miss Sally's house as their headquarters and it was Miss Sally that overheard the British Major Andre talking about Benedict Arnold's traitorous plot to surrender West Point to the British. She told her brother, who was one of Washington's spies, and they caught Andre and hanged him. Yes sir, Miss Sally knows everything that's going on."

A short while later, Joshua sat on the porch of Townsend Hall while Sally Townsend poured him a cup of tea. "Jonathan Hershberger. Yes, I know of him. He purchased a farm not far from here. I have not met the man, for it is said that he keeps to himself. I've heard that he is an excellent hunter and raises a few animals."

Joshua smiled at the lovely woman. "I was told that you had your finger on the pulse of Long Island, and now I see that it is true."

Miss Townsend took a sip of her tea and blushed. "When you are a girl who longs for adventure and yet you are frowned upon for any untoward behavior, you must use the gifts God has given you."

"You are a Christian, then?"

"Oh, yes, all my family are Quakers. And you?"

"I am Amish."

"Amish, how interesting. You don't have a beard."

Joshua felt himself blushing. "I'm not married, Miss Townsend, so I shave. I am Amish, however. My father, Jonas, came here on the Charming Nancy in 1737, seventeen years after the first group of Amish had settled in Berks County, Pennsylvania. I was born in the Northkill settlement in 1753. We moved to Fort Pitt when I was ten."

"Oh, the heart of the wilderness. Did you have trouble with the Indians during the war?"

A picture came into Joshua's mind, a picture of a beautiful Indian princess. She was seated on the grass beneath a spreading oak tree. He was seated at her feet, reading from the Bible. She was smiling at him as he read...

"Mr. Hershberger?"

Joshua turned to his hostess. "Excuse me?"

"I asked if you had trouble with the Indians."

Joshua thought for a moment and then answered, choosing his words carefully. "I had both trouble and blessing, Miss Townsend. My experiences with the Indians took me from the depths of despair to the heights of wonder. My whole life is a tapestry upon which the Indians of Ohio have woven their story."

Sally smiled. "My, a poet and a gentleman. Perhaps you could call on me in the future and share some of your experience."

"I would enjoy that very much, Miss Townsend, but I am on a mission. I am looking for my nephew who might have been one of the survivors of the terrible massacre at Gnadenhutten. I must speak with my brother, who was one of the militia who participated. He did not know that his wife and son were among the residents of the village until they had all been killed. When he found out, he was out of his mind for a long time. It has taken me months to find him. I have come to help him and to see if together we might find Matthew. If I find out anything I must return to Ohio to continue the search."

"His wife and son were there?"

Joshua set his tea down and looked away. "His wife was Opahtuhwe, the White Deer, the daughter of Wingenund, the most powerful chief of the Delaware Tribe and the fiercest enemy of the settlers."

There was a long silence. Then Sally spoke. "It seems there is a wonderful story here. Perhaps you might write me then and share it with me. It might help to relieve you of some of the memories that seem to trouble you."

"That is very kind of you. I will consider that. At the least I will let you know what has happened with my search."

At that moment a buggy came around the side of the house. Miss Townsend stood and offered her hand. "I have arranged to have Henry take you to your brother's farm and then drive you back to town. Please stay in touch."

Joshua took her hand and bowed. "You have been most kind. I will not forget you."

An hour later, the buggy pulled up on the road beside a field. Joshua could see a path that wended its way through the rush grass to a small shack set by a pond. Around the building stretched open fields marked by stands of pines and oaks. In the distance Joshua could see Long Island Sound. The driver pointed to the gate. "That's his place, sir."

"Thank you, Henry. Can you wait? I am not sure whether I will be staying."

The driver nodded.

Joshua walked up the path to the building. As he came to the porch, the front door opened and a man came out. The man was bearded, his clothing was rough-spun and his hair was streaked with gray. For a moment Joshua did not recognize him and then with a start he realized it was Jonathan. Jonathan stopped and stared at Joshua and then a half smile broke the set of the face.

"So, brother, you tracked me down. I thought I left word that no one was to follow me."

"Yes, I got that message, but what I have come for is too important. It's about Matthew."

"Matthew is dead."

"Jonathan, I know you believe that, but Heckewelder never found Matthew's body. If there is a chance the boy is alive—"

Jonathan took two strides forward and tried to take Joshua by the shirt, but Joshua grasped his wrists and held him. Finally, Jonathan went limp and sank down on the porch.

"Alive? You weren't there, Joshua. You didn't see what we did. I was there and the horror of it will never leave me. When I saw Scar, the madness came upon me and I killed him. I was drunk and urged the men on. They followed me and we killed all the Indians, everyone. Then in the midst of the madness I found

White Deer in the room with the women. I held her in my arms as she died. She forgave me! But I am guilty, guilty..."

"But if White Deer forgave you…"

"She may have forgiven me, but I can never forgive myself. I might as well have struck her down myself."

"But if you turned to God, brother, you could find forgiveness."

Jonathan looked up. "I will never serve the God who let this happen to me. No, never! I will stay here and rot in my sin and die and go to hell. And I will deserve every moment of torment. White Deer is dead. Matthew is also dead, I am sure of it. No one could have survived."

"But, Jonathan, two Indian boys lived through it. Matthew could also be alive. If Heckewelder did not find his body, there may be a chance. You must think. I can't find Williamson, but is there anyone else who could tell me anything? Matthew's life could depend on what you remember."

Jonathan looked up at Joshua. Joshua thought that for a moment he saw a gleam of hope in his brother's eyes. But then Jonathan's face set. "If you believe he is alive then find him. I know he is dead and will not waste what is left of my miserable life on such a hopeless search. Now get out of here and leave me to my ghosts."

"But, Jonatha—"

Jonathan rose up in a fury. "I said get out of here! If you're not off my land in five minutes, I'll kill you!"

Jonathan turned and went into the house. Joshua heard the latch close and the bolt shoot home. He stood for a long while staring at the door, and then he turned and slowly walked away.

Part Seven

The Unbroken Circle

Joshua never forgot White Deer. Eventually the Lord blessed him with a kind and lovely wife and his own children. But as the years rolled on, he always searched for any news about Matthew. Finally, in 1799, events unfolded that brought about a strange reconciliation between the brothers and the establishment of the Long Island branch of the Hershbergers—the family that gave me my Jonathan over 200 years later.

"O the depth of the riches both of the wisdom and knowledge of God! How unsearchable are his judgments, and his ways past finding out!"

The Unbroken Circle
From The Journals of Jenny Hershberger

Chapter Thirty-Four

A New Chapter - 1799

My Dear Sally,

As I promised so many years ago when you helped me to find my brother, Jonathan, I am sending along news concerning the search for my nephew, Matthew. When I spoke with Jonathan that day on Long Island, he was convinced that Matthew had died in the massacre. That has never been a settled issue in my heart, but I have not had much to go on these last fifteen years and up until recently my search for Matthew has been fruitless. I continued to search for Colonel Williamson when I could, but his trail vanished into western Pennsylvania.

But now, at long last, I have a good report. As you know, I married and settled not far from Fort Henry. The Lord has blessed me greatly and my farm and my mill have prospered and from them I have built a successful trade in grain and produce with the merchants in different villages of eastern Ohio. Recently, when I was in Zanesville, I learned that a man named David Williamson frequents a tavern there. I went to the tavern. He was not there that day, but I was assured that he often comes. I am going again this week to the village and will try to find the man. I believe he is the David Williamson who was the leader of the militia that

*perpetrated the massacre at Gnadenhutten. Perhaps he can tell me
more about Matthew's fate.*

*Also, I must advise you that I am very grateful that you have
allowed me to tell you my story in my letters to you over the years. It
has been a blessing and I doubt that I would have ever been free in
my heart to receive the love of my gentle wife, Sarah, had I not been
able to lay my feelings for the Amish Princess to rest by writing
down her story. Perhaps some day, future generations of my family
will benefit from hearing about Jonathan, Joshua, and White Deer
and the consequences that choices have in our lives. But for me, the
story will not be fully written until I have certainty about
Matthew's fate.*

*On another note, my wife and children have been greatly taken
with your letters detailing your adventurous role in the saving of the
Fort at West Point and the uncovering of the treachery of General
Benedict Arnold. You should most definitely put your
remembrances of that time into a book. I'm sure that many would
be interested in the tale.*

*I will say goodbye for now, but if I discover any news about
Matthew, I will most certainly inform you.*

Your Friend,

Joshua Hershberger.

Joshua paused before the swinging doors. He wondered if
this was the end of his search or just another dead end.
Williamson had disappeared after Sandusky. Some said he left
the militia and became a sheriff. Others said that he led the
survivor's of Crawford's defeat safely back to Pennsylvania then
died. Joshua had only discovered the whereabouts of Williamson
when, by chance, he overheard one of his customers remark that
the perpetrator of the Gnadenhutten massacre frequented
McIntire's Tavern in Zanesville, Ohio. So Joshua had come to
the village with new hope of finding his nephew.

He took a breath and pushed through the doors. His eyes
swept the room until he saw an old man seated in the corner at a
table. The man was quite different from the officer who had

arrested him twenty-two years before. That man had been a sharply dressed and focused leader of the militia, with a commanding presence. This man was overweight, bearded, and disheveled. A half-empty bottle and a glass sat before him. After so many years, he was barely recognizable. But it was Williamson.

Joshua walked up to the table. "Good day to you, Captain Williamson."

The man looked up with bleary eyes. "Colonel Williamson, sir. An who be ye?"

"Don't you remember me, Colonel? I'm Joshua Hershberger."

"Hershberger, Hershberger…I remember that name." He paused for a moment, looking at Joshua. Then the light dawned in his eyes. "Ah, yes, the coward I sent to prison…"

Joshua put a hand on the man's arm. He leaned over and spoke quietly to the man. "We both have things we wish to forget. You, for instance, may have been a hero when you massacred those Indians, but you are not one anymore. Public sentiment has gone against you over the years."

Williamson made a motion to silence Joshua and then motioned to a chair. "All right, all right, sit down." Joshua saw him glance furtively around the room, but the other patrons did not seem to have heard Joshua's remark and were ignoring the two men.

"What do you want of me, Hershberger?"

Joshua examined the man before him. The years had not been kind to Colonel David Williamson. Deep lines furrowed his brow and face. His eyes were sunken into hollow sockets and were bloodshot. His teeth were yellow and ground off and tobacco juice stained his beard and shirtfront.

"You've changed since my trial, Colonel."

The old man put his face in his hands for a moment and then looked up. "And who wouldn't change, carrying the weight that I have all these years."

"So you cannot forget leading the men that massacred the innocent Christians in the Village of Peace?"

Williamson looked around again. His face was agitated and his hands were shaking. He tried to keep his voice low. "Yes, yes, I led them. But those Indians were not innocent. We had reason to believe that they were aiding Wingenund and his warriors on their raids against settlers all along the border. The villagers even admitted to saving Wingenund's life after some of my men shot him. What else could we do?"

Joshua took the man by the arm. "They helped Wingenund the same way they would have helped you if you had been brought to them badly wounded. Zeisberger and Heckewelder were patriotic supporters of the revolution and often fed information concerning Captain Pipe and Wingenund's movements to the colonial forces. You were wrong to kill those people and history will bear me out."

Williamson took the bottle, poured himself another drink, and drank it straight down. He offered the bottle to Joshua, but Joshua shook his head. Williamson's jaw trembled and his hands shook even more. Then he laid his head on the table and began to sob. "You're right, you're right. It was terrible. I should never have allowed it. But your brother...your brother." After a long time, Williamson pulled himself together and looked up.

Joshua looked into his eyes. "What about my brother?"

"When Jonathan arrived on the morning of the massacre, he was drunk. He recognized one of the Indians, a man called Scar, and killed him. Then he got into one of his killing frenzies and urged the men on. They had been drinking all night and followed him. It got out of hand. It seemed like the right thing to do when we voted, but when the men started butchering those children...there was nothing I could do. I couldn't stop them." He stared blankly over Joshua's shoulder, and Joshua knew the man was recalling some fiendish scene, for Williamson's face was twisted in torment. Finally, Williamson focused his eyes and grabbed Joshua's arm. "I am beleaguered day and night. Help me...forgive me." The old man laid his head on the table again.

Joshua patted Williamson on the back, gently. "I am not the one to give forgiveness. You must seek the mercy of one much greater than I."

Williamson steadied himself. "God would never forgive me."

"Just tell Him what you said to me. You will find peace." There was a long silence. Then Joshua spoke softly. "Colonel Williamson, I did not come here to wring a confession of guilt from you. I have another question that only you can help me with."

"And what is that?"

"My nephew, Matthew, Jonathan's son, was with the Indians that day, but his body was not found among the victims. Do you know what happened to him?"

Williamson nodded. "Several of the men left after we voted to kill the Indians and refused to be part of what happened. Obadiah Holmes was one of them. He discovered that Jonathan's son was among the children, and he took him away."

Joshua's heart leaped. "Matthew is alive?"

"The last I saw he was. Holmes hid him in the woods, waiting for Jonathan to arrive. But then the slaughter started and before he could give him to Jonathan, Jonathan disappeared into the forest. Holmes looked for him but Jonathan had vanished. So Holmes took the lad with him."

"Where, man? Where?"

"To Pittsburg, he took the boy to Pittsburg."

Obadiah Holmes sat with Joshua on the porch of his small home on the outskirts of the growing town of Pittsburg. A small child sat on Holmes' lap and several others played in the yard.

"I had the lad for almost six months, Mr. Hershberger. I tried everything to find Jonathan but I could not locate him. Then after a year or so, I heard that he had gone to New York, but with my wife and a growing family of my own, I could not leave here to find him. You were in prison and I just didn't have the ability to do anything."

"Then what happened to Matthew?"

"I heard about a group of people in Youngstown that found places for the orphans of settlers killed in the war. They were kindly people, good Christians, mind you, and they took him in."

"Do you know what happened to him after that?"

Holmes hesitated for a moment. "No, I have never been back, but from what I heard, they often apprenticed the older lads or got them a place as an indentured servant. Matthew was a fine lad, and I am sure they placed him in a good home."

Joshua stood up. "Are you telling me that you took Matthew to an orphanage and simply abandoned him, knowing that he had living relatives? Why didn't you at least contact me? I have been searching for him for years."

Holmes stood also. "Now, Mr. Hershberger, don't be angry. I did the best I could for the boy. I had my own family to look after, and there was no pension for militiamen. You and your brother were both gone, and to be honest, I just wanted to put the whole thing behind me. After a while, I did not think about it anymore. At least Matthew had someone to look after him. And after all, I did save him from the scalping knife. That's got to be worth something."

Joshua took a calming breath. "Yes, yes, you are right, Obadiah. You did save my nephew, and for that, I thank you. Now, can you give me the name of the people that you left him with?"

"Yes, and I can tell you how to find them. They are well-known in Youngstown. Ask anyone there for the home of Mrs. Cowpers."

Joshua reached out his hand. "I want to thank you, Obadiah, for what you did for Matthew and for this information. You have given me great hope that my nephew can be restored to his family. I will bid you farewell." Joshua turned to go. He had taken a few steps down the path toward the gate when Holmes called out.

"Mr. Hershberger, wait. I forgot something." Holmes went into the house. When he returned he held an envelope in his hand. He came down the steps and handed it to Joshua. "She gave it to me."

"She?"

"Why, yes, Jonathan's wife, the Indian lady. The one they called the Amish Princess. She was a brave 'un. She tried to talk sense into Williamson and the men. She begged them to have mercy on the children. When I went to get Jonathan's boy that night, she wrote this letter. She asked me to get it to you, but you was gone. I've had it all these years."

Joshua took the letter. His hand shook as he stared at the writing on the envelope. It was Ruth's firm hand, and it was addressed to him. He stared at it for a long time and then slipped it into his pocket. He bid goodbye to Holmes and walked away. As he turned into the lane in front of the house, he was surprised to find that he was weeping.

Chapter Thirty-Five

Renewal

"Well, Mr. Hershberger, when Obadiah Holmes brought Matthew to us, he said that his parents were either dead or missing, and he needed a place to put the boy. So we took him in."

Joshua stared across the table at the elderly woman. "But don't you make an effort to find other relatives before you place children?"

The woman smiled. "Look around you, Mr. Hershberger. This was not an official branch of government. We were a small, private group of Christians who were trying to help the orphans of a terrible war find a place. If you didn't notice, you are sitting in my kitchen; hardly official, won't you agree?"

"Yes, Mrs. Cowpers, I understand. It is just that I have been searching for my nephew for fifteen years. And to find that he has been here in Youngstown, right under my nose, all this time…well, it is a bit disconcerting."

"Matthew has been well-cared-for and has grown into a fine young man. Mr. Andrews has seen that he learned a trade and has given the boy at least a basic education—"

"As an indentured servant working for a rich landowner with no hope for his own future. Am I correct?"

"Well, yes, Mr. Hershberger, but that was not our affair. Many orphans are apprenticed or placed as indentured servants, if they have no known family. As far as we knew, Matthew was exactly that, an orphan. In those days there was no official program for the care of orphans, so we, in local communities, did the best we could for them. Mr. Andrews is a prominent citizen of this village, and I can assure you that Matthew lacked for nothing."

"That's all well and good, Mrs. Cowpers, and I'm glad that Matthew had a place to live. But it appears to me that Mr. Andrews has taken advantage of the situation. A boy needs love, not just food."

Mrs. Cowpers shrugged. "I cannot direct the hearts of those who take in strangers, Mr. Hershberger. Matthew is not unlike hundreds or even thousands of other children who were displaced by the atrocities of warfare. We did the best we could. He may not have a loving family around him, but his basic needs were met. That's all I can tell you."

"Can you direct me to the home of Mr. Andrews, then?"

"I will, but I'm not sure Mr. Andrews will be willing to release Matthew to you. After all, he has a great deal of time and money invested in the boy."

"Indentured servitude is not for life, Mrs. Cowpers. Usually a contract runs four to seven years. The servant may live a harsh and loveless life, but at least they are released at the end of the contract. Andrews has done Matthew an injustice."

"Yes, but Matthew is an orphan, or at least we assumed he was. Mr. Andrews was willing to keep him as long as need be—"

"As one would keep a valuable slave, no doubt. Mrs. Cowpers, I am Matthew's uncle. Things are different now. If you will direct me to the Andrews farm, I will deal with the situation personally."

"Yes, Mr. Hershberger." Mrs. Cowpers took a pen and paper and scratched out a few directions. She paused for a moment and then added a few more words. She pushed the sheet across the table to Joshua. "This is the way to the Andrews farm. I have added a note explaining who you are. I hope everything works out well for you. But know this—Gordon Andrews is one of the wealthiest men in Ohio and has many powerful friends. If you are going to beard the lion in his den, I would find out a little more about him."

Joshua looked at the woman. "What do you mean, Mrs. Cowpers?"

"That's not for me to say. There are rumors in the village..." She stood up. "Goodbye, Mr. Hershberger. I must be about my day."

Joshua took the paper and bowed. "Thank you, Mrs. Cowpers. The Lord bless you." His mind was racing. He had found Matthew.

Joshua sat in the foyer of the Andrews house. He had been cooling his heels for over an hour, waiting for the owner to return from the fields. Finally, a maid came down the hall and beckoned to him.

"Mr. Andrews will see you now."

Joshua walked down the hall. The house was more a mansion than a house, with a sweeping staircase to the upper floors, oak floors and fine furniture. The maid led Joshua to a door at the end of the hall and opened it. She motioned for Joshua to enter.

The man behind the ornate desk was a well-fed gentleman dressed in the attire of a colonial landowner, complete with the curled wig and high, wrapped white collar. "Come in, Mr. Hershberger. Please sit down." He motioned Joshua to a chair. "Now what's this about Matthew?"

"I have come for my nephew, Matthew Hershberger, Mr. Andrews."

"Ah, your nephew, or so you claim. Do you have proof of this?"

Joshua reached into his coat. He handed a slip of paper to Andrews. "This is my nephew Matthew's baptism certificate. It has his date of birth and the signature of John Heckewelder of the Moravian Mission."

Andrews glanced at the paper and then handed it back. "This proves nothing, Mr. Hershberger. How do I know that you are indeed this boy's uncle? It will take more than a scrap of paper to convince me."

"But, Mr. Andrews, I am his uncle. I have traced him here from the Moravian Mission at Gnadenhutten. I can bring John Heckewelder and David Zeisberger here. They could identify Matthew."

Andrews laughed. "It's been fifteen years since the orphan society gave me the boy. How do you suppose anyone could recognize him after that long? Besides, I have come to think of Matthew as almost a member of the family."

Joshua leaned forward. "Have you given him your name and made him an heir along with your other children?"

Andrews fidgeted with his coat buttons. "Well...no, I have not. But I have given him a good position and treated him very fairly over the years. Why, I even gave him some basic schooling. The lad can read and write because of me."

"And what exactly is his position, Mr. Andrews?"

"Matthew is my assistant groom and in charge of the stables. He is a sharp lad and very good with horses."

"By being in charge of the stables, do you mean that he is the one who mucks out all the stalls and makes sure the horses are fed?"

"Yes...Matthew does those tasks."

"And where does Matthew sleep, might I ask?"

Andrews looked around and then adjusted his wig. "See here, Mr. Hershberger. I don't see what business that is of yours."

Joshua smiled. "I'm assuming by your response that Matthew has his bed in the stable with the horses. Am I correct?"

"Someone has to be on site, Mr. Hershberger. After all, I am the owner of some of the finest horses in Ohio, and I need to provide protection from thieves."

Joshua stood and went to the desk. "Here's what I think, Mr. Andrews. You got Matthew from the orphan society so your own sons could live a life of ease while Matthew did all the work a son should rightly do. I imagine that his clothes certainly do not match the quality that you and your sons wear, and that his bed is a simple straw pallet in a stall somewhere in your rather commodious stables. Am I right so far?"

"Really, Mr. Hershberger, you have no right to speak to me in such a manner. Do you know who I am?"

"Yes, Mr. Andrews, I do know who you are. You are Gordon Andrews. You helped to found the village of Youngstown. You have large land holdings, for which you paid cash during the Revolutionary war. That much is public information. What is not so public is the fact that much of that cash came from selling guns and whiskey to the hostile Indians, who then got fired up on your liquor and used the guns to murder innocent women and children all along the border."

Andrews stood up. His face had turned red and his hands were shaking. "How dare you accuse me of such a heinous crime? I am Gordon Andrews, and I am one of the most respected men in this entire state. You have absolutely no proof of what you are saying."

"Don't I, Mr. Andrews? When Mrs. Cowpers told me that you had kept Matthew all these years without giving him his freedom, I did some checking into your background. I heard some of the rumors that float about the village, and after a short investigation, I was able to verify some of them with the help of one"—Joshua reached into his pocket and retrieved another piece of paper—"James Garrison and one Meriwether Haraldson. Do those names sound familiar?"

Andrews' face went pale and he collapsed into his chair. He sat for a long time. Finally, he spoke. "You would have a hard time using those men to make a case against me, Mr. Hershberger. They are known criminals while I—"

"I might have a hard time, Mr. Andrews, but before I finished, I would drag your good name through the courts. You may have money, but you and your sons are not well-liked. There were many who were willing to speak to me privately about you. That is how I found Garrison and Haraldson. The rumors may or may not be provable, but in the meanwhile, there would surely be a public backlash, and guilty or innocent, I'm sure the good citizens of Ohio would not be as reluctant to judge you as some of the magistrates might."

Andrews started to speak and then changed his mind. He looked at Joshua with hatred in his eyes.

"All right, Mr. Hershberger, you've made your point. What is it you want of me?"

"Your past activities are not my main concern. If you are truly guilty of them, your sins will find you out some day. As for me, I want to see Matthew and I want to see him now. And I want him to be free to make the choice for his own life. If he decides to stay with you, I will go away and never bother you again. But if he decides for his family, we walk out of here, together, today."

Andrews nodded. "Agreed." He rang a bell on his desk and a servant came in. "Fetch Matthew here, at once."

"Yes, Mr. Andrews."

Joshua's heart was pounding. The servant was gone for quite a while. Then Joshua heard steps coming down the hall. The door opened and a young man came in. For a moment, Joshua could not believe his eyes. The boy was the spitting image of Jonathan—dark hair, piercing blue eyes, tall and obviously strong. Then after a closer look, Joshua could see White Deer in the young man—the skin a little darker, the white teeth, and the high cheekbones all declared his Indian blood.

The young man stood staring at Joshua. "What's this all about, Mr. Andrews?"

Andrews got up and stood by Joshua. "Do you know this man, Matthew?"

Matthew stepped closer. He looked at Joshua closely and then his eyes opened in recognition. "Uncle Joshua?"

"Yes, lad. It is I. I have found you, after all these years."

Matthew stood still for a moment and then stepped forward and took his uncle in a bone-breaking embrace. "I knew you would find me. I knew you would come."

Joshua felt the strength in the lad's arms, and he remembered the days of his youth when he and Jonathan had wrestled. The same strength was in Matthew. His shoulders were broad and strong, his arms muscled and powerful. Joshua felt tears in his eyes. "I have found you at last. Matthew...Matthew."

The young man stepped back. Joshua turned to Andrews. "It's up to you, Mr. Andrews. I do not want you ever to be able to say I used coercion."

Andrews coughed, then spoke. "Matthew, your uncle has come. He wants you to make the choice about whether you will stay here with us, your family, or go with him who has been absent these fifteen years. I leave the decision to you, but I want to remind you of the home you have here and the place you have in our household and our affections."

Matthew looked at Andrews, then to Joshua, and then back to Andrews. Then he laughed out loud. "Place? You say I have a place. I have no place in your family. I have been your slave since the day I came here. When your sons found out that I was half Indian, they beat me unmercifully every day until I was big enough to lick them. Then they finally left me alone. You gave me every dirty job on this farm; I slept in the barn; I ate the leftovers from your grand table. This was never my home; it was my prison."

Andrews paled. "But, Matthew—"

"Matthew, nothing. You are only anxious because you might lose a servant. If I have the choice…" He looked to Joshua once more.

Joshua nodded. "It is yours to make. Mr. Andrews has been…persuaded to abide by your decision."

Matthew looked around at the palatial setting and then turned to his uncle. "When do we leave?"

"Right now, if you wish."

Andrews stepped forward. "But you can't take your belongings. After all I paid for…"

A look from Joshua stopped him and he stepped back.

Matthew stepped forward until he was a few inches from Andrews. "Belongings? Belongings? You wretched man. You would strip me naked then, for the clothes on my back are all I possess."

Joshua reached in and gently pulled Matthew away. "Matthew, no."

Andrews shrank back, his face pale. He started to speak, then stopped himself. He took a deep breath and then waved his hand dismissively. "Go then, you ingrate. Never darken my doorway again."

Matthew bowed. "That, sir, is the first command you have ever given me that I willingly obey."

Joshua and Matthew turned and walked out of the room, leaving Andrews standing with his mouth open.

Chapter Thirty-Six

Decisions

Joshua and Matthew walked in the fields behind Joshua's house. The sun was setting and golden shafts of light from the west sent long shadows over the fields of hay and corn. The air was alive with the smell of harvest, and in the fields workmen bundled up sheaves of golden grain and laid them in rows to be loaded into the wagons. Above them, the clouds were tinged with the purple and rose of the coming dusk and away across the fields the broad Ohio wended its way through Joshua's farm. Joshua leaned against a fence and surveyed the land.

"Gott ist sehr gut zu mir, Matthew gewesen."

Matthew looked at Joshua strangely and then smiled. "I understood you, Uncle Joshua."

"So, you remember the German I taught your mother?"

"Yes, but why did Papa never speak it?"

Joshua sighed. "Your papa carried a great wound in his heart. When the Indians killed your grandmother and your aunts and uncle, something broke inside him. He rejected his Amish roots and all that went with them. So he never spoke German again. The last time I heard him speak it was just after we had been captured, and he didn't want the Indians to understand him. He was so filled with rage that he abandoned God and went his own way."

Matthew frowned. "The way I see it, Uncle Joshua, God abandoned him, and my mother."

"Matthew, that is not true—"

"Then why is my mother dead? She loved Jesus. And what about my father? What kind of God would allow such terrible things to happen to those who believe in Him?"

Suddenly, the frustrations of fifteen years were pouring out of the young man. "When the militia came to the Village of Peace, I remember the looks in those white men's eyes. They hated us. And yet they called themselves Christians. Brother David told us that all Christians were brothers, but those men weren't our brothers. I remember my mother, down on her knees in front of their commander, begging the men to at least spare the children. Did they spare them? Did they, Uncle Joshua?"

Joshua put his hand on Matthew's shoulder. "No, they did not, Matthew. They killed everyone except two Indian boys who managed to hide. It was a terrible thing. But don't you understand, boy? God did not kill your mother, wicked men did. They may have called themselves Christians, but a true Christian is one who obeys the commands of Christ. And Jesus said you know a tree by its fruit. Can bitter and sweet water come from the same well? It is why we Amish never raise our hand against another man, even in the greatest of trials. It is why my father watched as his family was murdered, even though he was in great anguish at the sight."

"He should have defended them, Uncle Joshua."

"And if he had, Matthew? You would not be standing here today for your father never would have married your mother. One of the things I learned when I was a prisoner of the Indians was that our trails are laid before us from the day we are born. I believe it is true. I believe that God knows everything that will happen in our lives from the moment we are conceived. The Bible says—"

"I know what the Bible says, uncle. But those empty words did nothing to save my mother and the gentle people in the

Village of Peace. No, do not quote the Bible to me. I have learned in these last years to depend on myself; my own strength, my own mind, my own abilities."

"But who gave you those abilities, Matthew? Was it not the Creator of all things?"

"You can believe that if you will, Uncle Joshua, but I do not. I believe that my mother and father created me, and through my own efforts and my will, I have survived. When the Andrews boys were beating me every day, I did not cry out to a distant God. I lifted more hay bales and dug boulders out of the fields until I surpassed them both in strength and skill. Then I beat them as they had beaten me. I was flogged for it, but they never bothered me again. I have come to rely on myself alone for anything I have."

Joshua's heart sank. To hear his nephew speak in such a way was heartbreaking. He was about to reply when he heard the voice of his youngest son calling. "Papa, Papa! *Maam* says to come to dinner."

"Yes, Ezekiel, we will be right there." He turned to his nephew. "Come, Matthew. Perhaps some of my wife's cooking will warm your heart and dispel the gloom from our conversation."

"I am sure that it will calm my stomach, uncle, but I am not so sure how will it affect my convictions."

"When you've rested here for a while, we will talk more about your future and your plans. Until then, let's put aside the troubles of the past and be thankful for your return to our family."

The two men walked back toward the house. The beautiful scene around them belied the shadow on Joshua's heart.

A few weeks later, Matthew came while Joshua was going over his accounts. There was a knock on the door and Joshua looked up as the young man entered. Joshua was always taken by the resemblance to Jonathan. Matthew had also proved that he was like his father in more ways than just his looks. He was a crack shot with the long rifle and skillful with knife and throwing hatchet. His days as a servant at the Andrew's farm had given him a love of the land and a great ability to handle animals of all kinds, especially horses. Joshua motioned to a chair by his desk. "What can I do for you, Matthew?"

"I've come to talk about my future, Uncle Joshua."

Joshua laid aside his account books and took the spectacles from his nose. "And what have you decided?"

"First, I want to thank you for never giving up on me, through all those years. I used to lie awake at night and dream of the day when you or Papa would come for me. It was one of the few things I had of my own, the memories of my days at the fort and in the village…before the trouble. These days with you have refreshed my soul and spirit."

"You are my kin, Matthew. I could do no less."

"That said, uncle, I want to talk to you about my father. I wish to see him."

"I was expecting that you would, Matthew. I have already arranged for us to visit him in Long Island. I have a friend in Oyster Bay, a Miss Sally Townsend, who knows all about you and that I have found you. She has sent a message to your father and has opened her home to us."

"Why would we not stay with Papa?"

Joshua stood and went to the window. Outside it was a cold, fall day. A light rain was falling, and the trees were almost bare of their leaves. The wind blew the colored bits across the yard in front of the house. In the distance, smoke rose from the fields as workmen burned the wheat and corn stubble. Joshua turned back to Matthew. "I must be honest with you. When last I saw your father he was a troubled man. He believed he was responsible for the death of your mother and could not forgive himself for that. Even though he had purchased a fine piece of land, he was not caring for it and it was run down. That was fifteen years ago. He came close to driving me off his land at gunpoint. I have not contacted him since because that is what he wished."

"Why would he think he was responsible for my mother's death?"

Joshua sighed and turned back to the window. "Your father was a scout for Williamson's militia. Even though he arrived after the vote was taken and Obadiah Holmes had hidden you in the woods, he helped to stir the militia into a frenzy."

"But why, uncle?"

"Jonathan found the man who had murdered your grandparents at the village. He was a Christian by then, but Jonathan flew into a rage when he saw him there. He was a tall man with a scar on his face, and he was the one who had come to our farm and taken us captive."

"Do you mean Jeremiah?"

"Yes, I believe that is the man."

"But he was my mother's friend and very kind."

"I'm afraid your father only remembered the cruelty Jeremiah showed when he killed our mother. As soon as he saw Scar, a killing rage came over your father and he struck him down. That was a signal for the men to begin killing the Indians."

"Did my father know that my mother was there?"

"He did not know that Ruth was there. He only discovered it after the women were killed. Your mother died in your father's arms. She forgave him, but he could never forgive himself."

Matthew shifted in his chair. "Then, if he did not know that Mother was there, he could not be responsible for her death."

"That is true. The sad part is that anyone would have to die in such a brutal fashion. The men were already angered when they found out that Wingenund had been nursed back to health at the village, and Jonathan's act was the spark that lit the fuse."

"Wingenund? You mean my grandfather?"

"Yes, Wingenund, the greatest enemy of the settlers."

"I remember him. He stayed in our cabin while he was recovering from his wound. He and I had many long talks. He was a gentle, kind man...at least to me."

Joshua stood for a long time at the window, silent. At last he spoke. "The history of the settler's treatment of the Indians is not a glorious one. When all is said and done, future generations will look upon these days with regret. Your grandfather was a man who saw his lands being stolen and his people murdered. As he was pushed further and further away from the Delaware homeland, I am sure his rage grew. He was a warrior and he only knew the way of the warrior. I do not blame him for his actions. He was defending his people and his home from those who could only be called invaders. How much better if greed and avarice had not ruled the settlers and we could have sat down and worked out an amicable agreement—if we could have lived in peace side by side as neighbors instead of enemies. I'm sure Wingenund would have much preferred to live a quiet life in his lodge, with his grandchild at his knee."

Matthew reached in his pocket and pulled something out. He stood and held it out to Joshua. "When my grandfather was at the village he gave me this. I have kept it with me always." In his hand lay a small piece of leather with a stylized wolf burned into it. "It is the totem of the Wolf Clan." Matthew looked at his uncle. "I am of both worlds. Perhaps I can be the one to bring peace to my father's heart. But I would also like to see my grandfather, if he is still alive, before we go to New York."

Joshua shook his head. "The Delaware continued to fight after the war was over. In 1794 General Wayne defeated them once and for all at the Battle of Fallen Timbers. They were forced to give up most of their land. Since then, Wingenund's whereabouts are unknown. I am sorry, Matthew."

Matthew shrugged. "I am sorry too, for I would like to see him one more time. If that is not possible, then when can we leave for New York?"

"I have arranged for transportation for next Monday. We will leave then."

Just then, one of the boys stuck his head in the door. "Come to supper, Papa." He took Matthew by the hand. "Sit next to me, Cousin, and tell me about hunting, for I would have you take me, if you will."

"If we can go before Monday, Ezekiel, I will take you hunting."

Joshua thought back to the day that he and Jonathan had hunted for a deer in the woods—that day so long ago, when his whole world had changed.

Chapter Thirty-Seven

The Homecoming

"Your brother has let himself go, Joshua, and it is sad to see." Sally Townsend poured another cup of tea for Matthew and Joshua. "When he came here sixteen years ago, he had enough money to purchase a piece of land. He built the small house that you have seen and some outbuildings, but since then, he has not improved the property."

Joshua set his cup down. "But how does he live, Sally?"

"He rents a portion of his land to a neighbor who farms it on shares, and he hunts. Other than that, he spends most of his time"—she looked at Matthew—"drinking."

Matthew rose and went to the window. "Does he know I am coming?"

Sally shook her head. "He is very reclusive. I sent my man to tell him, but he refuses to receive anyone. He does not know you are here."

Matthew looked at his uncle. "We have come all this way. We may as well go out to the farm."

Joshua took Matthew by the arm. "Do not expect too much, Nephew. He has been a hermit all these years. He believes his wife and son are dead. It may be a shock for him to see you. I know he will not be happy to see me."

"I must take the risk, Uncle Joshua. If he refuses to see us, I will return to Ohio with you and close this chapter of my life forever. But I must at least try."

The two men stood and bowed to Sally. Joshua slipped on his coat. "Thank you for all your help, Sally."

"I will pray that your meeting goes well. It would be a good thing to bring this story to a conclusion. Henry will drive you there."

Joshua turned to Matthew. "Ready?"

"Yes, uncle. Let us go."

The carriage pulled to a stop on the road. In the distance the two men could see Jonathan's house. A man was sitting on the front porch, but Joshua couldn't make out who it was.

"Shall I wait for you, sir?"

"Yes, Henry. We do not know if he will see us." Joshua nodded to Matthew, who took a deep breath. "Come, Matthew. Let us see what the Lord has for us."

The two men walked up the path from the road. They passed some outbuildings and a corral that were decrepit and falling down. As they came closer, the man in the chair rose and started to go into the house. Joshua called to him. "Jonathan, wait!" The man did not stop but kept moving toward the house.

"Papa, wait!"

The man stopped and turned. As Joshua and Matthew approached, he took a few steps forward. "What did you call me?"

The man in front of them was old beyond his years. His hair was completely gray and his features were lined and covered by a scraggly beard. A worn hat with a ragged brim was perched on his head, and his clothing was torn and unwashed. Joshua came closer. "Jonathan?"

The man ignored Joshua and pointed to Matthew. "I said, what did you call me?"

Joshua nodded to Matthew who stepped forward. "I called you Papa."

"And why do you call me that? My son is dead."

"No, Papa. I am not dead. I am alive. It's me, Matthew."

Jonathan turned to Joshua. "You always wanted to get the better of me, but you never could. Now you bring this imposter to torment me? Can you give me no peace, brother?"

Matthew stepped up on the porch and stood face to face with Jonathan. "I am not an imposter. I am your son."

"My son is dead. He died with his mother at Gnadenhutten."

"No, I did not. I was taken away and hidden by Obadiah Holmes. Before he could give me to you, you disappeared into the forest. He could not find you, so he gave me to a foundling home. For the last fifteen years I have been an indentured servant."

Jonathan stared at Matthew. "But how can this be? No one survived."

"I did, Papa." Matthew reached down and pulled up his pant leg. Along the back of his calf ran a scar shaped like a lightning bolt." Do you remember this?"

Jonathan stared at the scar and then knelt down and took Matthew's leg in his hands. After a long while he spoke. "You fell…"

"Yes, I fell from the top of a tree."

"You were only five and yet you managed to get fifty feet up that pine."

"I was showing off and I slipped."

"The branches broke your fall or you would have died."

"But I caught my calf on a sharp snag on the way down and tore it open."

"Your mother wanted to kill me; she was so angry that I let you do that. Your mother…"

"The wound looked like a lightning bolt coming from the sky. After it healed, you always called me—"

"Son of lightning." Jonathan stood. He stepped closer until the two were face to face. "Matthew?"

"Yes, Papa. I have found you."

Jonathan's arms shook. He started to reach for Matthew, but put his hand to his heart instead and staggered to the chair and collapsed into it.

"Papa? What is wrong?"

Jonathan smiled up at the two men, but there was no joy in the smile. "Too much red likker and too much heartbreak, I reckon. The village doctor says I have a bad heart; that it's pretty much wore out."

Matthew knelt by his father's side. "What can I do for you?"

"You've already done it, Son. You came back to your old *daed.*"

It was the first time Joshua had heard Jonathan speak German since the day they were captured. Jonathan looked up. "Surprised, brother? I guess that you can't cut yourself off from your roots completely. I see you have a beard now. Are you still Amish then and married?"

"Yes, Jonathan, I have remained in the church. There is a strong community of Amish in Ohio now. My wife and I have a farm near Wooster. I built a mill on a small creek there. It's called Apple Creek. I grind flour and trade with the villages around us. I met my wife fifteen years ago. She was a young widow who came out from the old Northkill settlement. We have two boys."

Jonathan smiled. "Always the good brother. Papa would be proud of you. But me, *Ich war immer das schwarze Schaf der Familie.*"

"No, Jonathan. You were not the black sheep. You were a good son. The trouble between you and Papa that day and after that only happened because you loved us all and wanted to save us. There is nothing wrong with that."

"But look at what my hatred for the Indians caused. I killed my own wife."

Matthew took hold of Jonathan's hand. "You did not kill her, Papa. You did not know she was there. How could you? It was Scar you killed. Mother loved you. She forgave you."

Jonathan put his face in his hands. "I miss her every day, Matthew. She was a wonderful woman."

Joshua looked down at the father and son.

I miss her every day also, brother.

Matthew stood up and walked to the edge of the porch. Joshua could see his gaze sweeping the land. Matthew turned to his father. "How much land do you have, Papa?"

Jonathan looked up. "What?"

"I asked how much land you have."

"It is over three hundred acres. I received a land bounty in Ohio for my service during the war and sold it to a settler out there. I used the money to buy this land."

"Is there water?"

Jonathan pointed to the pond. "The pond is spring fed. It's the freshest on the whole island." He stood up and walked over next to Matthew. He pointed to the fields beyond the pond. "I have never plowed the fields, but the soil is rich. I was never much of a hand at farming, though. Joshua knows that."

"You were ever the hunter, brother."

"Do you remember the day we both shot the deer and the master hunter gave the apprentice one more lesson in hunting?"

"I remember, Jonathan."

"That was the day that…"

The two brothers stood silently. Joshua knew that Jonathan was thinking of that day, as he was. The hunting, the meeting with Scar, and all that followed. "We cannot go back, Jonathan, nor can we undo the past. It is done. The best we can do is live life now to the fullest. With God's help—"

Jonathan raised his hand. "Do not go on, Joshua. I was done with all that long ago."

Matthew interjected. "The corrals and the barn need work, but they could be repaired. Miss Townsend said you rent out some of the land to another farmer."

Jonathan smiled a real smile. "That old busybody, she knows everybody and everything that goes on in this part of the island. Yes, there is a man who plants potatoes over in the back forty. He's been trying to buy the land from me."

Matthew turned to his father. "Do not sell the land, Papa."

"And why should I not sell the land?"

"Because even if you are not a farmer, I am. I learned much on the Andrews farm. I did all the work his lazy sons should have done while they lived a life of ease. I could make this farm prosper, Papa. I am also good with horses and livestock."

Joshua listened as they talked and even before Matthew spoke, he knew what the young man had decided. Matthew turned to Joshua.

"I will stay here, Uncle Joshua, with my papa. He needs me. You have your own sons, and they will take your farm, but Papa has no one unless I stay."

Jonathan turned to Matthew. "You would stay with me, even though I…"

Matthew shook his head. "We will speak no more about it. As uncle says, the past is past and cannot be undone. I am your son and I will stay with you, Papa."

Joshua saw tears start in his brother's eyes. He had never seen his brother cry. Jonathan's arm went around his boy. "Matthew, Matthew."

Matthew's arms crept around his father's shoulders. "Papa, I am home."

Joshua smiled and then he turned, stepped off the porch, and began to walk away.

Jonathan called after him. "Joshua."

Joshua stopped and turned around. Jonathan came off the porch and walked up to him slowly. "Joshua, I am sorry for all that has passed between us. You have brought me my son, back from the dead. You never gave up and I see now that you have always been my brother, even when I rejected you. I ask you to forgive me."

Joshua looked at his brother. The years fell away, and he was back in the woods of Ohio. They were crawling silently through the woods. They held their long rifles pointed ahead. Jonathan was in the lead and Joshua came close behind. A moss-stained rugged rock, trickling with water, lay to their left. On the right, a hillside covered with tangled ferns sloped down to a small pond surrounded by lush fronds and dotted by the swift movements of water bugs. The deer ahead of them had been drinking at the pond when she raised her head and moved off into the woods, disturbed by a slight scent on the wind…

"Joshua?"

Joshua stepped forward and took his brother into an embrace. "I forgave you long ago, brother. Now I can rest easy, for I know that you have someone to look after you."

Jonathan whispered in Joshua's ear. "You loved her, too, did you not?"

"Yes, brother, I loved her."

"And she loved you, too—I could tell. When I abandoned her, did you...did you...?"

"No, Jonathan. White Deer was always faithful to you."

Jonathan sighed and patted his brother's shoulder. "I know. You were always an honorable man, Joshua."

Joshua felt Matthew's hand on his arm.

"Thank you, uncle. I shall send letters and let you know how we are doing."

Joshua Hershberger walked away from the two men. Henry waited by the gate. As Joshua climbed up into the carriage, he turned to look one last time. The sun was setting. Long shadows crept across the fields. The breeze had died down, and the pond lay like a small diamond in the midst of a green tapestry. As the carriage rolled away, Joshua saw Matthew standing with his arm around Jonathan's shoulders. Matthew's hand lifted and he waved. Joshua waved back and then turned away. His task there was finished.

Chapter Thirty-Eight

Farewell

It was a bright spring morning in 1833. Joshua Hershberger drove into what had once been the Village of Peace. The primeval forest that had surrounded the village in silent majesty fifty years before was gone, replaced by spreading fields and farms. A small town had sprung up and a well-traveled road led through the cluster of houses toward the Ohio-Erie Canal that had been built only a few years before. Above Joshua, the Ohio skies were filled with a white rampart of clouds that were slowly moving west, signifying a coming change in the weather.

Joshua pulled the horse to a slow walk and looked around. The Ohio of his boyhood days had slipped into the past. A panorama of faces crowded his memory—his father and mother, his dear sisters and Aaron, his younger brother. He thought of Jonathan, now gone, and Matthew with his wife and children, prospering on the farm in New York, as he had promised Joshua he would. The lives of his own family had been planted in the deep, rich soil of Ohio. His wife was gone and now his sons ran the mill and carried on the trade that he had built over the years. And today, especially, his thoughts lingered on the beautiful White Deer.

As he drove by a house on the outskirts of town, the door opened and a man in simple garb came out with a broom. He saw Joshua and nodded. "Can I help you, sir?"

Joshua brought the buggy to a halt. He climbed out and walked slowly over to the fence that ran around the man's house. "Yes, my friend. I'm looking for John Heckewelder's house."

The man pointed to a sturdy building down the road. "Mr. Heckewelder lived there until he resigned his post and moved to Bethlehem, Pennsylvania in 1810. From what his church people say, he passed away about ten years ago. But many of the Moravians still remain in the village. They tend the grave."

"The grave?"

"Yes, sir, the grave of the Moravian Indian converts that were killed here."

"Ah, yes, the grave. That is the reason I've come. I was here once in 1783, but everything has changed so much that I'm turned around. Can you direct me?"

"Certainly, sir. It's not far from the old Heckewelder place. He built the first house here and then spent his days caring for the gravesite, along with the old one."

"The old one?"

"Yes, sir, that's what we call the old man who comes and visits here. He's an Indian and he comes two or three times a year. He cleans the debris away and makes sure the grass is cut and plants fresh flowers. I think he is visiting the village now, sir." The man pointed. "If you follow the road it will wind around Heckewelder's place. The grave is just beyond."

"Thank you, sir. May I tie my horse and buggy up here?"

"Yes, sir. If you wish, I'll unhitch him, let him roll in my pasture and feed him. He looks like he has come a ways."

Joshua nodded. "Kind of you, sir, very kind." Joshua walked slowly toward Heckewelder's house, putting his weight on the walking stick that had been his companion for the last few years.

So David is gone and now John. Life carries us along and before we know it, we have reached the end.

He walked down the road until he came to a place he remembered. A low mound broke the flat surface of a field. The mound was covered with grass. Around the edges some bright flowers were planted. As Joshua walked up, he saw an old man kneeling and planting some more flowers. Joshua came up behind the man. "Good morning, sir."

The old man turned and, seeing Joshua, he stood. He looked hard at Joshua and then smiled. "The yellow hair has turned white, but the man is still the same."

Startled, Joshua came closer. The Indian, though old, was tall and straight of bearing. He wore no shirt but had on trousers and a deerskin vest. Joshua could see the marks of scars and wounds on his arms and chest. He looked long at the face. "Wingenund?"

"The yellow-hair remembers. Wingenund remembers, too, when the one called Scar brought you to our village. Your brother, Black Eagle, wished to be a warrior, but you were the brave one with the true warrior's heart. You did not change from your ways and you cared for your father. There was much honor in what you did."

"You come here to tend her grave?"

"Yes."

"But I thought the Delaware left Ohio after the war."

"Many of the Lenni Lenape left to go north to Canada. Others went to the Spanish lands. A few remained in Ohio. I stayed"—he pointed to the grave—"to be near my daughter, to pray and to remember the old ways."

"To pray, Wingenund? Are you—?"

"A believer? Yes, Yellow-hair." The old chief laid aside his tool and motioned Joshua to a rough bench made of logs beside the mound. They sat quietly, looking at the grave for a long time. Then Wingenund spoke. "When I was a boy, before we left *Lenapehoking*, a great sachem of the Turtle Clan spoke over my life. He told me of the birth of my daughter, that she would be a princess of her people. He told me that this child would lead me to the greatest truth and, at a time when all seemed dark around me, a great light would shine in my heart." Wingenund's head bowed and he began to speak the words of the sachem:

" 'The arrow and bow shall fall from his hand and his voice shall be the voice of peace, for he shall speak the words of the greatest one who shines through all the darkness. And then this one shall use the truth as a hunter uses the sight on his gun. He shall aim his life by the truth. But before he knows the truth he will know great pain, sorrow and loss. For he is the 'willing one' and in time he will learn to be willing to bear the burden of his people with a true heart.' "

"And Ruth…White Deer, she led you?"

"When I was badly wounded, my warriors brought me here. I was near death and the people of this village brought me back to life. My daughter and my grandson watched over me. As I learned of her ways and talked with Glickhican, a great peace came into my heart. I could see that Opahtuhwe walked in a great light. The long years of battle had wounded my spirit, and I knew that I could no longer remain on the path of war. A few weeks after I left, White Deer and Matthew were killed. My heart was heavy with sorrow, but I knew that her life had meant something, for I returned to my tribe and shared the way of peace. Many came to know this Jesus and we laid down our arms."

"But Matthew is not dead, Wingenund."

The old man turned with surprise on his face. "My grandson is not dead?"

"No, he lives. He went back to New York and cared for Jonathan until he died. It was his greatest wish that he could see you again."

Wingenund smiled. "And so my seed lives on after me, and I am not the last of my line.

Black Eagle is dead?"

"Jonathan died three years ago. Matthew took care of him to the end."

"Did Black Eagle ever come back to your way?"

Joshua shook his head. "No, great Chief. Sadly, my brother never returned to the Amish faith. Matthew followed his father and closed his heart when I spoke of Jesus."

"So even in joy there is sorrow. And thus has it been since I was very young. The sachem also told me that through my daughter I would see both faces of the white man—the way of life and the way of death. Black Eagle showed my daughter the way of death, but you showed her the way of life, and in her heart, I think she loved you best." He paused and then spoke again. "I would go to see my grandson before I die. Eighty-nine winters have I walked upon the earth-mother and the end of my trail is soon upon me."

"I can arrange that. These days, with the canal and stagecoaches, it is only a few days' journey. When you are ready, I will let him know you are coming."

The breeze picked up a bit and Joshua looked up. The white clouds had turned to gray. Rolling storm ramparts moved across the sky. There was a flash of lightning and a distant roll of thunder. "It looks like we are in for a shower, Chief."

Wingenund smiled. "Yes, they come often here. Let us stand under the chestnut tree until it passes."

The two men stood up and walked over to a large chestnut tree that spread its many branches in a leafy bower beside the grave mound. In a moment, there was a thunderclap, much closer this time. A bright flash of lightning lit the sky followed by darkness and wind. And then the storm broke. Water poured from the sky in a torrent; the wind picked up and Joshua's cloak whipped around him as he held his hat to keep it from blowing away. For a few more moments, the storm raged and then the wind began to die. The rain, which had been coming down in sheets, turned to a soft shower and then the storm clouds rolled through. Behind them came a blue sky laced with high, white clouds. Bright sunlight streamed through the leaves of the trees, bathing the fields with a mystic radiance. As the two men watched, the sky above them was filled with a rainbow. To their amazement, it seemed to touch the ground right before them on the mound. It stayed for a moment and then, like a momentary vision, it faded and was gone.

Wingenund stepped out from beneath the tree. "Opahtuhwe walks the rainbow path. She comes from the distant forest to speak to us."

Joshua paused and then slowly reached into his pocket. "Perhaps she does, Chief, perhaps she does." He pulled out the letter that White Deer had written to him the night before she died. "I have had this letter for over thirty years. The man who rescued Matthew gave it to me. It is from White Deer, from

Ruth. I have never opened it because my sorrow was too great. Today seems like a good day to read it." Joshua pulled a penknife from his pocket and slit open the envelope. Wingenund's eyes were fixed on the sky. Joshua began to read.

> *My dearest Joshua,*
>
> *I am writing this letter because tomorrow I will be with Jesus. I will never see you again in this world, but do not sorrow, for I know that I will see you when we meet at the throne of our great God.*
>
> *If you ever see my father again, I ask you to give him this message for me. I love you, Father, with a daughter's great love. I love you even more because when you left the Village of Peace the last time I saw you, the truth of Jesus was in your eyes. You did not have to tell me, but I knew that the prophecy had come true and that you had seen the way of peace. I will look for you in the early morning sun at first light, when the mist rises in the forest and the earth spreads its life before us. Until then, may your trail be a trail of joy, not sorrow, for you are the willing one, the greatest chief of the Lenape and your people will know life through you.*
>
> *And as for you, Joshua, I love you with the love a woman has for the man who saved her. For surely you saved me. I was lost in bitterness and doubt, and you told me the words of peace. I turned from the path of death to follow your ways. I know you loved me, too, and that love held me in its embrace and kept me safe and warm when all else was hidden in shadows.*
>
> *I can tell you that I love you without shame, because I will rest in the peace that comes from knowing that I passed the test of honor and never defiled my marriage. I have you to thank for that.*
>
> *And so Joshua, my dearest one, I say this to you in parting; always remember the pure, holy love we shared. Hold it before you like a banner; let it guide you through the darkest night. Never forget your Amish Princess.*
>
> *Until we meet again,*
>
> *Ruth*

Joshua folded the letter and put it back into his pocket. A great silence gripped the world. Had anyone come down the lane they would have only seen two old men standing by a grave. They would not have seen the great battle being fought in the hearts of Joshua and Wingenund—a battle between sorrow and joy, anguish and peace. And, in the end, the memory of the Amish Princess, her beauty and her joy, her loving spirit and her great wisdom—that memory brought the tranquility to their hearts that only comes from knowing that God has worked all things together for good, once again.

Epilogue

The Rest of the Story

The tall writer stood with Jenny Hershberger in an Amish graveyard in Millersburg, just north of Apple Creek, Ohio. Jenny pointed to the name on the gravestone.

Hannah Hershberger — 1863-1941

"That was my great-grandmother Hannah. Her father came to Apple Creek with his father, Ezekiel, in 1860. Ezekiel was Joshua's son. It was Ezekiel who collected all of Joshua's letters and correspondence, including the letter from Ruth. He even traveled to Oyster Bay and met with Sally Townsend before her death and made copies of the letters Joshua sent to her."

The writer shook his head thoughtfully. "And that is how you came to know the story?"

"Yes. Ezekiel wrote it all down. He even wrote a shortened version of Jonathan and Joshua's story that my great-grandmother gave to my mother, Jerusha."

"And then you collected it all and wrote *The Amish Princess?*"

Jenny nodded. "Yes. And it was from these writings that I was able to share my husband Jonathan's history with him, the story that brought the wayward branch of the Hershberger family back into the Amish faith. Come, let's walk."

The writer looked down at Jenny. At seventy, she had lines and wrinkles, but she was still lovely. Her hair was snow white. The writer remembered the first time he had come to Paradise and met with Jenny. Her hair still had some gold in it then. The gold was gone now, but aside from that, she had not changed much. "And what happened to Matthew?"

They stopped at another site. There were two stones together.

Joshua Hershberger — 1753-1836
Ezekiel Hershberger — 1799-1860

"Matthew took care of his father until Jonathan died in 1830. He turned the farm into one of the most prosperous on Long Island. It was the land and the farm that was the basis for my husband's family's wealth. Joshua died on the farm near Zanesville, but when Ezekiel brought his family to Apple Creek, they brought Joshua's casket with them."

"And what about Matthew? Did he ever come back to the church?"

Jenny shook her head. "The Long Island Hershbergers were nominal Christians, I suppose, but never really knew about having a relationship with Christ or even that they were from Amish roots until Jonathan shared it with them on the last trip on their boat—the trip where Jonathan's parents were killed, and Jonathan was lost to me for eight years."

"And that was the story we told in *Jenny's Choice*."

"Yes. And now I have only one more story to tell." Jenny reached into the bag she carried with her and pulled out a manuscript tied up with a red ribbon. Like the others, it had been typed on an old-fashioned typewriter. She looked up at the writer as she handed it to him.

"I am grateful that you have helped me. Together we have told the story of the Hershberger women. When this one is published, my task will be finished. You have done my stories a great service."

The writer looked at the title. *The Mennonite Queen*. He smiled to himself. It had been a privilege to work with this little Amish woman, and he looked forward to reading the story and then rewriting it for Jenny.

Jenny pointed to another part of the graveyard and they walked together. They stopped at a section where three graves were clustered. The names were familiar to the writer—Reuben Springer, Jerusha Springer and Jenna Springer.

Jenny took out a hanky and wiped her eyes. "This is where it all began—Papa and Mama, and my little sister, Jenna. Without them, we would not be here and the story would never have been told. I still have the quilt my mama made for Jenna, the one she wrapped me in to save me from the great storm. I miss them, but I know I will see them again." Jenny smiled through her tears. The golden orb of the sun was sinking into the west. Long strands of sunlight picked their way through the branches of the tall chestnut trees around the graveyard, leaving a golden lattice of light on the ground. Jenny reached into her apron pocket and pulled out three yellow daffodils. She laid one on each grave.

Jenny spoke quietly. "I, too, was cast adrift. And though I was adopted and brought into the Hershberger and Springer families, I never felt at home until I discovered my own roots. And then when I married Jonathan, I felt like I was part of something so much bigger than myself—a plan that the Lord set in motion two hundred years ago to knit a sundered family back together. And now I can lay my pen down and put my typewriter in the closet and get about the task of finishing my days at the farm in Paradise." She looked up. "Ah, there is my cousin, Levi, come to fetch me. Until we meet again then."

They walked to the gate. The writer climbed into his car. He rolled down the window and looked one last time. Jenny stood looking out to the east. The breeze had picked up and was plucking at the unruly curls that peeked out of her *kappe*. Jenny turned and smiled, lifted her hand in farewell and then climbed up into the buggy and was gone.